DARK BROWN is the RIVER

an orphan's journey

DOROTHY TOOPER LUND

Gnarlywood Press
Hayward, Wisconsin

Gnarlywood Press
Hayward, Wisconsin

COVER AND INTERIOR DESIGN: Dunn+Associates, www.Dunn-Design.com
Cover illustration: Donna Post

Publisher's Cataloging-In-Publication Data
(Prepared by The Donohue Group, Inc.)
Names: Lund, Dorothy Tooper, author.
Title: Dark brown is the river : an orphan's journey / Dorothy Tooper Lund.
Description: Hayward, Wisconsin : Gnarlywood Press, [2020]
Identifiers: ISBN 9780578631769
Subjects: LCSH: Tooper, Wesley—Childhood and youth—Fiction.
Orphans--Québec (Province)—History—20th century—Fiction.
Families—Québec (Province)—History—20th century—Fiction.
Québec (Province)—Social conditions—20th century—Fiction.
LCGFT: Historical fiction. | Biographical fiction.
Classification: LCC PS3612.U535 D37 2020 | DDC 813/.6--dc23

Away Go the Boats

Dark brown is the river,
Golden is the sand.
It flows along forever,
With trees on either hand.

Green leaves a floating,
Castles of the foam.
Boats o' mine a boating,
Where will all come home?

On goes the river,
And out past the mill,
Away down the valley,
Away down the hill.
Away down the river,
A hundred miles or more.
Other little children
Shall bring my boats ashore.

—Robert Louis Stevenson

Author's Note

When I was young, I thought my father was the true author of *Oliver Twist*. Just as little Oliver was abused in an orphanage, so was my father similarly mistreated in such a place. "The food was terrible," he told me, "and sometimes it had green stuff floating in it. Once we did have something decent, so I asked for more. Boy did I catch hell."

As I grew older, I realized that Charles Dickens wrote *Oliver Twist* before my father, Wesley Tooper, was born. He never read the book, nor did he know it existed, but both he and Dickens knew what they were talking about.

Dark Brown is the River was inspired by my father's story. I have presented it as he, and others—my mother, Aunt Lilly, her daughters Wanda and Jackie, Uncle Cleve (who got my father out of "more jams than you could cover bread with"), and dear old Kate Tooper—told it to me in bits and pieces as I was growing up. What dialogue and events I created, I have done so with the knowledge of the characters in mind —how they would speak, act, and react under certain situations.

My other sources are letters I found in my mother's closet long after my father's death and shortly after hers. Some were written in the caboose of an Illinois Central steam train, others on a troop ship sailing "across the pond," others in the trenches of World War I and a French hospital for victims of mustard gas. I discovered other letters written in many locations and under different and sometimes dire circumstances. Those I have included in my book are exactly as they were composed.

—DOROTHY TOOPER LUND

Prologue

Around 1903, Edward Tooper, born Eioteeque Toupant in Quebec City, walked along the Kankakee River towards a stark, almost crumbling orphanage to visit his four sons. Looking over his shoulder, he side-stepped into a cluster of young maples to change from his brakeman's uniform into dark blue, serge trousers and his newest boiled shirt. Adjusting the knot on a borrowed silk tie, he congratulated himself for changing clothes. No one was going to take him for a stupid railroad cluck and pull the wool over his eyes. That was why he had dressed well when he brought his boys there, making it clear he didn't want them adopted out, just looked after until he could get a home together.

Avoiding a murky puddle, he glanced at his pocket watch. A home together. How? He hardly had enough time to see the boys and make it back to the train for work. Somehow he had to stop at his aunt's and then his sister's place to check on the girls—Hazel working like a hired hand, and Lillian only a few months old. As usual, thoughts of his children turned to their mother, Clara Saint-Jean Tooper, married to him at fifteen, bearing a son who died before the child was two, bearing six more and dying after the birth of her last. With such thoughts becoming too painful, Edward let his mind stray to the governor's mansion where his train often stopped. One of the cooks there liked him, giving him special leftovers and asking about his children. She was older than him, smaller yet stronger than Clara.

Suddenly he had a feeling similar to one that came upon him while he worked on the trains—that someone was going to jump onto the track. He would visualize a young girl with child or a despondent wife plunging down a steep bank and landing in front of the engine, too late for the brakeman and the engineer to stop it.

Forcing the thought from his mind, he focused on the building ahead where Cleve and Wesley, his two older boys, sat on a sagging porch, shoulders slumped, staring into space. Usually, all four came to greet him, Cleve carrying Willard, and Wesley holding Benny's hand. This time, when Cleve saw his father, he picked up Wesley and walked towards him, his younger brother's feet dragging on the ground. Edward ran and lifted both sons together, clasping them against him, shaking them back and forth, as if the movement itself would bring things to light. "Where are the little ones, Cleve?" he shouted. "Benny and Willard! My God, Cleve, where are the babies?"

When Edward set them down, Cleve squeezed his eyes shut and pushed his head between his shoulders like a turtle backing into his shell. "I told 'em not to take 'em, Pa, I told 'em! But Wes is still here. They didn't take him."

Starting Out

CHAPTER ONE

Orphans Exit

May 23, 1905

"I'm six years old," Wesley kept saying. "I'm too big to be carried," but Pa would not listen. He kept walking faster and faster, urging Cleve to hold onto his shirttail. "Stay with me Son," he kept saying. "Stay with me."

As foolish as he felt now, Wesley didn't think he looked as silly as when Cleve picked him up and took him down the lane to meet Pa. *Why did Cleve do that? Because he was always carrying Benny or Willard, and now they were gone?*

Pa stomped up the orphanage steps, his heels banging like steam hammers, upsetting a swarm of flies. He swung the front door open and slammed it so hard the porch windows rattled, one cracking, half its glass clattering to the floor. He marched through the front room where visitors sat with their children.

"If you know what's good for them," he yelled, "take 'em outa here while you still got 'em!"

Pa and the boys advanced down the hall, stopping at the room where the orphans slept. Leading with his free shoulder, Pa lunged at the door, but it opened easily, the force of his thrust propelling them inside. They landed in a heap on one of the narrow, iron cots that lined the room. At one end stood a row of cribs.

Pa looked around. "Where's your satchels?"

They pointed to two nearby cots, a wooden orange crate in front of each one. "Under our beds," Wesley said.

"Put everything you got in 'em. Make it fast now. We got a lot to do."

His voice broke for a moment. He held his hands over his face while Wesley and Cleve scurried around their beds, pulling clothes, books, and toys out of their orange crates.

A scrawny boy with pointed ears sat on the floor playing with little, round stones as if they were marbles. Wesley watched out of the corner of his eye as the boy got up, walked over, and tapped his finger on Pa's head. "Mister, you takin' Wessie and Clevie from here?"

Pa looked up. "You're damn right."

He narrowed his eyebrows and surveyed the boy carefully. "Look here, Sonny. Those marks on your face. What are they about?"

"They hit us sometimes. Hey, you know what? I'll miss them boys. They're funny."

Pa drew the boy nearer. "Who in the hell's 'they'? Do Wes and Cleve hit you?"

The boy flung out his hand like he would shake crumbs from a rag. "Noooo! They'd never do that."

Another boy, also very thin, appeared at his side. He held his hand over his mouth trying to suppress a giggle slipping out between his fingers like a musical scale. "Wessie and Clevie give people funny names," he trilled. "Father—they call him Fatso. And Head Sister— they call her Stringy."

Pa placed the boy's bony arm between his thumb and forefinger, his eyes focusing on black and blue circles and raised ridges of skin. "Who's hittin' you little fellers? Tell me."

"Father, the sisters, the monitors … somes of them that clean the place."

Cleve ran up with his hands full of nuts, bolts, and small gears. "Pa! Can I bring my motor parts? I'll wrap 'em in a rag so they won't get my clothes dirty." Pa nodded. Then he turned Cleve around, pulled his shirt up, and looked at his back. Wesley knew it was sprinkled with red, angry marks.

"Wesley," Pa said. "Come over here."

"Can I bring my figurin', Pa?" he pleaded. "I can roll the papers up real tight."

Pa wheeled him around and pulled up his shirt. Wesley felt his father's fingers running over his back, gently tracing over the raised marks, stopping longer on broken skin.

Pa released Wesley and staggered about the room, clutching his hair. "Clara. Clara!"

Then suddenly, as if a soothing hand of reason touched his shoulder, he strode towards his sons on steady legs, taking deep breaths, pulling his body up straight. "Just get them," he choked. "Just get your stuff into those bags quick!"

Glancing around the room, he called to anyone who could answer. "How about the rest of you? Do those bastards hit you too?"

Silence, and then a shriveled, red-headed boy curled like an unborn baby on a cot, pulled his thumb from his mouth and spoke. "'Cept for the little 'uns. They don't want no marks on them. They feed 'em real good too."

Pa rushed to the place where he heard the voice, knelt down, and looked at the boy's face. "But they don't mind marking you up, do they? For God's sake—why?"

The boy shivered. "Cause we're too old to 'dopt out. It don't matter how we look."

Pa hurried to the beds that had been Wesley's and Cleve's, jerked the blankets off, and covered the boy with them, gently tucking them under at both sides and at the foot of his bed.

He looked around the room again. "Anyone who wants to follow us, come on!"

He marched through the doorway and into the hall, one hand holding onto Cleve's arm and the other around Wesley's, with seven boys stepping into line behind them. When they reached Father Farellsi's door, instead of bashing it in with his fist or kicking it, Pa knocked quietly and waited.

A voice came creaking through like a door with rusty hinges. "Who is it?"

"I'm from the bishop's office, Father," Pa said, in a high-class voice. "I have an important message for you."

Wesley heard a smacking of lips, a loud gulp, then a scraping of a chair, footsteps, and a key turning in the lock. He'd been terrified his father would choke the priest to death, and the police would throw him in jail forever or hang him from the gallows. But now, as the door opened, he saw that would be impossible because Father Farellsi had no neck. His immense bald head sat on his shoulders like a jack-o-lantern on a fence, his huge backside and stomach announcing the outer borders of his black robe. His inflated cheeks and bulbous lips shone with grease. Drops of liquid hung from his multiple chins, descending onto his white priest's collar, staining it with spots of purple. When he saw Pa and the boys, he smiled through short, pointed teeth.

"Oh, Mr. Toopah, how nicccce to see you! And boysss, you've escorted this fine gentleman to my door. How consideratah."

Pa stepped back and leaned forward. Father Farellsi looked pleased, as if he were receiving a bow from a grateful parent. Pa bellowed and charged, his head hitting the priest full force in the stomach. Wesley pictured Father Farellsi flying across his chambers and out the window as far as the Kankakee River. Instead, he went bump, bump along the floor, flailing his arms like a man balancing on the edge of a cliff. Pa rushed forward and tackled him. The priest screamed, the sound reminding Wesley of a terrified rabbit.

Father Farellsi groped under his robes and pulled out a small silver whistle. Before he could put it to his lips, Pa batted it across the room. "Where's my two littlest boys, you devil's son of a bitch?" He tried to reach his hands around the priest's throat but could not find it. "Where's my babies, you filthy, rotten bastard?" He reached for the glistening, bald head and tried to bang it on the floor, but it slipped from his hands. Father Farellsi brayed like a donkey. Standing up, Pa searched for something to beat the man's head with, and then he saw the table in front of him.

Long enough for a dozen people, it had only one place setting, marked by the priest's half-empty plate. The rest of the table was covered with food—a roasted chicken, slices of beef, fillets of fish, grapes and pears, baked potatoes, squash, and corn. On one end of the table were two loaves of bread, one resembling a round, dark cushion, the other long and tube-like.

"Jesus Christ, Pa," Cleve cried. "Look at all that damn food!"

"And they feed us all that moldy crap," piped another boy.

"Take it!" Pa cried. "You kids, take it all. Take it to your beds, take it to the others!"

He sniffed the air and followed his nose to a closet and walked in with Wesley close behind. They saw rows of sausages hanging on hooks from the ceiling and jars of canned meats, pickled vegetables, and preserved fruits on shelves.

Pa threw the sausages to the orphans. "Come in here. Get it all!"

The boys swarmed into the closet, hands reaching outward.

Unable to get up, Father Farellsi wallowed on the floor like a pig in a mud bath, groping desperately for his whistle.

Spying the thick, velvet curtains on the windows, Pa flung himself on them. Ripping them free, he shouted, "Cover yourselves with these tonight, boys. They're warmer than those puny blankets you got."

His face red, jaw trembling, Pa turned again to the priest. "I want to know why. I always stuck by the church. I paid my tithes. Why?"

"But your wiiife," the priest whined. "She became a heeethen! She chose that science faith. The Lord let her bleeeed to death."

Pa grabbed a wine vial from the table and flung purple liquid at the priest's head.

"Liar, Liar!" he shouted, reaching for Farellsi with both hands. "Clara had more faith than anyone in this damn, stinkin' place!"

Cleve thrust a thick curtain rod onto his father's hand. "Pa, we gotta get the hell outa here. They're comin'—a bunch of 'em!"

Wesley looked where Cleve was pointing and saw a gang of men rushing to the doorway, a few white-collared, the rest in work clothes. "Pa," he pleaded, "we got the window open and our satchels out. Let's go!"

Some of the men ran to help the wailing priest. Others advanced towards Pa but stopped when he shook the curtain rod at them.

"Where's my boys? Tell me where my babies are!"

Cleve and Wesley pulled him backwards by his shirt. "Come on, Pa! There's too many."

"Don't you dare touch a hand to any of these little fellers again!" Pa shouted at the men. "I got friends at the governor's house, and … at the White House! Teddy Roosevelt has a heart for the railroad man. He'll throw you all in jail!"

They climbed out the window and Pa led the boys through the yard towards the trees. "We've got to keep moving!" he hollered. "Here, Wesley, get on my shoulders."

As they reached the end of the institution's property, the orphanage gardener stepped from behind a cluster of wild plum bushes. In one hand he held the sack Pa had hidden after he changed into his dress clothes.

"He's nice," Cleve whispered. "Gives us pears on the sly."

In his other hand, the man held a piece of folded paper. "Here, Mister Toops. Maybe what's wrote here might help you find your other boys."

Pa grabbed the gardener's offerings and pushed on, waving a hand in thanks. Soon they stopped and stuffed Wesley's satchel into the bag with Pa's work clothes and went on. They fled across a sun-blazed meadow, then slowed their pace and tramped into dark woods. Finally, along a secluded part of the Kankakee River near the railroad tracks, they stopped to catch their breaths.

Wesley had never seen Pa so distraught—so different from at his mother's funeral where his father's sadness had remained deep and quiet. Now he paced back and forth on the river bank, grabbing his hair in frustration, stopping in front of Wesley and Cleve, patting them on their heads, grasping them by the shoulders, and pulling them to him.

"Here, Wesley," he'd say, reaching into his pocket and coming up with nothing in his hand. "I should have a little something for you, Cleve," he'd go on, pulling the lining of the other pocket all the way out until it hung empty.

Swearing to himself, he took off his shirt and tie, handed the shirt to Cleve, and helped him put his arms into the sleeves and fasten the buttons. Walking over to Wesley, he draped the borrowed tie around his shoulders. "I'm sorry, boys," he said. "So damn sorry."

Wesley looked at the tie hanging past his knees and at Cleve with the shirt cuffs covering his hands. He tried to figure out what

his father was sorry about—their mother dying, for the beatings
they got at the orphanage, or for the shirt and tie being too long.

Far off in the distance a train whistle blew, causing them all to
look down the track.

"Jesus," Pa said. "My train comes after this one. I got to get back
to work. I got to find someone to keep you boys!"

"Pa," Cleve said. "We ain't lettin' nobody keep us again. Nobody."

"We ain't, Pa," Wesley echoed. "Not nobody."

Pa shook his head and blinked. "But … but, where will you go?
What will you do?"

"We'll hop trains," Cleve said. "We'll be hobos."

Pa got down on one knee and stared at the ground. Cleve walked
to the river and dipped a cloth in the water. Then he came back and
started washing the dust from his father's face.

"Remember when you told us how you rode the rails when you
was a kid? Me and Wes are lucky because you work on the trains.
Maybe we could go with you sometimes—in a boxcar."

Pa cocked his head. "Oh, I could teach you the tricks—how to
get on and off without gettin' hurt—keep my eye on you some of the
time. But what will you do when they send me on far-off runs and I
can't take you along? I can't give you money to tide you over. I gave all I
had for your sisters' keep and to that bastard priest for you four boys."

"We'll bum around," Cleve answered. "We'll find work on farms
and stuff. We'll get by, but nobody's gonna feed us rotten food or beat
us everyday again."

The approaching train bore down the track. "Come on," its
whistle sounded to Wesley. "Come on," it coaxed.

"Don't worry, Pa," he said, trying to make his voice rough and
raspy like Cleve's. "We're gonna be hobos."

CHAPTER TWO

Mother

1899-1902 Remembered

"I see you, Wesley," his mother would say at the cottage in Sheldon. "I know you're there." In the midst of babies, cooking and cleaning, she would wave her hand out to the side or behind her back, letting him know he wasn't lost in the shuffle.

"You're my little middleman," she told him when she had more time to talk. "You don't mind being the middleman, do you, Wesley?"

Once when Uncle Napoleon was visiting, Wesley had him look up the word "middleman" in his father's dictionary since Pa was away working on the trains. "See, Wesley," his uncle said, pointing at a word in the center of a page full of small print. "It says 'an agent or go-between.' Is that what you wanted to know?"

Wesley nodded and smiled, happily thinking of himself as his mother's agent: "Wesley, tell Cleve the pasture gate's open;" she'd say, or, "Wesley, please tell Benny I'll be right there; tell Pa to come down and eat. Wesley, tell Hazel to bring the baby to me."

At the time his mother called him a middleman, he was sure she meant things were even on both sides of him—Cleve and Hazel on his right and Benny and Willard on his left. She had put him in the middle, so the whole thing wouldn't tip on either side. When the new baby began growing in her stomach, she'd say, "You won't have to be in the middle anymore, Wesley, you'll be with the big ones— three big ones and three little ones, even Steven."

The baby turned out to be a Lilly not a Steven, but the numbers were still even, because if you took them apart, each side could be the same and add up to six—three big ones and three little ones, or two girls and four boys. If Clarence, the baby born before all of them had lived, they would add up to seven and wouldn't be even anymore.

Wesley liked it when his mother had him sprinkle clothes. He had to do it evenly, so she could iron out all the wrinkles. She placed a basket of clothes on the kitchen table next to a pan of water and had him stand on a chair. "Not too much water in one place," she'd remind him. "Just tiny drops all over."

She taught him to cup the water in the palm of his hand and use the space between his fingers like holes in a sieve. Baby Willard sat in his high chair and watched, his little brow wrinkled as if he were making sure Wesley did it right. After Wesley sprinkled each piece, his mother folded it into a straight line, rolled it tightly, and put it in a big washtub with the rest of the finished ones. Then she covered all the rolls with a cloth and put the tub in a cool place. The next day, she unwrapped them for ironing, and they smelled as if they'd been out in the rain for a short while. "Perfect," she'd say, giving him a hug like she did when she tucked him in bed under a warm, woolly blanket. "Just perfect."

When Benny and Willard took their naps, she worked on sheets of figures for the Grange, or for the feed store in town, or for the farm Pa managed when not working on the railroad. "Pa's good at figures, too," she'd say. "He's always helping with the books in the caboose at work. But he likes to play with harder ones, like geometry problems. Maybe that's what brought us together—numbers." And she'd laugh softly to herself as if it were her own private joke.

Her figures were small, slightly slanted, but large enough to read easily, standing out clear and black on the white paper. Wesley would try to copy them before he even knew what they were, wanting to make something orderly and unmixed-up like she did.

One day she said, "Look here, Wesley," and placed a piece of onionskin paper over one of her figure columns. "Now try and trace over mine. That would be fun."

He traced the numbers over and over, and soon he could write them freehand almost exactly like hers. Sometimes she'd write down little patterns for him to copy, things with + and - shapes, even though she didn't have time to explain them. He noticed whenever there was a 2 shape and another one under it with a line below, there would be a 4 figure under that line. Whenever there was a 3 shape with another one just like it underneath with a line below, there would be a 6 figure, and it all seemed so smooth and catchy, like music.

"I'll have Pa make you a writing desk and a bench," she said, "and make it high enough for you to use when you grow more. You can always sit on pillows at first."

Sometimes, before Lilly was born and when Cleve and Hazel were at school, his mother took the three youngest ones out to the orchard on a nice day. Wesley always reminded her to bring a pencil and paper and Pa's book, *Diseases of Horses,* along. He'd kneel in the grass with his paper on top of the big book and write down numbers. Willard, sitting on Mama's lap, leaned over and tilted his head so he could see the pencil lead touching the paper. Benny kept snatching the pencil out of Wesley's hand and tried to pull him away from his papers.

"He wants you to wrestle with him under the trees," his mother said, "or pretend the two of you are Teddy Roosevelt and his Rough Riders charging up San Juan Hill."

So Wesley put his paper and pencil inside Pa's book and played with Benny. Ever since Benny could walk, Wesley had taught him to run forward holding a twig in the air and hollering, "Charge! Charge!" Benny always hollered, "Carge! Carge!" which made Wesley and their mother burst out laughing. Willard too, who didn't know what he was laughing about.

The last time his mother took them to the orchard, she brought another book along, bigger but thinner than Pa's book, with pictures— *A Child's Garden of Verses.* When they became tired from play, she read to them, her voice soft as a pillow yet clear as a whippoorwill's call.

> *Dark brown is the river,*
> *Golden is the sand.*
> *It flows along forever*
> *With trees on either hand.*

Wesley crawled up on her lap and nestled against Willard while Benny slid under the curve of her free arm. The poem told about a boy sailing his toy boats on a river—the same dark brown color as the creek beyond the orchard. His mother took him there alone two times and made him paper boats to sail. The boy in the poem wondered, since his boat sailed past mills and valleys, how they would get back to him. Wesley wondered too, but just then a breeze, strong enough to fan the blossoms on the apple trees, blew over them.

His mother held them all to her like Wesley had seen a mother woodchuck do with her cubs in a den. Making happy tittering sounds, the three little boys huddled close to their mother as petals from the trees showered down. "When the breeze calms," she promised, pulling them closer, "we'll read the rest of the poem."

Benny and Willard soon fell asleep, but Wesley kept trying to figure out how the boy would get his boats back. Maybe he could run ahead of them on the bank and pull them in with a long stick.

Or he could shout to fishermen to catch them in their nets. Then
again, if the wind died down, the boats might drift ashore themselves.

He tried to guess the boy's name—Henry, Joseph, Charles,
Raymond, Thomas. Did he have brothers and sisters? Did he live
in the city or on a farm? Someone with a name like Henry probably
lived in a city, but maybe Charles lived on a farm and everyone called
him Charley like they did one of Wesley's uncles.

As the sun dropped lower in the sky, he couldn't stay on one
thought long enough to finish it. His mind jumped from picture
to picture—so fast he couldn't get a good look at them. He knew
he was falling asleep but kept his eyes open long enough to see his
mother's blue skirt sprinkled with apple blossoms as if someone
painted flowers on it with a tiny brush. And Pa's book, covered
with petals, looked like a pink and white gravestone in some far-off
fairyland his mother once described to him.

CHAPTER THREE

Nickle or a Doughnut

November 22, 1906

"Creamed corn and hogback," the Stanley Steamer, a horseless carriage, seemed to chug out on the rutted Indiana road as Wesley stood before the man who hired him. Becoming more aware of his growing hunger, he heard the machine change its tune as it climbed a nearby hill: "Maybe a dime too. Maybe a dime too."

The grim-faced farmer picked at his crooked, tobacco-stained teeth with a piece of fence wire, taking it out of his mouth every now and then and looking at it. Wesley puzzled over what the man would pay him for shelling corn all day. Twenty-five cents or even thirty? A chicken dinner with a piece of apple pie, or a warm hat or scarf thrown in? Or creamed corn and hogback along with a dime like the Stanley Steamer promised.

The farmer finally spoke, his voice high-pitched and scratchy, a sound that made swallows scatter. "Well kid, what do you want? A nickel or a doughnut?"

The words went right to Wesley's stomach. He blinked in surprise and despair, pushing his arms forward. "Look at my damn hands. They're raw!"

The farmer raised a wiry eyebrow. "That's why I'm givin' you such a nice choice. Don't know if I will now after hearin' you cuss like that. Where you from anyway?"

"Illinois."

"Where in Illinois?"

I'll tell a mad rat before I'll tell you—you devil's hinder. "I don't know."

"Oh, so you're lame-brained. Lame-brained and smart-ass like. If I knowed where you come from, I'd tell your pa, or don't you got a pa?"

"Sure I got a pa." *And he's gonna find a home for us all again. Even the little ones.*

The farmer made a sucking noise through his teeth. "He let you cuss like a heathen ever time you want?"

Wesley thought a minute. "He don't care—long as we don't say dirty words."

The farmer leered. "Dirty, eh? You talkin' about things that go down the privy? Or things you ought not know about. Things havin' to do with women?"

Wesley didn't answer. His stomach was growling, and he felt a little hollow of pain below his ribs, the size of the bowl his mother used to pour the cats' milk into every morning. It made him want to take the doughnut and eat it right away. But then maybe, if he took the nickel, he could buy a loaf of bread or some apples that would last longer. *But for a whole day's work with that slave driver at my back every minute!* He wished he knew what Cleve would do. He hoped his big brother had found a job further down the road. Maybe the farmer he worked for wasn't as rotten as this one.

"You're wastin' my time," the man said. "What'll it be? The nickel or the doughnut?"

Wesley's hand reached up to the top of his head, pressing down on an ever-present cowlick. Without thinking he said, "Can't I have both—the nickel *and* the doughnut?"

"Both?" The farmer flung his back into an arch and plopped his hands on his waist. "Well, here's a word you never learned, Skunky—piggish! Take your pick now or skedaddle!"

Desperately, Wesley took a step forward, his mind set against walking away with nothing. "How do I know you got either one if you don't show 'em to me?"

The farmer put his hand to his chest as if he had been injured. "Now you're sayin' I ain't got no honor. Well, I'll show you what honor is all about." He pointed to a rickety wagon standing about fifty yards away and stomped towards it. "I'll show you!"

As Wesley followed him, a flock of wild geese flew overhead, going south, their wings making soft, squeaking sounds as they headed towards a river beyond the fields. He remembered Cleve saying it was the Tippecanoe River right near where William Henry Harrison fought a battle with the Indians almost a hundred years ago. When they still lived at the cottage in Sheldon, their father told them how Chief Tecumseh tried to keep the land for his people, but his army was too small. Wesley had asked if the river was dark brown and Pa said, "Yeah, most are."

Wesley's eyes turned again to the farmer who reached into a brown paper sack and set a flat, stale-looking doughnut on the wagon seat. It reminded Wesley of one of the leathers on the pumps Pa took apart when they weren't working right.

"Looky here!" The farmer placed a worn nickel next to the doughnut. "And don't you try to take both, Skunky, because I'll catch you and get 'em off you if I have to pry your fists open with a pliers."

Wesley believed him. He wasn't big enough to outrun the man no matter how hard he tried. If he dared to argue, his voice would sound like a puppy when someone stepped on its tail. He wondered if any children sailing boats on the river would help him if he called but then gave up on the whole idea. Tears ran down his cheeks and his nose started to run. Looking up, he saw gloating, flaming eyes— a devil's triumph. Then anger pushed aside fear. He lunged towards the wagon seat, scooped up the nickel and the doughnut, and stuffed them into his mouth.

He had barely turned to run when the farmer tackled him and flipped him on his back. His echoing wail made Wesley's ears crack. "Give 'em back! Give 'em back!"

Fingers rougher than sandpaper pushed into Wesley's mouth. He bit down hard. The farmer screamed and pulled his hands back.

Wesley gulped down the nickel and some of the doughnut. "Here it is, you rotten tightwad," he choked, spitting out the rest of it. "You can have it!"

The farmer threw himself upon Wesley, digging his hands into his shoulders and bouncing his head off the ground. Wesley didn't care. He had the nickel where the man couldn't get it, and the doughnut was gone.

Suddenly he heard a whistle. It blew three times and pierced through the man's curses, through the starkness of the brown, stubbled fields, through the voices of the men who died at Tippecanoe. His head numb, Wesley expected to see William Henry Harrison standing over him with a fine uniform and gleaming saber, or maybe children bringing boats back to boys who lost them. Instead, through all the bouncing, he saw Cleve—hair slicked down and parted in the middle, a thin chain with a lock draped over his shoulder. He wore a grown-man's suitcoat over the top of his overalls, the sleeves hanging down past his wrists.

"Sir," Cleve addressed the farmer and blew his whistle two more times. "Sir, get away from that boy. He's a looney, and he can kill you!"

"Huh?" The farmer rolled off Wesley and stared up at Cleve. "Who in the hell are you?"

"I'm from the looney bin, Sir. This boy escaped from us. The guards are waiting down by the river. They sent me up here alone because I'm the only one who can keep him from getting riled. He can bite right through your skin into your arteries. Let you bleed to death right before his eyes."

"He was tryin' to do just that," gasped the farmer. "Bit through my hand like a saber-toothed tiger! Thank the Lord you got here. You from Indianapolis?"

"That's right, Sir. Indianapolis. I'll take him where he can't hurt anyone again."

Cleve wrapped the chain loosely around Wesley's neck and closed the lock. "Come along, my boy. You're not going to give me any trouble now, are you?"

As much as he ached all over, Wesley had to clamp his lips together to keep from smiling. *Why, Cleve looks like a bigger me— with his hair combed and a funny coat on!* Resisting the urge to giggle, he noted on his brother the same dark tuft of hair that wouldn't lie flat, the same square jaw like their father's, the same short, straight teeth, and the same mahogany-colored skin that made people ask, "Are you part-Indian or what?"

"Come on, now," Cleve spoke close to his ear. "Let's get moving."

Wesley sputtered and babbled like he thought a looney would do, waving his arms around in little spasms, and walked, half-stumbling, alongside Cleve.

"He swallered my nickel," the man called after them. "It was a liberty-head—the kind with stars on the edge. You oughta wrap that chain around him and throw away the key."

Cleve waited until they were out of hearing range before he spoke. "Damn fool don't even know his own stuff. That chain and lock musta been hangin' in his shed for years. So was this old coat."

Wesley gulped. He could feel the nickel, slightly slanted, slide down from the bottom of his throat towards his rib cage. "You swiped 'em," he half-whispered. "And the whistle? Is that Father Fatso's from the orphanage?"

Cleve shrugged. "I had a feeling it would come in handy some day. But listen, Wes, what are you gonna do about that nickel? Are you gonna try and find it? Are you gonna dig through your ... you know what?"

Wesley stared at Cleve. "Is that really where it'll go? Honest?"

"Yeah, in a day or two."

"Aw, Cleve, maybe I really am a looney. We coulda bought somethin' good with that nickel. Now we got nothin' after all that hard work."

*Cleve opened the lock and took the chain from around Wesley's neck. "Brother, you ain't worked for nothin' after all. Thanks to you, we're gonna have a feast tonight—chicken and potatoes and squash. Lots more too." He reached into his hip-pants pocket. "Here, have an apple. Don't gobble it, now. Your stomach's pretty empty."

Wesley spat twice and bit into the apple, letting the juice gush into his mouth and flow down his throat, washing away the feel of the farmer's fingers and the taste of the stale doughnut. It seemed the nickel was trying to stand up on its side but fell flat, scraping its way downward, causing him to envision the outline of stars on the top of Lady Liberty's torch. He took another bite and swallowed hard. "God Almighty, Cleve, where'd you get all that stuff? Where's the rest of it?"

Cleve draped the chain around Wesley's waist and led him off the road towards the railroad line. "In a hole down by the tracks, covered with a big rock. Wes, I stopped at a dozen farms today, and they didn't have no work or nothin' to pay me with, so I came back here. I could tell from the way that ol' skinflint watched every move you made, he wouldn't treat you right. While his eyes were glued on you, I grabbed a couple of his chickens pecking around by the road and some garden stuff from his root cellar. Then I stashed 'em and came back for you."

Cleve nodded at the chain around Wesley's waist. "Not bad, eh? Nice way to keep you with me when we're runnin' from the railroad dicks."

Wesley grinned. He liked the feel of Cleve's hand pushing gently against the small of his back and the little jingling sound as he walked. Inside him, the nickel budged grudgingly and, caught in the flowing river of juice and apple bits, descended into the depths of his stomach, disappearing from his senses forever.

CHAPTER FOUR

The Big Dinner

July 8, 1907

Wesley walked through the roundhouse at Springfield looking for his father. *Why isn't he here? He always stays at the roundhouse between train times—in case we need him.*

Through the steam and smoke, Wesley spied Bert, the foreman, and worked his way over to him. He made sure to sidestep Leo, the millwright, and his cronies. They'd labeled Pa a fool for trying to find Benny and Willard—two more mouths to feed. If they saw Wesley, they'd heckle him, calling him one of the little nooses around Pa's neck. Bert was nice and never bothered him. He sat on a high stool, his hands busy pulling levers as he switched engines on the huge turntable.

Wesley waited until the big locomotives moved out, and things quieted down enough to talk to him. "Mr. Bert," he said, reaching up as high as he could and tapping the foreman on the leg.

Bert looked down and smiled. "Hello, Little Feller. Long time no see."

Wesley stretched his neck and raised his voice. "You seen my pa?"

"He's not here right now." Bert took off his striped railroad hat and scratched his graying head. "Funny he didn't say anything about you coming over."

"He didn't know. Did his shift get changed?"

"No, he just left for a little while. I think you'll find him over by the governor's mansion."

Wesley frowned. "Governor's mansion? I can't go over there."

"Sure you can. Just follow the street out here to Old State Road. You'll see the big house right away and two buildings in the back— men's housing on the right, women's on the left. Your pa should be sitting on a bench in front of the left one right about this time. You'll find him alright, won't you?"

Wesley blinked. "I think so. I'm almost eight years old now. But what's he doing over there, Bert?"

Bert stepped down from his stool. He seemed as big as the picture of the giant in "Jack and the Beanstalk" and smelled like Wesley's favorite train engine, number 59, running to New Orleans. Bert placed his hands on Wesley's shoulders. "Son, it's an old story."

Without warning, a wave of harsh laughter flooded over them. It came from Leo and two other workers.

"Yeah," Leo sneered. "An old, old story, that's for sure." He bent his back and hobbled around in a circle like a hundred-year-old man. His sidekicks hooted with laughter.

"You hooligans shut up and get back to work!" Bert shouted. "Now listen, Little Feller, you just follow that path behind the fence going around the mansion, and you'll see those two buildings. There's like a little park with benches. You'll find your pa, don't you worry."

Wesley didn't worry as he walked along the avenue with all the buggies and horseless carriages whizzing by him. But when he saw the governor's huge mansion, he expected a guard to run him off any minute. Relieved when he found the trail Bert mentioned, he followed it with no trouble to the buildings behind the mansion.

Sitting on one of the benches, dressed in a black suit, a boiled shirt with cuff links dazzling at his wrists and shoes that glowed with spit shine, was his father—not eating, not writing something down in a little book, not even reading.

Wesley thought, at first, that Pa must be praying. But soon he knew he was listening to the silence around him, to horses hooves clomping, to birds singing, and maybe even to new spring leaves growing. Like trees standing firmly in the ground, he held his body as if there were no question why he was there. In his hands, he clutched a bouquet of purple flowers.

The big door at the back of the building squeaked open, and a woman in a long, black dress walked out on the lawn. She looked as old to Wesley as Grama St. John and shorter than Hazel. She moved carefully, as if afraid any quick movement would knock her off balance. Pa rose to greet her, holding out the bouquet. The woman smiled, took the flowers in one hand and Pa's arm in the other. Together they walked out onto the lane.

As Wesley followed, he wondered if Pa had ever extended his arm to his mother like that, his hand resting on his waist in such a fancy way. For a moment, he questioned if this man walking along as though time were no problem could be his father. Soon, the couple came to a building marked with a sign, "Finest of Foods," and went inside. Wesley walked over to where the carriages were parked, looked in the big front window, and saw his father pull back a chair for the woman. A man in a white jacket and black pants brought a vase for the flowers and placed them in the middle of the table.

Did Pa ever take Mama to a place like this? Who is this lady who looks like the smallest breeze could whirl her away like tiny bits of old newspaper? Was Pa, like Benny and Willard, adopted out when he was little, and now here he sits, back with his real mother?

As the waiter set two tall glasses on the table and poured dark, red liquid into them, Wesley remembered the only time in his life he had ever tasted grape juice. It was at his cousin Toussant's wedding. Now, he felt the sides of his mouth pull in and his lips pucker as the man and woman in front of him raised their glasses and took a sip.

Out on the street, a horse, frightened by a back-firing engine, let out a piercing shriek. His father turned towards the window, his eyes meeting Wesley's head-on. Wesley started to run, to lose himself in the traffic, but Pa was already out the door.

"Wesley! Wesley!" He reached him in three strides, picked him up, and clasped him in his arms. "How can I explain this to you? Your mother—when I first saw her—I couldn't wait to marry her. Each time she had one of you kids, she looked prettier than ever. She found things to laugh at when nobody else could. Always knew what I was going to say before I said it."

Wesley looked down and saw the two of them silhouetted in a large, mud puddle, Pa's broad back rippling in the murky water. The top of his own head looked like a bump on his father's shoulder, and the toes of his boots peeked out around Pa's hips like toadstools on a tree trunk.

"Wesley," Pa repeated. "I put you boys in that orphanage because I wanted to keep you together. Now two of you are lost, I'm away from you and Cleve most of the time, and the girls are with people who only put up with them." He shuddered and gave Wesley a shake. "But now, by God, I'm going to fix it!"

Wesley looked towards the restaurant where the woman in black sat alone, as if on a ship staring out to sea. His father nodded in her direction. "Her name's Kate. I borrowed money so I can court her. She's gonna help me buy a farm. It probably won't be until next spring, but that's not too far away. We'll pick up the girls, and then we'll get Benny and Willard back. You and Cleve can work the farm and Kate'll cook for us. Think of it, Wessie! All together again."

Wesley counted to himself. When Bennie and Willard were born, each time Pa said, "Wessie, you got a new, baby brother," and when Mama had Lilly, he said, "Wessie, it's a little girl." Now, when they were getting their own cook, he called him Wessie again. That made four times altogether.

"Do you know where they are yet, Pa? Benny and Willard?"

His father relaxed his hold on him and looked him in the eyes. "Your Uncle Napoleon and I checked into what the orphanage gardener wrote down for me. Benny might be just a state or two away. Every trace we find of him still has the name Tooper with it. If a child's last name isn't changed, he's a lot easier to locate. We're getting close, Wesley. We're getting close."

Wesley thought about the word "locate." It sounded like one a policeman would use or someone in a courthouse. He drew his father's face up with his hands. "And Willard, Pa? Will we locate him too?"

Pa took a deep breath. "Willard is going to take a little longer. He might have a different name now—just his last name, we hope. But I'm never gonna give up, Wesley, I promise."

Wesley leaned forward in Pa's arms and patted him on the back. He tried to think how the name Willard would sound with Jones or Zimmerman or Roosevelt. Even Washington.

Pa craned his neck and looked down the avenue. "Where in the hell's Cleve?"

Wesley continued patting as he answered his father's questions. "He went with some older fellers to Ohio. Those Wright Brothers are tryin' out their flying machine again, somewhere near their hometown. Cleve says they'll go higher and stay up longer than they did in that Kitty Hawk place."

"Huffman Prairie," Pa grunted, "near Dayton." His arms around Wesley stiffened. "He should've told me. He shouldn't go anywhere without you, damn it!"

"I told him to go, Pa. He's always watchin' out for me instead of doing things he likes. I wanted to make things even between us. See?"

As Wesley kept patting, his father's arms relaxed. "That Cleve. He'd rather watch an engine run than breathe. But do they know the right switches—the right cars to look for—the right train bosses if there's trouble"

"Yeah. Cleve knows it all, Pa."

"And you two boys would rather go on like you are than in a home with someone else, even if it's relatives?"

"Yeah, Pa. We would."

His father set him down and tousled his hair. "I'm going to have dinner with Miss Kate now, but I want you to come back in an hour. I'll have the waiter set you up with your own meal. Then I want you to go back to the roundhouse and look for the Memphis train. Wait for me by car 26. I'm gonna sneak you in and take you with me tonight."

Wesley felt himself smile so hard, the corners of his mouth hurt. "Oh boy, Pa! Can I have grape juice with my dinner too?"

"If they have it, you bet you can. Now listen. Down that street, about a half a mile, you'll see President Lincoln's house. Here's a nickel. Hand that over and they'll take you through with a bunch of other folks and show you everything. Then come back here and get your dinner."

"How will I know when the hour's up?"

Pa reached into his pocket. "Here, take my watch."

"But you need it for your job."

Miss Kate has one and there's clocks everywhere at the round-house. Take good care of it."

As Wesley walked out towards the street, both hands holding onto the watch, his father called to him.

"This woman wants to take care of you kids because you're mine. She'll go anywhere and do anything just to be with me, no matter how bad things get. It's hard to find someone like that, no matter how long you look."

CHAPTER FIVE

Moving In

March 22, 1908

The farm Pa bought was in the Kankakee River Valley, or, as the French Canadians called it, "Petite Canada." As he drove his wagon towards their new home, he told Wesley and Hazel how, seventy years ago, hopeful families followed a man named Noel LeVasser over half a continent to settle there.

"Hell, back in Quebec, the wheat midge and potato blight ruined all their crops. But here, the land was rich and full of timber, with open places for raising grain and streams full of fish."

He explained how some families thrived on their homesteads, and some barely made it. Others, like his own people, were lured to the railroad, by its steady income and strides made for workers.

"It's like coming home," he said, when they drove up to the two-story house with cracks in the boards and peeling paint. "We got another chance."

When Wesley first saw the fields surrounding the house, he thought they were as big as an ocean. Some were covered with stubbles of oats, alfalfa, and wheat plants, others with yellow-white corn stalks. The pasture lay off in a clearing near the woods. The next morning, he and Hazel helped Pa herd ten black and white milk cows through its gate. Some of them balked and tried to turn around, but Pa whacked them with a stick and told Wesley and Hazel to make a ruckus. Finally they got them all in.

Now the cows wandered peacefully, munching on piles of hay Pa put out for them or lying under the oaks chewing their cuds. Wesley loved the pasture, especially the trees, even though they didn't have leaves on them yet. They were bigger than those in the woods, and their branches curved upward gradually, so there was room to sit or hang a swing. He wanted to see how many he could climb, but Pa said he and Hazel should sweep up the house and look after Lilly while he went to town to marry the lady from Springfield. After that, he would bring her out to the farm along with the furniture he had stored in a boxcar.

Hazel was in the front room downstairs trying to clean. "We don't need a broom, we need a shovel," she said, picking up pieces of debris off the floor.

"Did Pa tell you he's going to teach us to milk tonight?" Wesley asked. "He says the cows at Sheldon were beef cows. That's why we never milked 'em."

Hazel sneered. "Well, he don't have to teach me. At Aunt Iris's I milked six of 'em every morning and night. My back was killin' me."

"When Cleve gets here, you won't have to do it anymore. Us boys'll handle it."

"He's been gone so long, I don't think he'll ever get here. Maybe he's not in Ohio anymore. Maybe he never even got there."

"Don't worry, Hazel, he'll come back. Then you can just help in the kitchen."

"If the great cook who's going to be our mother will let me."

"Pa says she's not gonna try to be our mother. She's just gonna raise us." Wesley looked at Hazel. She seemed bigger than he remembered—taller and wider. Her face was soft and pretty, but she had a way of walking that reminded him of the cleaning women at the orphanage.

Lilly called from her crib in Pa's room. "Want out, pease. Want out."

Wesley ran to where she stood in the crib Pa made the day before with boards and young maple trunks. "Here Lilly, I'll take you."

"Essie! Essie," she cried clapping her hands.

"No Lilly, say Wesley—WWWesley." He remembered how his mother taught him to say his name, and then he started teaching Benny the same way. Lilly was just a tiny baby when he had last seen her, getting her diapers changed and nuzzling against Mama's breast. Now she ran around and chattered like a magpie, even if she couldn't talk as good as the rest had at that age. Pa said Aunt Agnes hadn't spent as much time with her as Mama would have.

Hazel called from the front room. "Wesley, help me get this pile of stuff out of the doorway. Here comes Pa with that woman!"

Wesley held a piece of cardboard while Hazel swept the trash into it. He got it out the back door when Pa's new wife came walking up the front step. She looked like she did when he saw her in Springfield except for a long, heavy coat and a wide-brimmed hat, both black like the rest of her clothes. In her hands she carried a little, white cake with a smaller cake on top, and on that, a smaller one yet. When she reached the door, she didn't put the cake down and knock or hold the cake in one hand and try to turn the handle with the other. She just stood there.

"If she ain't got sense to knock," Hazel whispered, "she deserves to stand outside all day. Don't let her in."

Wesley couldn't bear the waiting. "Her hands are full," he told his sister and opened the door. He had expected a high-pitched, faint voice to come from such a thin, frail-looking person. Instead, he heard a sharp, grating sound shoot from her lips, as if she were trying to push her voice through but didn't have enough room, so parts of it slipped by quickly while others straggled along.

"Your pa's getting things out of the wagon," she crackled, looking around for a place to put the cake. The room had no furniture except for a piece of tree trunk Pa used for a stool. As she set the cake down on it, Wesley hoped it might make the room seem friendlier and brighter, but the cake with its plaster-white frosting and candy flowers made the chipped paint and cracked walls stand out more than they did before.

"I remember you from the eatin' place in Springfield," she said to Wesley.

Wesley nodded and pointed to Hazel. "That's the oldest girl."

The woman walked past them into the kitchen which held only a large, black stove. She opened the door and looked inside where a fire had burned down to red-hot coals. She turned to Hazel. "You know how to work in a kitchen?"

Hazel, sweeping vigorously, answered, "Enough to manage one myself."

The woman said nothing. Lilly ran up to her and pulled at her skirts. "You my mudder?"

The woman's voice spun out like a firecracker going off. "Who told her that?"

"Not me," said Hazel, sweeping harder than ever.

"Not me," said Wesley, keeping himself intent on gazing out the front window. He started to say he was going outside to give Pa a hand with the furniture but stopped before the words formed on his tongue. He wondered what was going on out there. He saw Pa run around the wagon picking up papers, darting off to retrieve those the wind caught, jumping up on the wagon, rummaging through things, pushing boxes and bags, reaching out for a runaway page, and shouting up at the sky. Wesley could hardly keep his eyes on him, his father moved so fast with so many sudden stops and starts. In a few minutes, he was at the door frantically kicking it. "Open up. For Christ's sake, open up!"

Wesley pulled at the door. Pa held the papers he had retrieved to his chest, some hanging over his arms, some climbing upward toward his throat. He let go, and they fluttered to the floor. He grabbed Wesley by the shoulders and brought him down on his knees in the middle of the pile.

"Look here! Tell me where these came from. Did Cleve steal 'em?"

Wesley didn't have to look. "They're my papers," he said.

"Don't cover up for him, Wes. They came from Cleve's satchel. It spilled over in the wagon." He let go of Wesley, clenched his fists, and flung his head back. "My God! I knew his stealing would come to something too big to handle!"

Wesley tried to explain that his own satchel was too full to carry all his papers from the orphanage, so he put some in Cleve's, but Pa wouldn't stop talking.

"Look here, Kate. Figures. Bookwork. How much they put out for the kids' food. How much they put out for the big shots. Just look at this! Kids' names with numbers after 'em with dollar signs." He fumbled through more pages. "Holy Christ. Look how much they got for my boys!"

Wesley kept tapping Pa on the back and calling his name, but his father raved on as if no one else were in the room.

"If only we could have found out some other way. But stolen papers? Stolen records? They'll have me arrested for illegal … illegal something or other, damn it. They almost had me thrown in the hoosegow as it is, and here it was them that stole my little boys. Those bastards! Those devils! Law can't touch 'em. I knew the truth all along. Now here's proof. But they'll turn it against me! They'll put me in jail. Cleve too. Then who'll take care of my family?"

Lilly started to cry, and Hazel and the woman in black got on their hands and knees gathering papers together and trying to smooth them out.

Suddenly Wesley let out a howl that made everyone's eyes pop open. He shouted so loud it hurt his throat. "Those are my papers! I copied them in Father Fatso's office when he locked me in there. Those are mine. Mine!"

Everyone else in the room sucked in their breaths.

Dumbstruck, Pa turned to his new wife. "But look at the writing, Kate. It's a bookkeeper's hand. Wesley couldn't have done that. He could hardly read or write then."

The lady in black shook her head back and forth. "I don't know, Mr. Tooper. I just don't know."

Wesley ran to a corner of the room and brought back a yellow tablet. "Look! Here's what I copied yesterday from your book about chickens, Pa. There's words there, but figures too—how much the chickens cost to raise, how much to feed 'em, how much you can get for the eggs, how much for the meat. It's the same writin' that's on the papers you found in Cleve's satchel. See?"

Pa took the paper and read it, his lips moving as he went over each line.

Wesley rummaged through the papers on the floor. "I didn't just copy those things you found, Pa! I copied anything I saw. Sometimes newspapers lying around the orphanage. Look, here's one I did. I musta copied the date, not knowing what it was."

Pa's eyes glistened. "How long did he lock you in that room, Wes?"

Wesley shrugged. "Sometimes just while the others ate. Sometimes longer. Once I fell asleep in the dark and woke up in the daylight."

Pa took the papers over to Hazel. "See how's he got your mother's hand."

Hazel nodded and tried to blink back tears. Lilly came and wrapped her arms around Pa's legs. The lady in black took a few steps back and bowed her head. After a while, Pa walked over to her.

"This really changes things, Kate. They can't arrest Wesley. He was just a little tyke then, and really didn't steal anything. Maybe this is better than gettin' the real records." He turned to Wesley. "Did the priest always keep that room locked?"

"Yes, Pa."

"No one could ever get in it unless he unlocked it himself?"

"No, Pa."

"And everyone knew he always locked it? Did the other kids know you copied things a lot?"

"Yes. Yes."

Pa started to pace the floor. "This is good—real good, but I've got so much to do. I need to find a lawyer right away. Damn. The wagon's full of furniture. It'll take forever to unload. Oh God, what time is it? I've got to get back on the trains tomorrow."

The lady in black walked up to Pa, and standing on tiptoes, reached as high as she could and picked a tiny piece of lint off the shoulder of the suit he had worn to bury his children's mother and to marry her.

"Mr. Tooper," she said, her voice not cracking at all. "It's Sunday. There'll be time enough when you get back from the trains. Plenty of time."

Pa took hold of her elbow and turned her around so they both faced the children. "Remember what I told you this morning, Katheryn Blelier Tooper? My name is Edward. Call me Edward, eh?"

The lady took a deep breath and cleared her throat. "Edward," she said, pointing a narrow finger in Wesley's direction. "If this boy with the fine writin' can get some wood on the fire and help you bring in a table, that oldest girl and I might be able to get some food on it. It never hurts to eat, now, does it?"

CHAPTER SIX

Benny's Book

May 30, 1908

"Pa! Wes! Paaah! Wehhhss!"

Wesley was dreaming. He dreamed Cleve had finally come back from Ohio, not knowing Pa married that Kate woman and bought the farm near Bonfield. He had searched for Wesley in the hobo camps, in all their hiding places along the tracks, through field after field, calling his name and looking for Pa in every train that went by.

Now he even called the girls too. "Pa! Wes! Hazel, Lilly!"

"Pa! Wes! Ma Tooper!"

Wesley sat straight up in bed. Ma Tooper. Who was Ma Tooper? Even though he was not asleep anymore, he still heard the voice. It sounded just like Cleve did in his dream, and it was coming close to the house. He pushed himself out of bed and came half-sliding, half-jumping down the stairs. Hazel and Lilly stood in their nightgowns, holding onto each other and looking around the kitchen. Then suddenly the back door opened and in trudged Cleve, wet to his knees, pieces of grass and twigs on his clothes, a dirty bundle over his shoulder.

"Where's Pa? For Christ sake, where's Pa?"

"He's on his way from the trains," Hazel said. "You think you can go away forever and expect everyone to be here when you get back?"

"Then where's Ma Tooper? Where the hell's Ma Tooper?"

So that's what we can call her, Wesley thought. The girls pointed to a closed bedroom door off the hallway. Pa didn't like them calling their stepmother Kate or "that woman" but didn't expect them to call her "mother" except for Lilly who never knew her real one.

The tiny lady with the new name opened the door. Hazel and Lilly jumped in front of her as if to keep Cleve's voice from blowing her over. As always, she dressed in black, this time in a sleeping bonnet and a nightgown with lace around the bottom, reminding Wesley of pictures he had seen of Hetty Green, the richest and meanest woman in America. The newspapers said Hetty never ate anything but dry oatmeal because it gave her strength to fight off the Wall Street wolves, and she looked and smelled so bad because she couldn't bear to spend money on soap. Ma Tooper, Wesley knew, kept herself clean, and even though her oatmeal tasted like soft paste, she always cooked it. Still, he had been waiting for Cleve to come home so they could giggle and whisper to each other, "Here comes Hetty Green," when she walked into a room.

And now, their own Hetty Green didn't waste any words. "You just wait 'til your pa gets home," she croaked at Cleve. "Running off and leaving us without sending word with planting about to start."

"Well, you just wait 'til you see this," Cleve said, laying down his bundle on the table and pulling out a faded, blue book. It was so worn and water-marked, all Wesley could see of the title was *A   oy's   cean Ad   ture.* Some of the letters had faded.

"What the hell's so great about that?" Hazel snorted.

"What da hell?" Lilly echoed.

"Don't you girls ever say that word outside this house," Ma Tooper shrieked.

"Wes, you should know," Cleve almost pleaded. "Don't you remember—*A Boy's Ocean Adventure?* It's the book we brought with us to the orphanage. The one I used to read to the little fellers. What I couldn't read, you and me made up. Benny loved it so much, I printed his name inside the cover. See here? It says 'Benny Tooper.'"

Awestruck, Wesley blurted out, "Where the hell …?"

"Where da hell?" repeated Lilly.

Cleve sat down at the table and ran his fingers through his hair. "Boy, I'm just lucky I got here in one piece."

"What happened?" Wesley demanded. "Did you fall out of the Wright brothers' air machine?"

"Talk sense, will ya, Wes. Those fellers that said they wanted to go to Huffman Prairie jumped me in a boxcar our first night out. They didn't give a hoot about seeing the Wrights fly. They wanted my money and the new shoes I bought after we planted tobacco in Owensboro. I made up my mind right then and there I wasn't gonna let 'em have it."

"What did you do?"

"I lammed two of 'em with a crow bar I had under my coat and pushed the devils off the train. The other one got scared and jumped off."

Wesley, Hazel, and Lilly cheered and clapped their hands like at a boxing match.

Ma Tooper squinted her eyes. "Did one of them have this book?"

"No, not them," Cleve said.

"Then why you telling us about 'em?"

"Because if I didn't go to Huffman Prairie by myself, I never would of run into this girl. If I'd been with those other fellers, her Pa never would've picked me up in their wagon. Those hooligans looked even rougher than me. So I'm walkin' along, and her father pulls up and says, 'Our boys are going up again, young man. Care to come along?'"

"What's the girl's name?" Hazel asked.

"What her name?" Lilly echoed.

"Francis. Francis Stanz."

"Tell us what she's got to do with all this." Wesley insisted. "What about the book?"

"It's all connected. This family lays out a picnic lunch right there on the grass and tells me to help myself to whatever I want. Then their neighbor, Wilbur Wright, comes over, grabs a piece of chicken, eats it, wipes his hands on a towel, and climbs into the flying machine. God, when I saw that metal bounce along the ground and slide up in the air with that thing called gravity trying to push it down, I knew nothin' would be the same for me again as long as I lived."

Cleve glanced at the kitchen stove, the long-handle pump by the sink, and the big oak table. He stared at Lilly and Hazel as if he'd never seen them before.

"This girl, Francis, sat right next to me watching the flying machine, and after Wilbur and Orville brought it down, I told her about Benny and Willard. I told her how we were lookin' for 'em and how we spelled our name like Cooper but with a 't' in front of it instead of a 'c'. She told me she was going to spend the winter with her grama in Pennsylvania and help her with the housework and babysit for some of the neighbor kids. Then she wished me luck and got in the wagon with her folks and they drove away."

"Why didn't you get on a train and come home right then?" Ma Tooper demanded.

"I was gonna, but I thought I'd stay a little while longer and ask the Wrights about the flying machine and how the parts worked. While I'm doin' that, this fella named Toby walks up and asks if I could come to his bicycle shop and work on auto engines with him."

"You shoulda wrote."

Cleve opened his bundle, took out four twenty-dollar bills, and laid them on the table. "Here's what I earned when I worked there. That and lots of good food and a place to sleep in Toby's shed with a stove to fire up when it got cold."

Wesley and his sisters sucked in their breaths. Ma Tooper walked over and picked up the bills, rubbing them between her fingers like she couldn't believe they were real. Cleve winked at Wesley and held one hand up with two fingers crossed.

Wesley put his arm on Cleve's shoulder and shook it. "The book! How did you get the book?"

"I'm gettin' to that. A few days ago, I told Toby I had to get back to Illinois or my Pa would skin me alive. He told me where I could jump a train, but when I got there, every one either went too fast or had lookouts. Finally, after more than an hour, I see one coming at just the right speed. I'm gettin' my stuff together, and here comes Francis runnin' like crazy towards me. I hadn't seen her in weeks."

"How in the world did she find you?" Hazel asked

"Toby told her. Here my train's coming, and the whistle's blowing and she takes this book out from under her sweater and shoves it at me. She says she found it in the house next to her grama's in Greensburg, Pennsylvania. Right after I jump on the train, she hollers, 'There's names inside!'"

Wesley, Hazel, and Ma Tooper stared at the floor and said nothing. Lilly came to the table and climbed on Cleve's lap. He reached his hand to her face and smoothed a wisp of dark curl back from her forehead.

"I sat up there on the freight car wanting to thank her," he continued, "but could only wave my hand as hard as I could until she turned into a tiny speck standing there in Ohio. I couldn't jump off and ask her all the questions I had because I had to get back as fast as I could and show all of you this book."

Laying his cheek on Lilly's head, Cleve sniffled back oncoming tears. "Here I was so damn mad … mad I couldn't catch a train right away. If I had, she never would've found me. We never would've known."

Lilly, Hazel, and Ma Tooper started to cry. Wesley wondered if Ma Tooper cried because here she was taking care of three kids, and in comes another one, Cleve, making four. And that fourth kid has news about another one that would make five. And, later, if they found Willard, that would be six kids for her to raise that didn't even belong to her.

"Praise the Lord," Ma Tooper rejoiced. "Praise the Lord!" And then Wesley felt bad for thinking what he did and cried right along with Hazel and Lilly.

Cleve raised his hand for them to be quiet. "Listen, everybody. Pa could write to the addresses in this book Francis found near her grama's house in Pennsylvania. Some of the neighbors might remember Benny. Maybe they can tell us things or give Pa other addresses. It might take a long time, but we've got something to go on. We've got to take patience. Do ya hear me? We got to take patience."

"Take patience," the rest of them murmured, even Ma Tooper. No one said he should have said, "have patience," because they knew that was just the way Cleve talked. Then they all got busy hauling water for his bath and firing up the stove so Hazel and Ma Tooper could fix him something to eat. Their new stepmother didn't talk any further about what would happen when their pa got home but kept eyeing the door with an anxious look. After Cleve had enough to eat, Wesley took him upstairs to their room.

"This is all ours?" Cleve asked, looking around as if in a cathedral. "The whole damn thing?"

Wesley giggled and pulled back the covers. "Get in, Cleve. You can have more than half the bed tonight, since you just got home."

Cleve crawled in and sighed with satisfaction. "I don't think I've ever laid on a bed with this much room before. Almost as good as seein' the Wright brothers fly." He let his head settle back into the pillow and sniffed the air. "What's that nice smell, Wes? It's like after a quiet rain."

"It's these sheet things we're sleeping between," Wesley answered, glad to know something Cleve didn't. "Hazel and Ma Tooper wash 'em every Saturday and hang 'em out on the line to dry." He raised himself up on one elbow and looked at his brother. "Cleve, how did you know Pa got married? How did you find us?"

"It was the talk of the tracks west of Toledo—how Pa got hitched up with this old woman who bought him a farm outside Bonfield. The telegrapher in town here told me where to find the house. 'How's old Ma Tooper doing?' he asks me. 'Fine,' I says, 'just fine.'"

They snuggled down into the mattress and listened to the breeze rustling through the elm tree outside their window, its branches scraping gently against the house.

After a while, Wesley said, "Cleve, what you gonna do when Pa gets home? Maybe the book and the money will make up for all the work you missed here, but you should've sent word."

"You know I hate to write. Words or figures."

"When we do something bad now, he makes us go out and bring in a stick for our own licking. Even if you get a little one, it can still hurt."

"Hell, if he does that to me, I'll bring in the whole damn tree."

"I tried that. It didn't work."

Cleve folded his arms behind his head and stretched out his legs. "Then I don't give a damn. I'm just glad to be here in a real house. What's Ma Tooper like, Wes?"

Wesley wondered if he should warn Cleve about Ma Tooper's cooking, since Hazel made most of Cleve's meal that night. Except for desserts, things she cooked that should be tender turned out hard and tough, and things that should be chewy or crispy turned out mushy and soft. Maybe she had been a cook who just made things like oatmeal cookies, cherry pie, and chocolate cake for the governor—nothing else.

"She's not as old as she looks," he said, "maybe ten years more than Pa at the most."

"I didn't ask how old she is," Cleve said, nudging him with his elbow. "I asked how she is, awful or what?"

Wesley opened his mouth to answer when they heard noises downstairs—Ma Tooper's voice, high and wavery, and Pa's, like rumbling thunder. Then they heard his footsteps crashing up the stairs.

"Cleve! Cleveland Grover Tooper!"

He opened the door and stood over them. Cleve and Wesley closed their eyes and tried to breathe as if they were sleeping. Pa made a moaning sound and fell down on the bed, his head between their backs, his arms draped around their shoulders. "My God, Cleve. My God!"

As the creaking house settled for the night, the breeze became still, and Wesley wondered if Cleve was asleep or still pretending. Daring to open his eyes, he saw the clothes he wore the day before all hanging in a small bundle by a hook on the wall. As time went on, he could make out the sleeve of his shirt, the glow of a button, the cuff of an overall leg. Gradually he recognized hints of color and readied himself for the crow of Ma Tooper's rooster, bursting through the dawn like an insistent question: "What ya doin' therrre? What ya doin' therre?"

Bed springs squeaked as Pa got up from the bed, casting a giant, gray shadow on the wall. Taking a few steps toward Cleve, Pa reached down where his older son lay. Wesley heard a crinkling sound from the other side of the bed and knew Pa took something out of his pocket and slipped it under his brother's pillow. It was the eighty dollars Cleve earned in Ohio.

Then he heard the footfall of Pa's boots on the floorboards as he walked out and closed the door.

CHAPTER SEVEN

High Hopes

July 7, 1909

Whenever he had a spare minute, Pa wrote to the names Ida Stanz had jotted down in the flyleaf of *A Boy's Ocean Adventure*. Mrs. Stanz wrote to Pa saying she remembered the family who had lived in the house where her granddaughter, Francis, found the book. It was Burnside. They had five or six children but she knew only the name of the younger one, Ella. She said the family had planned to move to Pottsville or Shenandoah where the father would look for work in the mines. If he didn't find work there, they would go to New York, but Mrs. Stanz didn't know where.

"Why would they want Benny if they already had all those other kids?" Wesley asked. "You wouldn't want to take in someone else when you already had us, would you, Pa?"

"I can't even find some of my own," Pa half-chuckled. But Wesley could tell by his father's next words that he didn't think it was funny. "If the Burnside family didn't have much money, they might put Benny down in the mines. He could become one of those Breaker Boys working ten hours a day pulling slate and rocks from rivers of anthracite."

The next week Wesley heard Pa talking to Uncle Napoleon over their weekly game of checkers. "I'll break that damn Burnside's neck if he did that to my boy. Those little Breaker Boys get all choked up with dust, and their backs get more curved and deformed as each day goes by."

The two railroad men bent over the checkerboard, their features rough cut, granite-like, eyes darker than ebony. Pa's were fitting to a brakeman's occupation—sharp, directed, as if fixed on couplings, cogs, and gears, towards throwing switches, and setting flares. Napoleon, the conductor, had a softer appearance, his eyes always scanning, as though he were keeping track of cars, checking on luggage, or making passengers comfortable.

"But Ed," he cautioned as he gently slid a red checker forward. "We don't know for sure if Benny is in Pennsylvania. The lady wrote you that the Burnsides might go to New York."

Pa jumped one of Napoleon's men, bringing his hand up sharply and slamming it down, scaring the cats out from under the table. "And how in the hell would I go about looking for him there?"

Napoleon pushed his chair away from the table and started filling his pipe. "There's a place in New York City called The Newsboys' Lodging House. It gives orphan boys bed, board, and hymn-singing for a dime a night. Teddy Roosevelt's father started it before the Civil War."

"Ol' Teddy's family, eh? Well, I guess it can't be half bad."

"That's right, not half bad. Horatio Alger boarded there with the newsboys from 1864 to 1894. Completely sold on the place."

Pa crashed his checker down harder than the one before and banged another one on top, making it a king. "I don't know why you get so wound up over that damn Alger. He's just a big phony."

"He's no phony. He graduated from Harvard Divinity School."

"Yeah, and when he was a preacher in Massachusetts, he monkeyed around with a young boy there. In a bad way, Napoleon, a bad way."

"Rumors, Ed. Ugly rumors."

Pa knocked the ashes from his pipe. "Makes you wonder don't it? Why would he board with all those young newsboys for thirty years?"

"Maybe because he wanted to help them stay on the straight and narrow and advise them about their futures. Please, Ed, let me get in touch with the newsboys' house. What can it hurt?"

"I won't stop you. But, why would he be there? Those newsboys are on their own. Benny would be with the Burnsides, especially if they wanted him to earn money for them."

But by the time Pa got the names of the Pennsylvania mining companies and sent letters to them, Uncle Napoleon had already received a letter from the newsboys' home. They had a boy there named Benny Tooper, a boy eager to come back to his family.

Pa was paralyzed with amazement. He had never been visited by such a miracle before. He sat frozen while his children jumped up and down hugging each other, hooting and hollering, racing around to find things to save for their brother's homecoming. Then he went down to the cellar and stayed up all night building a bed for the son he hadn't seen in years.

The next day Cleve and Wesley helped him carry the bed up to their room. Ma put a quilt on it that her mother had made for her years ago, and neighbors on both sides of their road brought hand-me-down clothes and toys for Benny.

Everyone agreed that Uncle Napoleon should go to New York and pick up Benny since he was the one who found him. Napoleon, a railroad man, could ride to New York for free in the caboose. Pa, Uncles Clifford and Joe, and some of the grown cousins chipped in for tickets back to Bonfield, including Pullman berths and dining-car meals. They wanted Napoleon to bring Benny back in style.

• • •

When Uncle Napoleon got off the train in New York, he took a horse-drawn jitney to the Newsboys' Lodging House. As he stepped down onto the street, a boy rushed up to sell him a paper. He told himself he wouldn't have time to read it and didn't want to carry it around with him. But when he looked into the newsboy's friendly, expectant face, he couldn't resist buying one. "I don't know why I'm doing this," he said, handing over the money. "I'll only be here long enough to pick up one of your boys and take him back with me."

The newsboy's face brightened like a newly-cleaned railroad lantern and asked, "Would that boy's name be Benny?"

"Yes."

The boy put down his papers, saluted, and clicked his heels together. "I'm Benny, Sir, at your service."

Amazed, Uncle Napoleon exclaimed, "Benny Tooper?"

The boy grinned and said, "That's me."

Together they walked into the lodge. Benny had no valise to put his things in, so they stuffed them into a laundry bag the housekeeper gave them. Benny talked constantly in a New York accent as though he'd been speaking it all his life. A true Tooper, Uncle Napoleon told himself, able to fit in anywhere.

Napoleon was perplexed at Benny's milky-white complexion and short, turned-up nose like a ski jump, not like a French Canadian's, looking as though it were heading straight downhill. Then he remembered that Clara St. John, Edward's first wife, had some English blood in her as well as French. This boy could have been the only Tooper child to inherit features belonging to British offspring and, because of this, turn out different than his brothers and sisters. Napoleon also hadn't expected the boy to be so tall, much more than Cleve and Wesley who were older than Benny. Then again, he told himself as he walked to the office to sign the boy out, a far-back ancestor's traits could show up anytime during a family's lifetime.

About an hour later, a telegram came to the Bonfield train station from New York: "Boy not ours Stop. Name Benny Cooper not Tooper Stop. Napoleon."

Everyone at the Tooper farm fell into despair, except Cleve. "Hell," he grumbled to Wesley, "why didn't he just bring him home and not say anything? Everyone would've been so glad to have him, they wouldn't have wondered if he was ours or not, and you and me wouldn't have to do so much work on this farm by ourselves."

"But what would happen then if we find the real Benny?" Wesley asked.

"I don't think we'll have to worry about that."

When Pa heard the news, he walked back and forth across the kitchen with his hands to his face. "You can get the two names mixed up when you say them," he kept repeating, "but we had them in writing. Napoleon wrote to them, spelled out the name, and they wrote back and spelled it out. How could this happen?"

Ma Tooper scurried into the front room and came back with a note Napoleon had written to Pa and the letter they received from the Newsboys' Lodging House.

"Look Edward," she crackled. "Napoleon's 't's. They seem awfully like 'c's. Especially the capitals. When you look close at the note from the newsboy's home, the last name does look more like Cooper. We wanted to believe it was Tooper, so we just saw what we wanted."

"Those crooks," Pa said. "They tricked us."

"We should have made sure," Ma said. "We should've said our name starts with 't' as in Tom—just like Cooper only with a 't' instead of a 'c.'"

"And we should have known anything having to do with that Horatio Alger would be crooked as hell."

"I want Benny," Lilly cried.

"The poor little guy," Hazel sobbed. "His heart will break in two. Just think, getting all ready to come to us and then be told he's not ours. Can't we take him anyway?"

Back in New York, Uncle Napoleon was thinking the same thing, except Benny Cooper did not look like his heart was breaking, nor was he little. Still, Napoleon felt sorry for the boy and offered to take him to Illinois.

The young newspaper salesman politely declined and asked if he could have the ticket money instead. "They told me you were going West," he said, "but you're not."

Napoleon assured him that, indeed he would be going westward, to Illinois.

"But I thought you meant really West. Like where cowboys chase Indians over mountains and deserts. That's where I want to go. You know what everybody's saying these days? They say, 'go West, young man, go West.'"

Napoleon gave Benny Cooper the money from his ticket, cashed in his own, and rode the train back to Bonfield in a boxcar, as the caboose was already full of railroad men.

As the days passed, Pa started writing to more addresses from Benny's book. A man who lived across the street from the house where Francis found it, wrote back. He said that many families had moved in and out of that house, but he didn't remember a Burnside family. In another letter, a lady wrote that she remembered the family as well as a little boy, but the little boy wasn't Mr. and Mrs. Burnside's son. Then the man who owned the house wrote that the boy belonged to Mrs. Burnside's sister, Henrietta Clark, whose husband died in a mine explosion the year before. When the Burnside family left Greensburg, Henrietta planned to go out west and become a Harvey Girl.

"Maybe this Henrietta and her husband couldn't have kids so they took Benny, and then her husband died," Pa said. "But I don't think Fred Harvey would let a girl with a kid work in one of his places. But then again, if he knew she was a widow and not an unwed mother, he might give her a chance."

"Or maybe she's hiding him out," Wesley said. "And no one knows she has him."

"What's a Harvey girl, Pa?" Hazel asked.

"It's a girl who works in one of those eating places called Harvey Houses. They're all over the country, even in God-forsaken places like New Mexico, right next to the railroad depots. Hell, they've got mahogany counters, chrome-plated coffee urns and crystal glassware. But you can get a steak, eggs, a big pile of brown potatoes, a stack of pancakes with fresh butter melting on top, and pure maple syrup spilling down the sides for thirty-five cents. Before Fred Harvey started those places, a passenger couldn't find a decent meal in time to make it back to his train."

As Pa discovered, Henrietta Clark did work at the Harvey House in New Mexico, even though she was a mother. Fred Harvey even arranged for someone to take care of her boy while she was at work. He made it clear that he required his girls to act like dignified young women at all times. Henrietta fell short of the mark, her weakness being gum-chewing. Harvey, on an inspection tour of his restaurants, saw the Clark girl chewing gum while she waited on tables. "You're a waitress, not a cow," he told her. "Don't do it again."

Henrietta got rid of the gum, but a few weeks later the manager noticed her take a new stick out of a package and start chewing away while she filled the salt and pepper shakers before the restaurant opened in the morning. Even though there weren't any customers in the place, he fired her on the spot. No one knew where she went, and Pa stopped trying to find her after he learned that the boy she had with her was about four years old—too young to be Benny.

Pa had no more addresses to write to and no new leads about Willard, his other lost boy.

"I sure wouldn't mind being one of those Harvey Girls," Hazel said. "They would never catch me chewing gum."

CHAPTER EIGHT

The New Door

September 8, 1909

One day Pa came home carrying a new door made of golden oak with a frosted, glass window etched with a picture of a cardinal, the state bird of Illinois. It had been lying around the Decatur train yard for over a year with no one claiming it, so the railroad let Pa have it for two dollars. As fancy as the door looked, he insisted he bought it because it had a strong lock. "That's to keep some son of a bitch from getting into the house," he said, "someone looking for the records Wesley copied at that institution from Hell."

"That's a bunch of bull," Cleve whispered to Wesley. "If someone wanted to get in, all they'd have to do is break the glass."

"But if someone does try to get in," Wesley whispered back, "they won't want us to know they've been here. If they'd break the glass, we'd sure know it."

"It's still a bunch of bull. He got it 'cause it's dressy."

A week later, Wesley came home and found the door locked. Pa was off on the trains, Cleve was working on a road crew near Union Hill and Hazel was in school. When he knocked and hollered for Ma and Lilly, no one answered. Fresh buggy tracks in the yard told him that their neighbors, the Heelers, probably took them to town.

Instead of going to school that day, Wesley stopped at the Thibault farm. Marcel Thibault had asked him to drop by so he could tell

Wesley how his boss at the flour mill had been cheating him on his wages. "That devil's been doing this for at least three years," he said, handing Wesley a sheaf of wrinkled papers. "If you can go over these figures and prove it for me, I'll give you a fiver."

Wesley marveled at the sound of it. Five dollars for just a few hours work! If he could just get in the house now and sit at his writing table with everything fresh in his mind, he could come up with the answers Marcel wanted.

Then he remembered he had left the upstairs window slightly open. He found a ladder in the wood shed, set it against the side of the house, and climbed up on the first-floor roof. He looked in the window. The quilt Aunt Jo made covered the double bed where he and Cleve slept, and a carved elephant and metal spinning top sat on their own chest of drawers. Uncle Napoleon had given him the elephant telling him Teddy Roosevelt brought it back from Africa. Near the bed stood the writing table his mother had Pa make for him at the cottage in Sheldon. Above it, a shelf held his papers on one half of it and Cleve's collection of gears, pulleys, and small motors on the other.

After a while he found, if he sat quietly and looked through the window a certain way, he could see himself and Cleve inside the room, moving here and there, puttering with their favorite things, crawling into bed whispering and laughing. How different to sit outside looking in. How different he felt about the things he saw every day, the things he regularly used and touched. Too old to play with the top anymore and no longer believing Uncle Napoleon got the elephant from Teddy Roosevelt, he told himself it didn't matter.

"I love that top," he said out loud. "I love that elephant." His eyes moved to a rag in a corner that Cleve used to clean his motor parts.

"I love that rag."

Suddenly he felt so lucky living in a house with Pa and his brother and sisters, and with Ma Tooper, who backhanded him sometimes but sewed his buttons on tight so he never had to wear a shirt with a space where a button belonged. And sometimes at night, if he couldn't sleep, he'd go downstairs to the kitchen for a drink of water, and he'd see a piece of cherry pie sitting on the table that seemed to say, "Here I am, Wesley, just for you."

He felt so grateful he forgot to open the window and go inside and so happy he started to cry. He wanted to grab everyone he loved and go dancing around on the other side of the window. And then he realized he would have plenty of space to dance because the room only had one bed in it. There should be another bed there, but he, Pa, and Cleve had taken it out because the boy they thought would sleep in that bed had the last name of Cooper instead of Tooper.

Wesley remembered how Father Fatso locked him in his chambers when Benny and Willard were taken away. Cleve fought and tried to stop it from happening, but locked in that room, Wesley, could do nothing but sit on Father Fatso's cold floor copying numbers that looked neat and safe.

He felt sorry for his little brothers, torn away from their family to live with strangers, and for Cleve who had to watch them go. He felt sorry for Lilly, never knowing their mother, and sorry for Ma Tooper who came to raise a mess of dirty kids in a run-down farmhouse with cracks in the walls and nothing in it but a stump on the floor. And he felt sorry for himself. Sorry because Sister Stringy kept hitting him on the back when he couldn't eat the moldy food on his plate. And the more he threw up the more she kept hitting him.

He heard a voice yell and saw a fist go through the window, and realized the voice and fist belonged to him. He pulled his hand out of the window and watched blood seeping out of his cuts like water seeped from the ground when you dug a deep hole. He kept crying. It didn't hurt as much to cry about a cut hand as it did about things that happened long ago when it was too late to change them. Then he heard the thump, thump of feet on the floor inside. He looked up, startled to see Cleve standing in their room talking to him through the hole in the window.

"What in hell are you cryin' about?"

Wesley sniffled back his tears. "I'm not cryin'. How'd you get in the house?"

"Through the front door."

"But the front door is locked."

"I got a skeleton key, and yeah, you were cryin'. I heard you when I came up the lane and saw you break the window."

Wesley wiped his eyes with his fists. "Where … where did you get a skeleton key?"

"I don't remember. Come inside, now. That's what you climbed up here for, isn't it?"

Wesley crawled into their room, and Cleve wiped the blood off his hand and placed a square of folded cloth on it telling him to hold it there. Wesley lay down on the bed and closed his eyes. The throbbing in his hand slowed gradually and stopped. The comfort of being in his own room and hearing Cleve moving about almost soothed him into sleep until he realized what he had done, and he sat straight up.

"Cleve, I gotta run away. Pa's gonna kill me when he sees this window. Do you know how much that glass costs? I'm gonna get some money pretty soon but I don't have any now. I'm not supposed to open that window, but I get so hot at night and need air comin' in. I gotta get out of here fast. I gotta start packin' now!"

Still holding the cloth to his hand, he looked around for something to carry his clothes in and saw Cleve out on the roof setting a new pane of glass into the window frame. "God Almighty," he hollered, "where'd you get that glass?"

Cleve rolled his eyes. "Maybe I found it a long time ago and stored it."

"How'd you get the right size?"

"I cut it to fit."

"Where'd you get the thing to cut it with and the stuff to hold the glass in?"

"Maybe I found those too."

Wesley lay back again and watched the late afternoon sun splash Aunt Jo's quilt with gold. Cleve finished puttying the window and came inside. He picked up one of his motors from the floor and sat down at the foot of their bed.

"How's the hand?"

"Better. How come you're home early?"

"Crew got rained out, but now it turned nice."

Cleve turned a little wheel on the motor back and forth with his finger and squinted at the line of light bouncing off the metal spinning top on their dresser. "Wes, I got a letter from Francis Stanz in Ohio, and I wanna write back to her and tell her thanks for runnin' like hell to the train tracks that day and givin' me Benny's book."

"Pa already wrote her grama a long time ago and said to tell Francis thanks."

"Well, I thought I'd thank her myself. And, I'd ask her if her Grama knows any other ways we can look for Benny. Could you help me write the letter to her, Wes."

Wesley thought he'd burst with pride. Here Cleve was fourteen years old and asking for help from his nine-year-old brother—the brother who he whisked out of trouble more times than a leopard frog had spots. Finally he was giving him a chance to even things up a little.

"Sure, I will, Cleve, but I thought you always said it wouldn't do no good to keep looking for him."

"Oh, you never can tell. But I do know one thing for sure."

"What's that?"

"It's a good thing you didn't break the glass on the new door."

"Why"

"Because I don't have one of those."

CHAPTER NINE

The Ice Cream Cone

June 15, 1910

Mrs. Ida Stanz of Greensburg, Pennsylvania, could not lift herself from despondency. For months she believed that the book her granddaughter, Francis, found in the attic next door would unite a missing boy with his family. To think that Francis would learn the name of the missing boy from his brother, a young man among many young men traveling to Huffman Prairie, Ohio, to watch the Wright brothers' second air machine tryout. To think that while Francis visited her in Greensburg that winter, while she played with other neighborhood children in the vacant house next door, she found a book with the name of that same boy, Benny Tooper, written on the inside cover! And to think, some months later, she would get back home to Ohio with the book before the young man jumped on a train to Illinois, just in time to give it to him.

A few weeks after that, Mrs. Stanz received a letter from the boy's father. He said he wrote to the families who had lived in the house next door and to those living near it. He went on to tell her how he followed every lead he could think of, but all paths had turned into dead ends. He appealed to her to suggest any other direction he might take.

After racking her brain, Mrs. Stanz had decided to put an ad in the town newspaper:

*Anyone knowing of the whereabouts of Benjamin Tooper
please contact Ida Stanz at 212 Washington Street in
Greensburg.*

Weeks had turned into months, and not a soul contacted her—
not even friends who might be curious about the ad. They probably
figured she met a gentleman somewhere, and not wanting to be a
widow any longer, was trying to locate him. As much as they might
be dying to know the details, their better selves cautioned them to
say nothing. Too late, she realized she should have given Benny's age
in the ad.

Throughout her life, she had assumed that help and comfort would
come to the poor, hard-working creatures of the world, but with every
line she read of Mr. Tooper's letter, she became more disheartened.
His last two sentences saddened her the most. "Hope the drought
isn't getting to you. We are cooking and so's the crops."

She walked out to her yard where every grass blade, every tree
leaf, and every flower petal lay dying of thirst. With each breath she
took, she could smell the smoke-stacks from the Pittsburgh mills.
The bone-hard ground her made her heels click like they did when
she walked on concrete.

A little girl wailing on the sidewalk interrupted her depression.
Instinctively, she pulled out her handkerchief and hurried to her.
"Oh, little sweety, what's wrong?"

Sobbing, the child gazed at a pink puddle with strawberry bits
floating on top. "It's Benny's fault! He put too much ice cream on my
cone."

Mrs. Stanz's hand flew up to her chest. She felt the same flutter in
her heart she felt two years ago while falling down her cellar steps.
She would have tumbled to her death or been crippled for life had

her right hand not curled around a spike in the wall just enough to slow her down so she could steady her feet. The nail had probably been there for years, but she had paid no mind to it.

"Benny?" she asked, gently wiping the girl's hands with her handkerchief. "Benny who, dear?"

"Over at the store." The child pointed her finger to the streets behind Mrs. Stanz's house. "I gave him my money and he piled the ice cream too high."

Mrs. Stanz took the little girl's hand and began walking through her backyard. "Well, let's just get another one for you. Will you show me the way?"

The child nodded happily and directed her, three blocks away, to a small store marked by the sign, "Whitehouse Grocery." As they walked through the door, Mrs. Stanz saw a tall, thin woman with gray hair standing behind the counter separating pennies from a small mound of coins.

"Hello," Mrs. Stanz said, "do you still have ice cream?"

The woman smiled and reached up to the shelf for a box of cones. "We're lucky to have enough ice," she said, pushing a lock of damp hair off her forehead with the back of her hand.

Mrs. Stanz glanced around at the flour bins, the ice boxes marked Milk and Meat, and the aisles of well-stocked shelves. "I'll have to shop here sometime," she said. "My son-in-law owns Pitts' Grocery downtown, so I hardly ever get to any other stores. I just live over a few streets."

The woman lifted the ice cream maker onto the counter, her breath becoming visible in faint, white puffs as she bent over it. "Well, it might be handy for you to run over here for last-minute things. We'd love to have you as a customer. I'm Imogene Whitehouse and my husband's name is James."

She picked up a large, round scoop and began filling the cone with thick, pink ice cream, patting it around the edges. "This should help get rid of her tears."

Mrs. Stanz saw her opportunity. "I found her crying her eyes out in front of my house because the ice cream fell off her cone. She said Benny put on too much."

"Oh, that boy. He means well but overdoes it sometimes."

Turning to the little girl, Mrs. Whitehouse said, "That bad ol' Benny. If he wasn't out playing soldier somewhere we'd give him a good scolding, wouldn't we?"

The child squealed happily at the sight of the new cone.

Mrs. Stanz wasn't sure how to continue. "I suppose," she ventured, "he just wanted to give her as much as he'd like himself. It's hard to find such a thoughtful worker."

The store owner handed the child her frozen treat. "Well, he's more than a worker. He's ours."

Mrs. Stanz found it necessary to steady herself against the counter. Noting again the woman's gray hair, she asked, "Is Benny your grandson?"

Shaking her head, Mrs.Whitehouse rinsed the ice cream spoon in a bowl of water. "You'd think so, wouldn't you, at my age? James and I couldn't have children of our own. Benny looked so cute, and his ma and pa were dead, so we took him in."

Mrs. Stantz handed her the money, reminding herself that Benny was a fairly common name, and the Benny she was looking had a father. "Did you get him from the children's home here?"she asked,

"Oh goodness no. We got him from an orphanage in Indiana when he was two years old, right near the Illinois line where we used to live. James's sister paid the fee for us. We couldn't afford it ourselves."

"That's a shame, because, you sure work hard enough. Everything looks so clean here. I'd suppose you hardly have time to read a newspaper."

"Oh, I don't need to," the lady at the other side of the counter chuckled, "my customers give me more news than what the paper gets out."

The little girl left the store, and the sound of the slamming screen door remained hanging in the hot, summer air while Ida Stanz pondered her next question.

"Did … did Benny ever lose a book?"

"Books, ball bats, even his toy guns. That boy loses more things than James and I lost in both our lifetimes."

Mrs. Stanz thought a moment, cleared her throat and spoke. "When my granddaughter was visiting me, she was playing in the old Collins house. She found a book with the name Benny written inside."

The woman put the money Mrs. Stanz gave her in a drawer. "I've never known him to write his name in a book. He's not that careful with his things."

Mrs. Stanz suddenly lost hope. It wasn't the same boy after all. How could it be? But then she felt the unseen hand of her late husband Donald gently touch her shoulder. "Slow down, Mama," he used to tell her. "Don't go rushing ahead now."

"It had another name after it," she began cautiously. "Not Whitehouse. This was Hooper or Cooper. My granddaughter said it had pictures of the ocean all through it."

The store owner put her hands to her face. "*A Boy's Ocean Adventure!* The oldest Burnside girl used to watch him for us when we got busy. I never thought to look in that house. They'd moved away by the time he started missing it. He used to carry it around everywhere, even though he couldn't read yet. You mean you have it?"

Mrs. Stanz struggled to take a breath. "Oh, good Lord, it is the boy. It's him! What if he wants his book right away? What if he cries for it at night? But Francis took it to Ohio and gave it to the young man who took it to Illinois who gave it to his father.* "My granddaughter," she said thinly, still short of air, "my granddaughter lent it to someone. I could get it for you, if … if he wants it."

Mrs. Whitehouse smoothed her dress with both hands—a dress faded but clean and starched. "Oh, it's been so long now, he's forgotten about it. Maybe it's better not to bring it up again."

"Up again," Mrs. Stanz repeated and glanced again at the store's shelves, this time without seeing them.

The store owner picked up a rag and began wiping off the counter with long, sure strokes, her eyes fixed on what she was doing. "He might not remember that book but he still remembers his real name. I started him in school as Benny Whitehouse because it makes things less complicated. Everyone around here calls him Benny Whitehouse, but he understands his last name is still Tooper. When James and I get enough money to make everything legal, we'll let him decide which name he wants. That's what it comes down to, doesn't it? Which name he wants."

Mrs. Stanz started to agree but couldn't get the words out. Then she decided it didn't matter because the pleasant store owner with a friendly ring to her voice already knew the answer.

Flies buzzed around the window panes above the ice boxes. The child's chatter as she skipped down the street grew fainter. A dog barked. The air, seething with heat, remained motionless. Mrs. Stanz listened to the cicadas' incessant buzzing outside and thought for a moment she heard something beyond it. Could it be thunder? Taking her handkerchief out of her pocket, she patted her forehead, her cheeks, and her throat, even though her skin didn't have a bead of moisture on it. She didn't know why she did such a foolish thing or why her skin would be dry on such a sweltering day, but she did know that the sounds of that afternoon would always be with her, as long as she lived.

CHAPTER TEN

The Homecoming

July 11, 1910

"Now you kids get down to the road and stay there 'til he comes," Ma Tooper scolded from the front porch. "And don't you sneak up and snatch any of my bakin'.'"

"Cripes," Wesley grumbled as he followed Cleve and his sisters down the lane marked on each side by drooping and yellowing crops. "When are we gonna get any?"

"When Benny gets here," Hazel reminded him.

"We've been waiting for three days. You think, at least, Ma would give Cleve some sweets. If he hadn't met that Francis Stanz in Ohio and told her about Benny, her grama never would've heard about him and she never would've found him for us."

"You're just saying that because you think Cleve would give you some of his goodies."

"Don't worry, Wes," Cleve said, reaching into his biggest overall pocket, "I got cookies for all of us—ginger, molasses, and maple sugar."

"I'm tellin'," Lilly said.

"You do and you won't get any the rest of your life," Hazel chided. "And Wesley, if Benny takes too long getting here, we'll still get some pie today. I cooked an extra gooseberry while Ma took a nap with Lilly."

"I don't see," Cleve said, his mouth half-stuffed with cookies, "why Uncle Napoleon didn't go after him, like he did the other Benny. Or Pa. Or even me. I coulda brought him."

"He don't want nobody to bring him," Hazel said. "He says he wants to do it himself."

Wesley shook his head. "He musta been a pretty rotten kid for those Whitehouses to let him go like that. Maybe they couldn't wait for him to get the hell outa there."

"It ain't so," insisted Lilly. "The lady wrote Pa that it was a terrible mis … mis … "

"Misunderstanding," prompted Hazel. "They really love him, Wes, but they felt so sorry for Pa. Anyway, they're moving back to Illinois, just over in Gilman, to be close to him. Pa says he can go see them anytime he wants. He can even go back for good if he don't like it here."

"If he has to work as hard as we do," Cleve said, "he won't be here more than a few days. Hey, Hazel, did you ever say where you got that pie stashed?"

Before going back to the house that evening, they ran to the haymow where Hazel had her pie hidden under an over-turned apple crate. The pie's tart-sweet taste, their full bellies, and the satisfaction of pulling the wool over Ma Tooper's eyes, curbed their disappointment of having no long-lost brother to greet.

But after another day of no-Benny-yet, the Tooper kids' outlook took a downward plunge. Standing by the road the fourth morning, Wesley wondered if his own face looked as gloomy as his brother's and sisters'—Hazel's pale and downcast, Cleve's clouded with surliness, and Lilly's, like Uncle Napoleon's barometer, forecasting a downpour at any time.

The Whitehouses had sent word to the Bonfield telegraph office with reasons for Benny's delay, ranging from extra goodbye parties to train layovers. Pa changed shifts with another worker for two days, but after that, he had to leave on the Carbondale 400. Ma Tooper stayed in the kitchen baking pies, cookies, and short breads which she guarded with a hickory switch.

Although Pa had dropped the possibility of someone forcing Benny into a life of horrible labor, Wesley could not forget the pictures he saw of the Pennsylvania mining boys, their skin covered with coal dust, their faces gaunt and stoic.

"Maybe he is a Breaker Boy, after all," Cleve said, as if reading Wesley's mind. "Maybe someone scooped him off the train in Cleveland or Ft. Wayne."

Wesley wrinkled his brow. "And those fellers got it a lot tougher than we do working outside and not worrying about the ground cavin' in on us."

"Maybe someone stuck him in one of those cigarette factories, pasting tiny signs on cigarette boxes," surmised Hazel. "'Cork tips, cork tips,' the same words all day long."

"Oh," said Lilly, perking up, "I like to paste."

"Shut up," said Wesley, "here comes a wagon."

When they saw him sitting next to the driver, full of confidence and lacking even the tiniest thread of self-consciousness, they thought he belonged to a family in another house, another town. Surely, the wagon would go on down the road, and they would continue their endless watch. But the driver reined in the horses and pulled a traveler's trunk onto the road. A boy in a three-piece suit with a handkerchief in its breast pocket and shoes without a mark or a scuff on them climbed down from the wagon. As the wagon rumbled away, he began pacing back and forth in front of them on the powdery, dry road, his hands curved around his jacket lapels. Wisps of dust sneaked out from under his polished shoes, circling above his ankles like tawny ghost-snakes.

Then he stopped, brushed off his trousers, and said, "I'm Benny Tooper."

Lilly clamped her hand over her mouth.

No one spoke. Wesley thought he could hear the corn withering, the grains of oats shriveling on their stalks.

Finally, comparing the new suit and shoes with his own faded overalls and bare feet, Wesley said, "You sure don't look like a Benny Tooper."

"That's right," Hazel burst out. "You look like a ... a midget preacher."

Wesley winced. He had noticed right away the inch or so extra bestowed on the brother born a year later than himself. If this Benny was a midget, then what in God's name was he?

"What took you so long?" Cleve rasped. "We've been waitin' for days."

Benny took an exaggerated step towards them. "I've been busy lately. Very busy."

"Busy!" Wesley gasped. "We've been worrying all this time that you might be a Breaker Boy with your back all bent over and your face black with coal. Or ... or maybe in a cigarette factory mumbling 'cork tips, cork tips' all day long! And now you tell us you've been busy?"

"What in the goddamnest day in hell," Cleve snapped, "would keep a shrunk beetle in a suit busy?"

Benny held up his hand, signaling them into silence. "Matter a fact," he said, looking each one in the face, "I've been helping Will Rogers."

"Will Rogers?"

"Yes. My friend, Will Rogers. He asked me out east to go on his vaudeville tour. I helped him with his roping tricks at Madison Square Garden. Had me ride his horse, Teddy, while he threw two ropes at once." Benny laughed as if remembering the occasion. "Yes sir, caught me and the horse at the same time."

"You can ride a horse?" Hazel asked, looking him up and down.

"Oh, sure. I can do rope tricks good as ol' Will himself."

"That's dandy." Lilly piped up, getting a threatening glance from everyone but Benny. "What else can you do?"

"Well, I can do lots of things, little girl. I ... I can do a song and dance number, but this road's too sandy for that."

"There's a big, flat stone right over there," said Lilly pointing her finger to a gray rock surrounded by yellow grass. "When it's muddy everywhere else, we all stand on it together."

Benny put one foot up on the stone as if testing it—looking back, Wesley thought, to see if anyone else would urge him on. But all this new brother saw were blank stares coming from faces with noses straight and eyes dark as his own.

"You know," he said, "Will likes to do jokes and songs about dogs. He just loves dogs."

Then, jumping onto the rock, with the dust and dying crops of Bonfield around him, he shuffled out a dance step, and in a voice as flat as Ma Tooper's pancakes, he sang a ditty new to everyone watching:

Everytime I go downtown,
you're always kickin' my dawg around.
Dawg around, Dawg around.
Everytime I go downtown,
you're always kickin' my dawg around.

Lilly laughed and clapped her hands, and Hazel's mouth flopped open and stayed there.

When Benny finished, he clutched his lapels and rocked on his heels, smiling proudly. "You wanted to know what I can do. Well, that's one of the things right there."

Cleve, legs apart and arms folded, looked at Wesley. "We wanta know somethin' else he can do, don't we?"

Wesley looked knowingly back at Cleve. "We sure do."

"Oh, there's lots of other things I can do. Being you're my brothers and sisters, I can let you in on 'em. Why, I can .... "

"No, no," Wesley interrupted. "What Cleve's talkin' about is whether you can swim or not."

Benny stroked his chin and looked at the toes of his shoes as if trying to see his reflection. "Swim, you say?"

"That's what I said—swim."

"Swim? Oh, yes, course I can swim. Matter a fact, I swam the Hudson."

"Hudson? You mean that big river out east?"

"Yessiree. Right across it."

"Well, that's just first rate," Cleve said. "Because me and Wes been talking about taking you swimming in Horse Creek. Hazel, you and Lilly go up to the house and tell Ma Tooper that Benny's here, and we're gettin' the travel dirt off him before supper."

"That's not fair," Lilly said. "I wanta swim too."

"We can't," Hazel said, grasping Lilly's hand and turning toward the house. "They're gonna take their clothes off. We'll swim tomorrow, Lilly."

"Benny's not talking anymore," Lilly said, looking back at her brothers.

"That's right," Hazel agreed, "Benny's not talking anymore."

Benny wasn't talking when Wesley and Cleve walked him along the bank to the deepest end of Horse Creek or when they helped him out of his clothes. But when they threw him in the water, he hollered in midair, "I can't sswwimmm!"

He didn't thrash around like Cleve did when Pa threw him in or like Wesley did when Cleve threw him in. He didn't swim to save himself from drowning like every Tooper boy for generations did when he learned to swim. Instead, he blew all the air out of his lungs, went straight to the bottom, and stayed there.

"Good God!" Cleve shouted. "The damn fool's gonna drown." He dove down, brought his arms under Benny, and carried him up. "Now you got another chance. Swim, damn ya, swim!" But Benny went straight to the bottom.

"This time I'm not lettin' him do that!" Cleve yelled. After bringing Benny up he stayed under him, keeping him from going down.

Swim," Wesley hollered at Benny. "Swim!"

Benny didn't move.

"Benny!" Wesley yelled, "you can breathe. Cleve can't. You're gonna drown our brother. Swim. For God's sake, swim!"

Benny's eyes bulged. He jerked his head up and down like he finally understood and whirled his arms and legs around like blades on a windmill.

"That's right," Wesley cheered, "swim to me, swim to me!" He stretched out his arms and saw huge drops of water bouncing off them. Rain.

When Benny reached him, Wesley grabbed and held on. The rain came down in kegsful, plastering their hair against their heads and drenching their eyebrows and lashes.

"You did it, Benny, I knew you could!" he hollered through the roar of a million raindrops tap dancing across the creek. Cleve came to the surface, and Benny and Wesley each flung an arm around him. They all began to shiver.

"W-Where'd you learn to stay d-down like that?" Cleve stammered.

"Read it in a b-b-book."

As the sky blackened, the wind picked up. Wesley's lower lip trembled so much, he could hardly get the words out. "W-why would you d-d-o that?" he shouted through the downpour.

"C-c-ause when I'm a soldier, I … I might be c-c-captured. They torture you and hold you under, so you give up s-s-secrets. I w-won't g-g-give 'em up."

"Did you ever see the Hudson River?"

"N-No."

"Did you know Will Rogers?"

"N-No."

"Where'd you get that song and dance?"

"M-made it up."

Their hair, molded and pasted by the rain, made them resemble statues. Almost facing Benny nose-to-nose, Cleve spoke through lips tight and close together so the water wouldn't fill his mouth. "Listen, you. We won't let nobody pick on you as far south as Bloomington and as far north as Fargo, but don't you lie to us again. Not never!"

"I won't," Benny promised. "N-not n-never."

Ten Years Later

CHAPTER ELEVEN

A Cockeyed Brother

October 22, 1917

96 Co. 6th Regiment

Quantico, Va.

Dear Brother:

I am writing this at the Y.M.C.A. and there is a heavy wrestling match on. They have been wrestling twenty minutes and neither one of them has went down yet, so I guess they will both have to give up. It is causing a lot of excitement in here, all kinds of yelling and hollering going on.

There is a big bunch of Marines leaving here tomorrow. Oh, how I do wish I was with them but it cannot be. You know if one stays in one place too long it becomes monotonous and he wishes he was back home. Well, that's the way with me now, so I do wish we would move from here, but there is no more encouragement, so I guess we will stay here til spring.

I had a wonderful dream last night. I dreamt that I was in Chicago with you and we were just fixing up to go to a show downtown and Hazel and Dan came in. They had brought Dan's car so instead of going to a show we went auto riding and on our way we met and got acquainted with two beautiful girls and we took them riding. You and I were in the back seat with 2 girls and were having a H—of a time. Oh Wes! You don't know how disappointed I was when I woke up and heard the old bugle blowing reveille and instead of it being really true it was nothing but a dream.

Oh yes! I forgot to mention the girl I was telling you about. She came down to camp just to see me the other day and she is a very nice looking kid. Her folks are moving to Washington so if we do stay here all winter I know where I will spend my Saturdays and Sundays from now on. She seems to think quite a bit of me, for when she left she kissed me goodbye and started to cry. But I finally got her on the train promising to go see her next Sunday and you may know I am going unless we are on guard and if that's the case I am out of luck then for another week. She is a respectable girl, so she is no flirt, for when some of my friends would try to talk to her she would give them the cold shoulders.

I wrote a letter home yesterday and I wrote one to Hazel about a month ago and never heard from her so I am not going to write to her any more until she writes to me and if you ever see her and she asks you about me, tell her you haven't heard from me since I was home on furlough. If she wants to be so independent to me for not going to Palmers when I was at home it is going to be her hard luck not mine. So do as I tell you, won't you please?

Well, Dear Brother, I expect you are getting tired of reading this nonsense so will close with love from yours.

Brother Ben

• • •

Wesley sat at the lunch counter at Woolworth's eating the newly-advertised sandwich, corned beef on rye. He ran his finger around the inside of his white, starched collar, loosened his tie, and undid the top button of his suit coat. *When will I ever get used to wearing this damn armor?* He knew the answer—never. But if he wanted to get anywhere with the work he did best, he would have to wear what successful men wore.

Taking a large bite of his sandwich, he began reading parts of Benny's letter again. Although he found it in the mailbox the night before, he didn't have time to open the envelope until today's noon hour. After getting back from his classes at LaSalle Business College at 10:00 PM last night, he did his homework until after midnight. He couldn't read the letter in the morning as he had to look over a pile of invoices before going to his office job at Westchester's Department Store.

His eyes scanned the paragraph where Benny explained about his "wonderful dream." *God, after everything the kid's been through, and all the people who treated him a damn sight better than I have, who does he pick to dream about but me?*

Wesley's mind flashed back ten years—to the first night Benny stayed with his real family. After supper Benny wanted to go to bed right away so he could wake up early and learn how to milk cows and work in the fields. Wesley and Cleve looked at each other dumbstruck. Each day they complained about all the work they did. Wesley made it a habit of reminding everyone in the family that he was shorter than many boys his age because he worked like a coolie before he was full grown. And, lo and behold, along comes a kid a year younger and a couple inches taller who wanted to do farm chores more than he wanted to spend a day at the circus. How cockeyed!

Then instead of crawling into the bed Pa built just for him, with Ma Tooper's quilt making it look like you wanted to lie there for the rest of your life, Benny ran over to Wesley and Cleve's bed, jumped right in between them, and fell sound asleep.

The next morning at the breakfast table, they could hardly wait to tell Benny what they did with the eggs Ma Tooper cooked for them.

"She says she worked as the governor's cook," Wesley whispered. "Either she just helped the real cook, or the governor liked his eggs fried extra hard. She makes good pies and cakes though."

"She won't give us dessert at suppertime if we don't eat everything she gives us during the day," said Cleve. "We can get everything down but the eggs—even the mushy oatmeal with lumps. Those damn eggs are harder than auto tires."

"What do you do?" Benny asked.

"After she goes back to the kitchen, we take 'em into that closet there and hang 'em on hooks. She checks the waste baskets and even our pockets. Once she looked in the closet but just down on the floor. Me and Wes knew our goose was cooked if she just glanced upwards. We almost heaved up our lumpy oatmeal. But she didn't see 'em and went out to feed the chickens like she always does. Then we took the eggs off the hooks and fed 'em to the pigs like we do everyday."

But after Ma Tooper put their breakfast on the table, Benny didn't want to hang his eggs in the closet. "I'll just eat mine," he said to his brothers. "And yours too, if you don't want 'em."

"Why in hell would you do that?"

"Because when I'm a soldier, and if I get captured, I'm gonna have to eat stuff nobody else would put in their mouths. This way I'll get used to it. Besides, her stuff don't taste that bad to me in the first place."

As the days went by, Benny's brothers and sisters stood agape as he gobbled with gusto food they barely cared to swallow.

"Maybe because he lived close to Pittsburgh for so long," mused Hazel, "his stomach is as strong as the steel they make in the mills."

After harvest time, Pa and Ma Tooper went on a trip to Champaign to see a special doctor about Ma's bad back. The Tooper kids saw this as their chance to eat as much whipped cream as they always wanted. Wesley and Cleve brought in all the cream from five days of milking, and Hazel whipped it all in a big washtub and put sugar in it. Lilly kept saying she would tell Pa when he got home, but she ate almost as much as the rest. They all threw up except Benny.

"I never seem to get sick," he said, finishing what the others left.

When Wesley read the part of the letter about Benny's new girlfriend, he smiled. Girls fell for his kid brother as fast as bass went for night crawlers on a hook. Wesley reflected on the girls he himself had known. Maybe he had taken more girls out for a good time than Benny had, but they slipped through his fingers like water.

Finishing his corned beef, Wesley glanced at the paragraph where Benny mentioned Hazel. "If you ever see her and she asks you about me, tell her you haven't heard from me since I was on furlough."

Damn it—right smack dab in the middle again! Wesley put the letter back into its envelope, paid his lunch bill, and walked out onto State Street. He couldn't blame Benny for not wanting to go over to Dan Palmer's house with everyone screaming and hollering and Dan's folks never liking Hazel. With all the good men after her, why did she have to fall for that bastard?

"He's so exciting," she always said. Yeah, so exciting he chased after other girls whenever he got the urge, and when he did that, Hazel could not concentrate on anything else, including writing to her little brother who could be shipped off to war any day.

Each time she caught Dan red-handed with someone else, she kept ranting on how she'd never go back to him again, even if he begged on his knees. But if she thought she heard his car drive by, she would start wailing and crying about how much she loved him no matter what he did. If it turned out not to be Dan's car, she would get someone to drive her around Kankakee so she could look for him, moaning over and over that if he only knew how much she loved him, he would come back to her.

On top of it all, Pa wanted Wesley to try and talk some sense into Hazel—make her see that Dan would never stop running around no matter how good she cooked or kept house, and maybe he would catch one of those sexual diseases and give it to her. And now Benny asked Wesley to tell Hazel he hadn't gotten a letter from him.

His mother had been right. "You're our little middleman, Wesley." Back then he felt privileged because he helped move things along for someone he loved. Now he felt hopelessly mixed up in other people's lives.

As he waited for a policeman to stop traffic on Dearborn Avenue so pedestrians could cross, Wesley realized it wouldn't do any good to talk to Hazel about what a mess she'd be in if she married Dan. But then, if he didn't try, it would always be nagging at him that he should have. So he decided he would. And if Hazel asked if he received a letter from Benny yet, he would say he hadn't. After all, Benny, a serviceman representing the whole family, asked him to do this favor for him.

Benny itched to go overseas and get into the war action, but what did he dream about at night? About being with his brother, the one closest in age to him, dreaming about being together with two beautiful girls and having the time of their lives. When you had a brother that loyal to you, even in his dreams, how could you say no?

CHAPTER TWELVE

Horse Apples

November 15, 1917

96th Co. 6th Regiment

Quantico, Va.

My Dear Brother Wes:

I read your two letters and was very glad to hear from you. I had a letter from Hazel also, stating that she is now married. I wonder if she and Dan are going to run the place all alone or is old Dan going to stay with them. I bet Mrs. P. is raving yet for she never did like Hazel and neither did old Dan.

You ask me if I had a watch. To tell you the truth, I have none. You remember the one that I bought in Chicago. I sold it when I was at Paris Island and I would appreciate a watch as you describe. It is handy for knowing the time, but it is also handy to designate targets with. I will not have a real lot of use for it here, but after we get across the pond, it would be more of a comrade than a watch.

You remember the ring that Whitehouses sent me for my birthday. I lost it the other day while washing my clothes. It slipped off my finger into the pail and I threw the water in the river, ring and all. I saw it as it fell, but the water was too deep to get it.

The Y.M.C.A. has a vaudeville here every Wednesday night and it is generally pretty good, and it is all free for us. As it is quite an entertainment, they always have some very pretty burlesque girls, and you'd ought to see this bunch rave. They nearly go nuts, but at that they hold their respect and never do anything out of the way.

And Wes, if you have some more of those little diaries, send them to me to sell for you. I can sell anyway 10 of them, but if you haven't 10, send what you have for the first of the year. Everyone will want a diary. I am going to start mine from Jan. 1st and keep it going all year and later on it will be very interesting.

You spoke of that girl and want a picture of her. Well, I haven't an extra one at present, but when I do get over I will send you one. But do not think that I am going to marry her yet. I told you I wouldn't marry a girl unless she was nice and pretty and could cook real good. Well, she is everything in that line, just my style. But I wouldn't marry her now, but if she will, I may after I get out of Service.

Well, Dear Brother, I wish I could be talking to you instead of writing but as it is, a letter is all the best I can do, so will close hoping to hear from you soon.

I remain as ever, your loving brother, Ben.

• • •

Wesley's spirits always lifted whenever Benny wrote to him about his girlfriend—a nice girl, crazy about him, who didn't look at other men. Could it be, he wondered, that war brought couples together, even those who might otherwise stay apart? That had been the case with Cleve, thanks to the trouble in Mexico.

Sitting on the trolley with Benny's letter on his lap, Wesley thought back to a certain day when he went home to Bonfield for a weekend visit with the family. He had been working in Chicago and Cleve had full charge of running the farm for Pa. When Benny wasn't helping on the farm, he worked as a salesman for anyone who had anything to sell, his reputation growing as far as Joliet. But the Germans were in the midst of launching attacks on French fortresses in Verdun, and Benny itched for the United States to get into the War so he could join the Marines and go overseas.

As Wesley stepped off the train at Bonfield station, Cleve and Benny drove up in a fancy-looking buggy with red, velvet cushions and a fringe on top. "Thanks to the squirt here," Cleve said, nodding at Benny, "I got a great deal on it. He talked Jake at the livery down to less than half of what he wanted. Jeez, the kid's good!"

Benny smiled proudly. "I got him down on the price because of so many people buying motorcars now. He even gave me a commission for getting Cleve to buy the buggy."

"I'd of saved my money for a motorcar," Wesley said, tickled at Cleve calling Benny a squirt when Benny was the tallest of the three. "That's what everyone wants."

Jake's getting in a whole bunch of 'em," Benny said. "He wants me to sell the rest of his buggies and start taking orders for the motorcars too."

"I wouldn't mind having a motorcar," said Cleve, "but they cost too much. Now, let's go home and change into our Sunday best. I want you two to go with me to Mary's."

"Why?" Wesley asked.

"I think she'll accept an invitation to go riding with me when she sees this fancy buggy. Her fussy, old aunt won't let her go out alone with me, but if you two are along, she might say it's okay."

"I'll go," said Benny. "Maybe she'll want to order a motorcar or one of Jake's fancy buggies, cheaper than cheap can be."

"No, you don't," Cleve said firmly. "This ride will be strictly for pleasure."

As they drove up to the farm where Mary lived with her aunt and helped with the children, Wesley realized she always made him a little nervous. He had a hard time understanding her Danish accent and felt she wanted everyone to know she came from a well-to-do family and had the best of schooling. Although Cleve was so shy around her he could hardly talk, he couldn't seem to get enough of her.

Cleve parked the buggy, got out, and walked up to the farmhouse.

"Maybe I should go in with you," called out Benny. "To see if her aunt wants to buy a motorcar."

Cleve turned and shook his fist. "Will you quit talking about those damn things? Stay put!"

After a few minutes, Wesley saw Mary standing in the doorway, turning her head and looking at the buggy. Soon Cleve returned and said, "Wes, get in the back seat with Ben. She'll go if her cousin, Helen, can come along. You remember Helen, Wes. She went to school with you."

The girls came out of the house, and Cleve handed Helen up to Wesley and practically lifted Mary up to the front seat. Sitting behind him, Wesley could tell from the way Cleve's ears set on his head that he was grinning so hard his cheeks probably hurt. Mary talked to him more than usual, and the sun shone down warm and steady for early spring but not too bright or hot. The first robins of the year pecked for worms along the roadside and white, downy spikes appeared on pussy willow branches as if announcing green leaves would be coming soon. Best of all, no motorcars came by that might remind Mary she wasn't riding in the latest. The more they drove along, the more Cleve seemed to relax. He could even talk now.

"Say, fellers, maybe the ladies would like to have lunch at the Bonfield Inn."

Mary said, "Won't that be awfully expensive?"

Cleve snorted. "Who can't handle lunch easily for five people at such a small-town place?"

"I can help pay," chimed in Benny. "I just made some nice money for myself." He started to say more, but Wesley's elbow jabbed him in the side.

In voices low enough so they wouldn't offend Mary, the three began talking about the days at Bonfield school.

"Remember the time Wesley settled the score with that snooty Gerald Foyer?" Helen asked.

"How could I forget?" Wesley guffawed, thinking back to that particular day. Gerald Foyer always bragged about the high-class foods he had in a wicker lunch box with wooden handles and how his family had its own cook. The Tooper kids brought their lunch in one tall lard can. Ma Tooper made sure they had plenty to eat in it, even enough for the poorer kids who sometimes had only bacon grease in their pails. They would all sit under a big butternut tree and tell jokes and riddles while they ate, not paying any attention to Gerald. Then one day, as soon as the teacher rang the lunch bell, Gerald ran out ahead of everyone, took the lid off the Toopers' lard bucket, sat down on it, and made a big loud "whoops."

"I'll never forget the look on Gerald's face," Helen laughed, "when Wesley yanked him off the bucket and threw him in the mud."

"And Wes took Gerald's lunch for our family and anybody that wanted some," added Benny. "Then he made Gerald eat all the food in our bucket."

"The bucket with the farty taste," Helen tittered at Wesley. "And while you were stuffing all that smelly food down Gerald, Benny stood by with his fists clenched. 'I'm coverin' for ya, Wes,' he kept saying, 'I'm coverin' for ya.'"

Wesley and Benny looked at each other in shock. They couldn't remember anything Helen said after she uttered the word "farty." They had never heard a young lady say such a thing before, not even their sisters. Ma and Pa let them say damn and hell, but nothing close to fart. Wesley tried to talk but couldn't get a sound out. Then Benny snickered, and Wesley felt spasms of laughter rising inside him so hard, he could barely breathe.

"Ben ... Ben thought he'd stand watch," he gasped, still hearing Helen saying farty taste over and over in his mind. "In ... in case Gerald's friends might jump me."

"Friends?" Helen quipped. "Friends?"

"Gerald didn't have any!" Benny sputtered. Then he, Helen, and Wesley covered their mouths with their hands and laughed as hard as they did as when they were guileless children in a one-room country school.

The road ran down a steep hill and curved sharply just before crossing a bridge. Seeing this, Wesley wanted to kick himself for not insisting that he and Cleve try out the buggy before they took the girls out. Cleve's attention was more on Mary than on the road, and when the horse got to the bottom of the hill, it reared up nervously and made a complete stop, causing the front of the buggy to come almost right under its exterior. Letting out an angry neigh, the horse lifted its tail and held it there as if to scorn the passengers in the buggy and their lovely day. All five young people stared in disbelief as a dozen, golden horse apples magically appeared under the bright, afternoon sunshine directly over the thick, velvet upholstery of Cleve's new buggy and Mary's delicate, lace stockings.

Helen screamed, and all Wesley could do was shout, "Do something!" Cleve thrust his hands out in front of him, leaned over and caught the whole squishy pile, except for parts of it that ran down his sleeve and onto his lap.

Mary pulled her shoes up on the seat and looked at Cleve with as much horror as if she walked into her aunt's house and found the whole family butchered by a crazed intruder.

Cleve got out of the buggy and tried to wipe his hands in the grass, but that only smeared the gooey liquid around more, and the manure that fell onto his clothes now dripped down his pant legs. He fixed his gaze on Mary, saw her look of disgust, and gave up.

"Take the girls home, Wes," he said, walking across the road toward the fields. "I'm done—done with the whole mess."

He didn't come home that night and left a note that he went to Chicago. The next day he came back announcing he enlisted in the Army. He would be in Texas for training and then sent to Mexico because of Victoriano Huerta trying to take over as leader.

"The Mexican Army arrested a bunch of American sailors when they went ashore at Tampico for supplies," he told the family. "President Wilson told Huerta to salute the American flag and apologize for the arrests. Huerta refused, so Wilson's getting forces ready."

"Humph," Pa scoffed. "Back when our Mr. Wilson was Ambassador to Mexico, he couldn't wait to raise a glass toasting Huerta and his new cabinet."

"That was before Huerta ordered Francesco Madero, the best president Mexico ever had, shot to death," Cleve retorted. "Europe's trying to pressure Wilson into recognizing Huerta, and he won't do it. Goddamn it, I'm going."

"The bravest of all Mexican rebels," Benny said, "was Fortino Samano. He refused a blindfold when Huerta had him in front of the firing squad. Then Samano asked for a cigar, and guess who gave the order to fire. He did."

"Don't you get any crazy ideas about being a hero," warned Pa.

"Don't worry, I'm not going to Mexico. I'm waiting to enlist and go across and fight the Germans."

"Don't get your hopes up too high, Squirt," Cleve cautioned. "We might not get into the War until Wilson loses the election in November. Right now the action is in Mexico, and that's where I'll be."

"What will you do if you run into Pancho Villa?" asked Wesley. "He's been giving Huerta hell."

"You know what I'll do if I see him? I'd tell him if things get too bad for him there, he should go to Ohio. That's where I had it the best. Remember?"

And Wesley did remember—a Cleve bursting into the farmhouse at midnight carrying a book with the lost Benny's name scrawled on the inside cover. He remembered a Cleve full of tales of the Wright brothers' flying machine, of his one-in-a-million job working on motor cars, and of a girl named Francis. He remembered a Cleve eager for help writing letters to Francis until he received her last one saying she was recently married.

A few months later, on another weekend visit, Wesley saw Mary at a horse-pulling contest in Mantino. He tried to slip away, but she ran up and asked how Cleve liked the Service. Wesley didn't tell her how disgusted Cleve felt at not being sent to Vera Cruz when the Marines took over. Cleve wrote him that Germany was sneaking arms in for Huerta, four men were killed and twenty wounded, and the Army couldn't give its men anything better to do than camp along the border.

"I'll never forget the last day I saw him," Mary said.

"Neither will he," Wesley said, remembering that afternoon.

Then Mary asked if she could have Cleve's address. "I've never known anyone to sacrifice himself so," she said.

Wesley didn't know if she meant Cleve volunteering to help with the problem in Mexico or catching the horse apples so they wouldn't get on her best shoes. "He's got more guts than anyone I know," he said.

"Oh, he does, he does!" Mary almost squealed. "Thank you for the address, Wesley. Thank you so much."

After Huerta resigned and left Mexico because the Navy stopped his supplies from coming in, the trouble between the two countries died down. By that time, Pa had sold the farm and moved the family to a house on Schyler Avenue in Kankakee. "I can't keep the farm anymore with both Cleve and Wesley gone," he insisted, "and Benny's probably going to enlist as soon as Charles Evans Hughes takes the presidency away from Wilson and gets us into the War. The papers say he's got the election in the bag."

What the family didn't know was that the Army gave Cleve an honorable discharge because of weak eyes. He didn't write Pa or Wesley about this but sent word to Mary. She had her cousin, Harold, drive her to Momence to meet him, and then she and Cleve got on the train to Crown Point, Indiana, and got married.

• • •

Wesley put Benny's letter in his pocket and pulled the cord for the next trolley stop. Two brothers, he mused, were both set with someone they wanted to spend the rest of their lives with. And neither one would have his girl if it weren't for the Service. "Am I a fool or what?" he asked himself as he stepped off the trolley. "Maybe I should join."

SOMEWHERE IN FRANCE

Mr. and Mrs. Ed Tooper of this city received a letter from their son, Corporal Ben A. Tooper, who has just arrived safely "Somewhere in France". He stated that he was "happy as a lark in the summertime".

He also mentioned the beautiful scenery while crossing the pond and that he did not get seasick.

France is a beautiful country, he said, if it was not for the war, which has ruined it terribly.

A favor he asked of his mother was to send him some of those good home-made cookies she used to make and some salted peanuts. This will be granted him soon.

He wishes all his friends and relatives of this city the best of health and happiness.

An article published in the Kankakee, Illinois newspaper concerning a letter from Ben to his father and stepmother telling them he had arrived safely in France.

CHAPTER THIRTEEN

The Trenches

May 7, 1918

96th Co., 2nd Battalion, 6th Reg.,

U. S. M. C. American Expeditionary Force

Somewhere in France

Dear Brother,

I rec'd your letter sometime ago and have just now a good chance to answer it. I am in good health and spirits which is quite natural for me. Well Wes, I am writing this letter to you and the Germans are sending regards by way of shells to me. Sometimes we have to do a lot of lively moving, dodging shells from the Germans' big guns. We have been in a few bombardments but I have gone through lucky so far. We have spent a number of days in the front line trenches and it is quite an experience for me and I guess it is for everyone else.

When we are in the trenches we have to sleep in dug-outs and the water and mud is knee deep, but the bunks are out of the water so when one is tired it seems a fine place to sleep. We also see a lot of aeroplanes and observation balloons, but as many as I have seen I have never seen one shot down yet. I guess they are pretty hard to hit, much harder than those jacksnipes we used to hunt down at Bonfield.

Oh, Wes, I forgot to tell you that before we shipped over we had been shooting on the range and. I shot for record with a revolver. I shot 87 out of 100, so you see I was shooting pretty close but for expert you have to make 96. I couldn't quite make it, but I can shoot better with it than I used to with our old 22 revolvers, but I think I would shoot good with them now unless they don't shoot straight.

I was with Alva Heeler and Melvin Hixon last night and we had a grand talk. You remember when Larry Kline was driving that milk wagon and we were going swimming in Horse Creek and Cleve and you was going to fight Kline and Heeler. Well this is the Heeler it was and he spoke of it last night. I wish we was living out there yet and having a good time hunting, trapping, and all that stuff, don't you? We had a good thing there but didn't know it.

I had a letter from Clara Mair. Henry and Fred have been drafted and also old Carroll Dummir.

Well Wes, have you seen the play of *The Unbeliever* yet? Our company helped make that picture, so go see it if you get the chance.

One can never tell how soon this war will end, but as soon as it does, I think I will be able to get out, but if it lasts for four years more I am good for it all unless I get shot and then my worry is all put to an end.

Well, dear Brother, I do not know anymore to write. I will close hoping to hear from you soon.

I remain your affectionate Bro Ben.

ok Lt. C. B. Cates

• • •

Flooded with guilt, Wesley slapped the letter down on his desk. *Oh Christ, I should have gone with him! For God's sake, why didn't I go with him?*

Echoing through his mind came Ma Tooper's words on the day Benny enlisted, "Go with him, Wesley! Take care of him."

"No," Pa had declared. "Wesley's starting to get somewhere in Chicago, and we need him close by. They don't have to register for that selective service 'til they're twenty-one. The War'll be over by then. It's all politics. Politics!"

Wesley picked up Benny's letter and reread it. The kid was selling again. Ever since he'd promised his brothers at Horse Creek he would never lie to them again, he put all his steam for spinning yarns into selling. He sold the two worthless revolvers Pa had found in a boxcar as Civil War relics and got enough money for a brand new .22 rifle.

He sold the fancy buggy Cleve left at the farm when he went to Mexico, swearing up and down the auto rage would fall dead in its tracks any day. He got more than Cleve paid for it, giving his oldest brother enough money to get married and move to Chicago with his bride. Then if Benny didn't turn right around and sell an auto to their cousin, Chester, declaring the days of the horse and buggy were over for good And now he was making a pitch that life on the front was a bowl of cherries, just like he eased some sucker into a sale. His reason? To keep Ma and Pa and the whole bunch from worrying about him.

Wesley's eyes zeroed in on the letter's third line. "The Germans are sending regards by way of shells to me." Wesley shook his head in dismay. Yesterday he witnessed the results of such regards while visiting Leonard Bonet at the soldiers' hospital on the south side—

both legs blown off. He and Leonard had been in the eighth grade together at Kankakee Elementary when Leonard won the award for the fastest runner in the school.

"When those shells hit," he blurted out as Wesley lifted him from his bed to a wheelchair, "the whole ground opens up, and you think you're going to Hell for good. You see bodies all blackened and twisted and rifles and … and helmets and backpacks flyin' through the air. And the screamin', Wes. Men moanin' and cryin' for their mothers or their sweethearts. Beggin' the medics for water. 'Water. Please, water.' And the trenches. They're covered to keep out some of the rain, and you think you're gonna suffocate if you don't get more air."

Wesley ran his finger under the line where Benny described the trenches as "a fine place to sleep." *Selling again. The kid can't stop selling.* He tried to imagine himself standing in a hole with water up to his knees. He might be damn glad he had a bunk high enough to give him a dry place to nap, but would he call it a fine place? Maybe, if he was dead tired. But what did Benny leave out of his letter?

"Hell," said Cleve when Wesley showed it to him. "We don't know how much of this was censored. He couldn't tell us the whole story if he wanted to."

I should have gone with him! I should have gone with him! The words wouldn't stop inside Wesley's head. *How come I'm not drafted yet?* Maybe some of the forms had stuck together at selective service when he signed up on his twenty-first birthday. "I didn't see you, Wesley," Ma Tooper always said while he was growing up. "I skipped over you." Well, maybe the Army skipped over him too.

Lying in bed that night, Wesley thought back to the week before Benny enlisted. As if someone waved a magic wand over his head, Patriotic Steel, one of the biggest manufacturing companies in the

Midwest, hired him as supervisor of their accounts receivable division. He'd been working at Westchesters' Department Store ever since he finished his basic accounting courses at LaSalle Business College and had completed a whole load of advanced accounting classes— four hours every week, Monday through Thursday. He worked out a new inventory method that saved Westchester's time and money, and Patriotic Steel got wind of it. How could he leave everything and go off and join the Service?

Unable to sleep, Wesley remembered back to when he first came to Chicago and how he couldn't get any kind of office job. Companies hiring bookkeepers or accountants weren't impressed by the experience he had at little dabbler jobs in farm towns.

"Go to the stockyards," the bosses told him. "You might get in there."

Thank God Uncle Napoleon talked him into going back to school after the family moved to Kankakee. He had quit the little school in Bonfield to work more on the farm and take bookkeeping jobs in Bonfield and Momence, but Uncle Napoleon kept after him for a whole year to finish elementary school.

"A diploma will mean more from Kankakee than Bonfield, Wesley," he said. "You got to get a good education."

So he started the eighth grade over, older than most of the other students—and Benny already done with school. After graduation he left for Chicago. At the stockyards, the men in charge of hiring said he could have a job taking care of the animals designated for slaughter.

Wesley told them they were crazy. He had a diploma from Kankakee Elementary School and could add a column of figures a mile long in two seconds. They set him down at a table and had him work six pages of figure problems. Duck soup. They gave him a job posting figures and the address of LaSalle Business College. "Get yourself in school," they said.

He sailed through the accounting courses easily, and enjoyed the course he opted to take in proper English and speech so he wouldn't sound like a hick when he got a decent office job. Even so, it seemed like he spent his whole life on the trolleys—going to the stockyards early in the morning, downtown to LaSalle at the end of the day, and then back to his room at Cleve's as late as midnight.

The smell was terrible in the stockyards, but he got away from it somewhat in the offices. He felt an ache in his heart for the skinny, sickly-looking boys who took care of the animals—up to their shins in two city blocks of manure, their ears hearing nothing but cows bellering like hell because they knew in their bones what would happen to them. As much as he hated the yards, he'd stop by sometimes on his way to his workplace and catch a glimpse of the boys' faces. Was he searching for Willard there, his youngest lost brother nobody talked about anymore?

In his first accounting course at LaSalle, he saw a fellow who looked about two or three years younger than him sitting in the row ahead. He had black hair slicked up in a pompadour, like many of the Toopers, and he reminded Wesley of Pa or Cleve because he looked at the instructor as if he didn't believe what he said. On the way out of the classroom, Wesley asked him if he knew where he could buy the accounting books second-hand. As soon as he heard the kid's voice, slurry and kind of lazy, Wesley knew he couldn't be Willard.

Within the next year he got a job in the bookkeeping department at Westchester's Department Store. He received raises and promotions quickly and made more money than he ever dreamed he could. He sent some home to Pa and Ma every month with an extra envelope for Lilly. He started a savings account at Chicago First National Bank hoping some day to buy an auto—not a Ford that just any fellow with a steady job could buy, but one of those Studebakers or

Oldsmobiles. It would take longer to get the money together, but he'd rather ride the trolleys and have no car at all than buy a cheap one.

Still, even after he took the job at Patriotic Steel, he kept half hoping he'd be drafted. He missed Benny so much his chest hurt. If he got drafted and shipped over right away, maybe they could see each other. Everyday someone would ask him, "Why aren't you overseas fighting for us?" Christ, he'd just reached twenty-one a few months ago, even though he looked closer to thirty.

Last week, the War Department changed the draft age to eighteen, making him feel more like a moocher than ever. Here he had a soft, safe job, getting promotions and saving money, while men younger were getting killed or their legs blown off like Leonard. Cleve couldn't go because of his eyes, but he looked old enough that people didn't ask him why he wasn't in Service. Besides, married men didn't usually get called up as soon as single men. That's why Wesley felt so sheepish whenever a married man or an older fellow like Carroll Dummir back home got a draft notice. But he looked everyday in the mail and never found one. The bosses at work told him if he got drafted, his job would be waiting for him when he got back. But if he enlisted, it would be gone for good.

Pa said he would be nuts to give it all up and enlist. "Look how I sweated all those years to get a brakeman's wages. Here you wear nice clothes, never get your hands dirty doing something you could do in your sleep it comes so easy for you. Your wages are higher than I can count. Then you take a few lessons and get an even better job. What luck."

What luck? After all the hours I put in on the job and in school— the homework taking almost all night sometimes, and he calls it luck. Still, he had to admit much of it came easier and faster than he'd expected. But no matter how many hours he worked, he never

felt that pleasant tiredness like he did on the farm—when you worked
'til you almost dropped. Even Ma Tooper's cooking tasted like the
best in the world. You fell asleep as soon as your head hit the pillow
with pictures in your mind of the hay safe and dry in the barn loft,
the corn in the silo, and the cows all milked and contented.

As bad as he could imagine it overseas, maybe he could sleep
like that over there, just thankful to be alive for another day. But
why in the hell wasn't he drafted yet anyway?

CHAPTER FOURTEEN

Gas Bombardment

June 19, 1918

96th Co., 2nd Battalion, 6th Reg.

U. S. M. C. American Expeditionary Force

Somewhere in France

Dear Brother:

I thought I would answer your letter of the 5th of May.
This is the first chance I have had to answer you as I have
been on the move and on the front for so long. I have
been up on the real battle throng for 16 days and believe
me I have seen some hard fighting. But the Germans could
not whip us or make us retreat. I am in Base Hospital 17.
But I am not severely wounded. We were in that gas
bombardment for 8 hours. My eyes and lungs are inflicted
pretty bad and I have a few bad burns on my body. Our
whole company was gassed. Some of the boys are very
severe cases.

Well Wesley, are you still a civilian or a soldier? I
hope you are a soldier by this time but then Wes it is hard
footing now-a-days. It isn't like Cleve did, go down to the
border and lie around. When you move to France you
can say, "Here's where I get them or they get me." It's one
of the two. I had a bayonet fight with one big old husky

German and all he said was "ugh." He never had a chance to say no more. The Germans will not fight wih their bayonets or any other way in the open. They will give up as soon as you can see them, but as long a they can hide in the brush they are good fighters. They sure did make the French retreat though on their last drive, but when they met the Americans they stopped. I expect you have seen by the papers what the Marines have been doing. We are all proud to have been in the thickest of it.

My lieutenant and 24 of us went into the town of B_____ and drove out a machine gun company. The machine gun bullets were flying as thick as an Illinois hail storm but some of those bullets were shot for nothing for they only got 2 men out of those 24 and we got a good deal more than that. Altogether we counted 83 Germans dead and 12 wounded and we also took a bunch of prisoners. These prisoners wanted to know what we were, and when we told them that we were Americans, they would not believe us. They said that we were not Americans but Canadians in different uniforms.

Well, Dear Brother, I hope to hear from you soon as I will close with love to you and also to Uncle Ed and Aunt Jo.

I remain Bro Ben.

ok C. B.

• • •

After Wesley read the first paragraph of the letter, he raced through the rest of it and uttered, "I'm coming, Ben. I'm going to find you again!"

He made up his mind what to do. He would tell Pa and Cleve he received his draft notice. Lucky for him he no longer lived with Cleve and Mary, or Cleve would have picked up his mail and known he didn't get drafted. This way Cleve wouldn't have to lie to Pa for him. Wesley had moved in with Uncle Ed and Aunt Jo because Mary and Cleve wanted to start a family and would be needing Wesley's bedroom for a child they planned to have.

On the trolley the next morning, Wesley read Benny's letter over three times. He wanted to sob like he did when Cleve came home from Ohio with Benny's book. The name on the inside cover proved that they had a little brother, Benny Tooper, and there was hope of finding him some day. This letter made Wesley want to reach out for Benny, put zinc ointment on his blisters and castor oil on his eyelids. But now, he seemed farther away then ever.

The trolley pulled up to the enlistment center where a band played "Over There," and little boys in army uniforms waving miniature flags marched back and forth. When Wesley walked to the front of the trolley to get off, the driver tapped him on the shoulder and nodded to the letter still in Wesley's hand.

"Bad news, son? You lose a pal or a brother?"

"Gassed," Wesley said, barely getting the words out.

"You go over there," the driver hollered out as Wesley walked away, "and you make 'em pay!"

When Wesley tried to enlist, he found that the Army had no record of him.

The recruiting officer blamed it all on him. "You're twenty-one years old. You should've been drafted by now but how can we draft you when you don't register? You could go to jail for this."

Wesley brought out a copy of his selective service form. Pa always told him to get a copy for himself whenever he filled anything out.

He shoved it at the officer. "Look at this. Is this proof enough for you that I registered?"

The officer, hardly old enough to ask Lilly out on a date, looked at the form and shook his head. "There's something fishy here. We never lose a form."

Wesley reached over the table and grabbed him by the shirt front. "Listen, you yellow son of a bitch! If your office did its job right, I would be with my brother now. And he's not dishing out forms somewhere like a coward. He's lying in a hospital burned from mustard gas."

As Wesley's grip tightened, the officer's face turned as red as the stripes on the American flag hanging from the ceiling. "Listen, Mister," he croaked, "you put twenty bucks on the table, or I'll call the MP's and have you thrown in a cell."

"You bastards don't have me yet."

"Then I'll put a civilian assault charge on you, and you'll never see your brother."

Wesley released his hand and reached into his pocket. He had a twenty-dollar bill and change for trolley fare—enough money to last him all month, if he didn't have to hand over the twenty dollars to keep himself out of trouble. Now he'd have to withdraw money from his savings account. But he had to get into the Army. He had to get across.

"Here," he said, throwing the bill on the table. "Now where do I get my orders?"

"Two doors down on your left," the kid said, moving his sore neck back and forth and smoothing his shirt front. "You got off easy treating an officer like that."

"You're right," Wesley snapped. "I got one hell of a bargain."

When he announced at work that he was in the Army, his supervisor acted as suspicious as the recruiting officer. "This doesn't sound right," he said, pulling at his chin, "you better go see the president."

Walking to Charlie Kylie's office, Wesley remembered how the president of Patriotic Steel was impressed with what he knew about accounting at such a young age. He hired him on the spot, waiving the requirement of an interview with the board of directors. He also waived the requirement of a chaperone when Wesley drove his niece, Marjorie, around in her fancy, little car on Sundays or taking her to dances and clubs on Saturday nights.

It seemed to Wesley that Marjorie had picked him before he realized he was out of her class, and he wondered if Charlie Kylie hadn't set it all up. A lot of fresh men chased after Marjorie because of her money, her wildness, and her desire for a good time. Wesley wouldn't have put it past Kylie to introduce her to someone he thought would keep the treasure hunters away and not step over the line— until the right man with the right background came along. Marjorie liked to go to places Wesley couldn't afford, and she insisted on paying the bill from an extra purse she brought along, complements of Uncle Charlie.

When Wesley walked into Kylie's office, the president of Patriotic Steel greeted him with a big smile. "Why hello, Wesley. Nice of you to drop in. No problems, I hope."

"Not one. I'm in the Army."

Kylie sat up in his chair and reached for the phone. "You've been drafted? That's impossible. The War Department's going to hear what's good for it. My company supplies most of the parts that keep things going over there."

Wesley knew the jig was up. "I enlisted, Mr. Kylie."

Kylie held the phone receiver in mid-air. "You're signed up, you say. You've been accepted?"

"That's right. I leave for Indiana day-after-tomorrow. From there I'll probably go to South Carolina."

"You're a fool, Tooper!" Kylie slammed the receiver down on its hook. "You could have gone far here. You never would have been drafted."

"What makes you so sure of that?" Wesley knew right down to the bottom of his gut something rotten was going on, but he had to leave it alone. He had to get out of there and across the Atlantic to Benny.

Kylie answered Wesley's question. "Because you're a member of a company that plays a key role in keeping this war moving in the right direction." His voice softened a bit and he leaned forward. "Wesley, the fact that you work here makes you a soldier. You're a part of the great cause. Maybe there's still something we can do."

Wesley couldn't keep from laughing. "No, Mr. Kylie, my brother was the soldier all this time. Me? I sat behind a desk helping you fellas make money. He's lying in a hospital somewhere in France. His company withstood a gas bombardment for eight hours. You know what mustard gas does to your lungs? It dissolves them so when you try to take a breath, there's nothing there."

"And you think you're going to help by going over and have the same thing done to you?"

"I don't know, but I've got to try. Goodbye, Sir."

He was cleaning out his desk when Marjorie stormed in and threw her hat with a big ostrich feather in his face. "You rat!" she screamed. "Take advantage of me, spend my money, and sail off across the high seas. You dirty rat!"

"I never took advantage of you—not for a minute." Wesley straightened the feather on the hat and set in on a chair. "You think I'm going on some high-class cruise? I could be killed."

"I hope so. I hope you die! We treated you so damn good. You could have gone all the way to the top here."

"Not by a long shot. You have to be a certified public accountant with a fancy education to get to the top of what I'm in. I'm not a CPA and never will be."

"Uncle Charlie would have sent you to the university."

"That's crazy. I've never even been to high school."

"Uncle Charlie knows how to get around all that. We could have gone to Champaign and had a grand time. Now you've ruined it all."

"You mean I could've tagged along after you to rich kids' parties while my brother and his friends are dying overseas? I go to LaSalle Business College at night and work during the day. I'm from the farm, Marjorie. I rode the rails since I could walk. I lived in an orphanage."

"That's what you are. A farmer. A tramp. I was just biding my time until someone better came along."

"Me too. Bye, Marjorie."

• • •

Aunt Jo and Uncle Ed took him to the train station.

"Oh, Wesley," his aunt cried, we wanted so much to get to know you better. If only you could have stayed with us longer."

"I know, Aunt Jo, Thanks for having me."

"Don't ever forget this one thing, Wesley. Your mother watches over you night and day. I always knew deep in my heart you were her favorite."

"You're right," Wesley said, kissing her on the cheek. "Me and five others."

CHAPTER FIFTEEN

Soldier's Sacrifice

October 4, 1918

Headquarters Supply Co.

10th Reg't. F. A. R. D.

Camp Jackson

Columbia South Carolina

My Dear Bro. Ben—

Your letter dated Sept 1st. reached me yesterday. Of course, it was long looked for. Say Ben, I've written 4 letters in the last 2 months to you. I guess you have perhaps rec'd a couple of them now. I am tickled to death to hear that again you are out of the hospital in good health and back on the firing line again.

Ben, I guess the folks are very much worried over you. Try and write to them at least every two weeks, Ben. You know how Pa is about worrying.

I get very anxious also at times for you and would like to hear from you as often. The picture of your Nellie came in good condition and I thought she was very pretty. Where does she live Ben? You bet I'll take good care of the picture and have it for you when you return. Perhaps you will bring her along. Eh? Ha! The girls are not very thick around here Ben, but there are some.

I've been in the Army over 2 months now and of course like it fine. I have it pretty snappy here at Camp Jackson. Easier than in civilian life and a whole lots better eating too. Anything I want to eat, I get. I do the buying of food for Mess in my company and the officers put no restrictions on me whatever. A man is allowed 52 cents a day now for a ration and for that much I can feed the men real good. I gave up the job as Mess Sarg't and was transferred and then went here as head cook and at the same time I am breaking in a new man as Mess Sarg't. I'd rather cook and have every other day off and not so much responsibility. I get the same pay also.

Well, Ben, as yet I have no idea how soon I will go across. Some men get a chance to go over as soon as they are inducted into Service, but I was unlucky in not being transferred to a regular Reg't. But I really think I'll see France yet.

There is good encouraging news from the front now, Ben. Bulgaria surrendered! I think Turkey will fall soon and then Austria can soon be overcome. At any rate, the Huns' days of brutality and plunder are nearing an end. It makes one proud to hear and read the reports from the American fighting line where the Yanks are fighting so valiantly and heroically. Never driven back! Each man seems to cast all thoughts aside except to fight and to secure victories and give help to France, the allies, also whose victories will insure victory and peace for all. But the fellows over here are anxious to get over to do the same.

Uncle Ed and family are all well. They send your letters here, also a package of candy. Yes, Ben, I certainly stuffed myself at home. So would you. Ha! Pa is getting very fat now. He can eat me to death. He eats more than ever before. Well, it shows good health. Ma and Lill are also fine and dandy. Hazel and Dan also. Dan was put in Class 4. Also Cleve is in the same class. They will never have to go, I don't believe. Dan is moving on a grain farm 25 miles away. Some move!

Say Ben, do you realize that Willard is 18 years old now and in the draft? Of course, we are ignorant of him, but he may be in Service now. I hope he is not for he is too young. I want to see the day when he and the whole family are reunited once again. It will be a joyful day for Pa.

That stuff you rec'd from home must have been good, was it not? I'm surprised it was in good condition. I got a big cake from home. Believe me, it was good!

Cleve works for the government in Chicago now and makes from $45 to $50 per week. It is pretty good for him. Clifford Tooper had to go to war lately. Three LaCosse boys are in Service but I lost track of Joe's address. I presume he is over now. Uncle George St. John also is now in Service.

Well, Dear Old Bro, I've written all I can think of so I'll hush, I guess. Now Ben, do not forget the brotherly spirit in which I send my letters and answer as soon as you get them, and with brighter prospects for an early termination of the war. Yet I hope to meet and embrace you on some battlefield of France or Berlin. With much love. I am as ever your Bro, Wes.

• • •

Wesley managed to slip out the side door of the latrine where the loud-mouth sergeant dragged the men with the purpose of giving them cleaning instructions. He had decided to mail his letter to Benny while the bully barracks leader shouted that his men didn't know crap about cleaning a toilet. Damn it, the guy was bullying the Mexican kid again, degrading him in front of the whole bunch. "Filthy Mex," he called him, "yellow chicken-shit," and that poor kid kept himself and his bunk as clean as the next fellow, maybe even cleaner. What did he ever do to the almighty Sergeant Denser? Nothing. It made you sick to think some bastard enjoyed mistreating people and had the authority to do it—so men had to bow and scrape to him or get into serious trouble.

Wesley had been lucky most of the time. Just like at home on the farm with Ma Tooper, he managed to slip through without being noticed—until last week. He was pulled out of regular detail to help with bookkeeping problems in the business office, and Denser noticed him simply because he wasn't there. It must have riled the bastard that a non-commissioned man would be given special privileges to be in a position where the great Sergeant Denser couldn't pick on him or humiliate him whenever he felt like it.

Hell, Wesley wished sometimes that he had never been handy with figures, never gone to business school. If it hadn't been for that, and he had been just a common laborer, he would be in a regular regiment and sent across already. If the Army hadn't assured him he would still have the same training as any combat soldier, he would have refused his placement no matter what happened. The smartest thing he ever did was turn down the mess sergeant's job and just be head cook. The men really liked his cooking, and he ate better than he had before in his whole life. Except for not being sent across yet, and Denser giving him trouble the other night, things were pretty rosy.

On the night of the day he'd been excused from Denser's detail to do accounting work, he was having a beer with a couple of friends when Denser walked up to the bar. Without saying hello or even nodding to anyone, Denser turned to Wesley and said, "What are you, Tooper?"

"What do you mean, what am I? What are you?"

Denser looked at the other men knowingly like everyone knew what he was talking about.

"What I mean is why are you so dark? That's what I mean."

"Probably for the same reason you're so light." Wesley knew all the answers to those kind of questions. He was never asked things like that in Bonfield where most families came from Quebec, never asked them in Momence or even around Kankakee. But anywhere else, sooner or later, he'd be talking to someone and realize after a while that the person wasn't listening to a thing he said. "Where did you get that dark complexion?" they'd ask or "what nationality are you?"

"What I'm sayin', Tooper," Denser said, "is are you a Mexican, a Wop, an Indian, or what?"

"What I'm sayin' is I'm French Canadian."

"Oh, that's what you are. Well, Tooper, say something in French Canadian. Come on now, say it for us all."

The beer glass Wesley was holding was extra tall with a handle big enough to grasp it with his hand in a tight fist. The handle was cold and acted like a center, pulling all his frustrations of the moment towards it. He raised the glass up in front of him as if preparing to make a toast. "How about ... how's about ... GODDAMN SON OF A BITCH?" Then he brought the glass down on the bar with all his might. It shattered and then crumbled into a small pile on the bar, but the handle remained in his clenched fist.

He stood up and set the handle on Denser's shoulder, the arms facing downward. It rocked up and down like a little teeter totter. "Is that French Canadian enough for you?" he asked. Nobody said a word as he laid money on the bar to pay for the glass and walked out. He was sure Denser would really give him hell as soon as they were both back in uniform and the sergeant called the shots in the barracks. Pa would have told him he was taking a big chance, that he should have just laughed and kidded Denser out of it. "Your temper's gonna ruin you, Wesley," he'd say. But as the first few days passed by after the incident in the bar, Wesley felt invisible again, and Denser acted as if he didn't exist. Still, he remembered to carry a certain piece of paper in his back pocket at all times, in case he ever needed an ace in the hole.

After mailing his letter to Benny, he ran back to the barracks, opened the latrine door enough so he could slip inside and quietly took his place in one of the lines.

"How's it going?" he whispered to the man next to him.

"Rotten. He's really givin' it to the Mexican kid. He's makin' him clean the toilet with his own toothbrush."

"Oh God."

"Scrub it good, you lousy little piece of filth!" Denser hollered at the kid. "Get it under the rim where the stains and the crap crumbs are." The kid was down on his knees, his back to the other men. They could see the deep crimson color spreading over his neck and ears like blood from a fatal wound.

"Oh my God," the voice deep inside Wesley kept saying. "Oh my God, what am I going to do?"

"Don't do anything," his father's voice kept telling him. "Stay out of it. Stay out of it, Wesley."

"Now stand up," Denser ordered the kid. "Stand up and face your buddies."

The kid stood up and turned, his face burning red, his eyes searching the rows of men for some sign of compassion, for help.

"Stand up straight!" Denser kicked him in the rear.

"You bastard," the voice inside Wesley said. "You're what we should be fighting in this War too. The kaiser's a bully bastard and so are you. It's you. It's you!"

"Stay out of it, Wesley," his father repeated. "Stay out of it."

"Now," Denser said to the kid. "You're gonna take that nice little toothbrush that scrubbed that shitty toilet and you're going to give those dirty yellow choppers of yours a real good cleaning."

Wesley could hear gasping sounds from some of the men in the lines.

"Jesus," the man next to him whispered between clenched teeth. "Jesus." Denser started screaming at the kid, calling him a string of names one after another.

Wesley took the folded paper from his pants pocket and shoved it in the back pocket of the man in front of him. "Give this to the company commander for me, unless I take it back from you soon." The man nodded.

The kid's face was turning gray now, his eyes reflecting the nightmare he was living. "Sarge," he pleaded. "I didn't do nothin'. Don't make me. Please!" A tear of agony and embarrassment stood out on his face like a cruel scar.

"Pa," the voice inside Wesley said to his father. "I can't stand this! Remember at the orphanage? Remember when you knocked the wind out of the priest and poured wine all over his head?"

"That was for family, Wesley," he heard his father say. "Stay out of this. Stay out."

"And remember, Pa, remember when that school master broke my finger with a ruler, and Cleve turned over his desk on top of him and smashed his spectacles?"

"That was different. Stay out, Wesley. Stay out."

"Do it! Do it!" Denser shouted at the kid. "Put that toothbrush in your mouth and scrub!"

The kid hung his head and moved it slowly from side to side. The toothbrush fell from his hand to the floor.

"Do it, you piece of slime!" Denser yelled again. "Do it and say, 'yum, yum good,' ya hear? Yum, yum good! Do it, or I'm gonna throw you in the clink and you'll never get out."

"No," the kid sobbed. "I didn't do nothin'."

Wesley pushed through the lines of men in front of him. He snatched up the toothbrush lying at the feet of the weeping soldier. Taking it in both hands, he turned and faced Denser, holding the brush outward and snapping it in two.

"No one's ever gonna use this dirty, rotten toothbrush again!" he shouted, throwing it down and stamping on it with his boot, grinding it into the floor. "Never again. Never again!"

Each time he said it his voice got louder and higher until it was a frantic croak. "Never again!"

He thought those two words would never stop spewing out of him until he lunged for Denser. It took at least three men to hold him back.

CHAPTER SIXTEEN

Jailbird

October 12, 1918

The next thing Wesley knew, his eyes were watering from the sun's
rays shooting onto his face between the bars of a window. He moved
his head out of range and realized he was sitting on the floor with
one of his hands cuffed to a ring in the wall. He wiped his eyes on
the back of his free hand and looked around. Was this the dreaded
stockade he had heard about since he was a little boy, where trouble-
some soldiers got sent and never came back? He didn't remember
being brought here, but he couldn't have been thrown in too hard
or beaten up because he didn't have any pains or bruises. Instead, he
felt like a huge weight had been lifted from his chest—as if he had
landed in a cool, quiet haven of peace.

The guard who brought him his supper apologized that he couldn't
unlock the handcuff until he received further orders. Wesley told
him not to worry about it. He and his brothers, when they were
young, liked to see who could eat for the longest time with his left
hand before spilling on himself. Besides, someone else's cooking
always tasted better than your own—one handed or two.

He wasn't surprised when Benton, his company commander,
came to see him. Wesley saluted but couldn't stand up straight so
Benton sat down on the floor next to him and rested the back of his
head on the rough, gray concrete.

"Well, Tooper," he said. "I knew when they put you to work on the books, they probably picked the only man in the United States Army who might figure out what I've been doing. But I never thought you would use it against me."

"I don't want to," Wesley said. "You've treated me and the rest of the men more than fair. There's just some things I need, and I don't know any other way."

Benton motioned for the guard to unlock the handcuff. "You want out of here? I can claim you fell apart under pressure. You can have a nice, soft hospital bed and an open door out of the U. S. Army."

"I don't want out of the Service," Wesley snapped. "I want you to get me shipped over now. You hear me? Now."

Benton took his hat off, ran his fingers through his hair and sighed. "That's going to be a tough one. Denser's probably going to insist charges be brought against you. From what I heard each time you yelled 'never again' about the toothbrush, he kept shouting out the military code you were violating."

"What happened after I left?"

"He dismissed everyone."

"Including the Mexican kid?"

"Yes."

"Good. That's the other thing I want. I want the kid transferred to where Denser can't get at him, to another regiment. Better yet, to another base where nobody knows about this thing—so he can hold his head up again."

"That's fairly easy, Tooper—a lot easier than it will be doing something about you."

"Don't hand me that. I know how these things work. You've got people above you who owe you favors for things you can hold over their heads. What'll happen to you if I turn you in?"

"The worst. My career, my family—everything." He gave Wesley a side-long glance. "But maybe not if I give the word in here not to let you talk. Ever."

"I don't think you're the kind who would do that. And even if you were, I've taken care of it. If anything happens to me, you can bet your shenanigans will be all over the newspapers. Now for God's sake, cut out all this damn talk and get busy. Give Denser a promotion that'll shut him up."

Benton thought for a minute. "Now that's a possibility. An office job, maybe."

"Yeah, that's right. Where he can't lord it over people again."

"Would you be willing to do any kind of duty if I got you shipped over with a battalion? Ship administration problems, more accounting?"

"Anything. Just get me over. Give me a little time with the books, and I'll fix your little embezzlement all up. No one will be able to put the clamps on you like I did."

Benton sighed as if he'd come to the end of a long journey. "I probably knew this would catch up with me sometime. As long as it was going to, I guess it's best you were the catcher. I knew it was wrong. I got in a bind and I couldn't stop. I did it for my family, for my kids." He looked down at the floor. "Most of the other officers have a wife and kids. They didn't resort to this."

"You owe me a favor," Wesley said, "but, you don't owe me any explanation. Your little pilfering is nothing compared to the thievery that goes on in this War and to all the dirty tricks and unfairness—people getting fat from other people's sweat and suffering. Hell, I work with the figures. I've seen in black and white where the money comes from and where it goes. Before I joined up, I worked for one of the biggest suppliers for the war effort. What you did was harmless next to what they pulled off."

"But the worst of them all," he said, slamming his open hand down so hard on the floor, the guards outside could have heard it, "is a guy like Denser. Dirty rotten bully. Making men so miserable they wish they were dead. Shaming them day after day, and they can't fight back because they don't have the power. Dirty, rotten bully. He should pay. He should pay!"

Benton placed his hand on Wesley's shoulder. "Easy. Take it easy." He moved closer and spoke in almost a whisper. "We don't want those guards coming in here. Look, Tooper, things just might work out. I'll look into the Mexican boy's transfer tomorrow morning. With some finagling, maybe we can get you on a ship."

Wesley placed his hand on the commander's arm. "Thanks."

"It's probably going to take longer than you like, maybe over a month."

Wesley sighed. "I figured as much."

"If you want, I can try and fix it so you'll work your regular job during the day and come back here at night. The men miss your cooking already and the kitchen is in chaos. I could get you back there during the day in about a week."

"If you don't mind, I'll just stay here until I go across. I've got a lot to think about."

When Wesley woke up the following morning, he walked to the window and looked out. How different a military base seemed when he was isolated from it than when he was a part of it. He tried to picture himself walking among the servicemen there, but he couldn't. Maybe that's why he landed in jail.

Then he saw Denser. He emerged from a building where other men with sergeants' insignia came and went, disappeared between two long buildings, and reappeared at the end of them. Then he kept walking until he was a little speck merging into other little specks.

That's all Denser would have been to him if not for the bullying of the Mexican boy. He would have been an insignificant speck passing uneventfully through the life of Wesley Tooper and then forgotten.

That night, with the base grounds in front of his cell window illuminated by one lone gaslight, Wesley saw him again. Denser came out of the same building he had in the morning and followed the same route he did then—disappearing between the two long buildings. Because of the darkness, he could not be seen at the other end.

The next day, Wesley watched him at the same time as the the day before—just like clockwork coming out of the sergeants' building. What was it about his walk? He lifted his legs and arms as if pulling some weight along. His rear end. He wasn't overweight but his rear end stuck out and shook a little when he walked like the gelatin Ma Tooper made from boiling cows' hooves. Of course Denser would have such a butt.

Long ago Wesley and Cleve discovered that kind of butt on railroad cops who cracked the skulls of hobos riding the freights, on school masters who broke your finger with a ruler because you picked up a penny someone lost and then lied and said you didn't. Father Fatso had that kind of butt, although it was hard to see with all those robes he wore. A bully but. That's what Wesley and Cleve had called it. As old as they were now, how they would laugh if Cleve were here to see it too.

The next morning, when Wesley saw Denser walking between the two long buildings and coming out farther down, he realized this particular sergeant could be identified from everyone else on the whole base because of his rear end. Even as he got further and further away and became just a dot walking among other dots, Wesley could pick him out because of his bully butt. It faithfully bobbed along behind him, powered by the steady pumping of his arms.

From the stories Wesley had heard about military prisons, he expected to receive a number of beatings. That would be all right. His pa had dished out punishment to his sons when they disobeyed him. Wesley figured because he was smaller back then, his bigger size now might make up for it if the guards swung harder than Pa did. The nuns at the orphanage, mean field hands, and warehouse bosses roughed him up whenever they felt like it before he reached ten years old. He became toughened and used to it. He would take the beatings in this prison just fine.

As the days drifted by, the beatings never came, although he noticed the guards picked him out for hard labor more than the other men. This was because his records showed he did office work before he got into Service and got away from "real work" in the guards' eyes. Chained to prison mates, he'd be hauled in a wagon to a work-site where he loaded bricks or rocks, railroad ties or pieces of stumps.

"Little heavier than a pencil, ain't they, Bookkeeper?" the overseers chided, or "lots harder on your back than shufflin' papers, ain't it, Mr. Accountant?"

Wesley would answer, "Yes, Sir," and wrinkle his face and grunt when he lifted a load to make it look like he was straining terribly. But hell, he could lift twice that much. Those laggards didn't know what work was. Why, he and his brothers could clean up the whole site in one third the time as this prison work detail did.

They liked to lord it over him at mealtime because he'd been head cook before he got thrown in prison. "Can't put special food aside for yourself now, can you, Cooky? No special treatment, huh? Think you can get it down?" He'd make it look like the food was hard for him to swallow, but when they weren't looking he'd smack his lips. Pretty damn good.

CHAPTER SIXTEEN Jailbird 137

His favorite pastime was lying on his bunk listening to the trains. He had listened to them ever since he could remember, but it wasn't until his mother died that he thought they were chanting to him: "There there, Wesley, there there, Wesley; go to sleep now; safe and sound now, safe and sound now." He hadn't lived near any train lines since he left Kankakee County, but he could still tell the sound of a freight from a passenger train, an express from a milk train. Just by listening he knew which trains had the heavier locomotives, which freights pulled more cars, even what kind of loads they carried—coal or wood or oil. He could even tell close to the mile how far away a train was when he first heard its whistle or how fast it went.

As soon as it got near to the city of Columbia, he let the wheels tell him by the way they rolled over the track when would be the best time to jump on—if the train slowed down, rounded a curve, or chugged uphill.

"Not yet, Wesley," he'd whisper to himself, hearing the popping of the wheels and a long, low whistle in the background. "Wait a bit. Run along side. Easy. Easy does it. There now! Grab it, fella. Climb up. Keep your head down, ol' boy. Head down."

Thanks to Pa, when he first came to Camp Jackson he made a point to pick up the latest train schedule. "As soon as you get to a place," his father always told him, "find out when the trains are going in and out, where they come from, and where they're bound." From what he remembered from the schedule and what he learned from merely listening, he came to know the trains and their destinations, their departures and arrivals.

The more he watched Denser through the window and the more he listened to the trains and learned their schedules, the more he felt these particular circumstances were coming together for a purpose. An opportunity was within arm's length of him, if he would only know how to use it. But it wasn't until the night guard started getting friendly that he actually made a plan.

The guard patrolling his section of cells at night was Mexican. As the time grew later, he'd stop at Wesley's cell and talk. He said he was born in Nuevo Laredo but enlisted in the American Army at a recruiting station in Corpus Christi, Texas. Sometimes he'd take a deck of cards out of his back pocket, and they'd play five card stud between the bars, and a game the guard learned growing up in Mexico, a game something like rummy. Sometimes Wesley noticed the guard staring at him as if trying to figure him out and a few times letting a hint of a smile creep out from a corner of his mouth. Wesley wondered if the guard knew why he'd been thrown in prison and if he was being friendly with him because he'd helped one of the guard's own. He wondered too how, being a Mexican, the guard was able to get one of the better jobs in the Army. Maybe he was lucky never to run up against someone like Denser.

Wesley liked his accent, and when he lay on his bunk after the guard left, he'd whisper certain words and expressions over and over that sounded to him like "Meh-hee-ko" or "ze weendow" or "ze du-orr". The next night, he'd listen again and try to get closer to the way someone from Mexico would pronounce them.

As his plan came together he worked on the exercises he learned in basic training. He concentrated mostly on the push-ups, twice as many as they did in the barracks. When he stood at his window waiting for Denser to make his routine appearance, he grabbed onto the bars and squeezed as hard as he could, then released, squeezed and released back and forth so his hands got stronger and his grip unbreakable. He watched Denser more carefully at night noticing that even if he walked out of the sergeants' building with someone else, he was always alone when he turned and walked into the darkness. Wesley counted the steps it took him to get to the long buildings and when he couldn't see him anymore, he estimated the number of strides it would take him to get to the end.

"My God, I'm crazy," he told himself. "Tooper, you're buggier than a damn bedbug."

CHAPTER SEVENTEEN

Farmboy Justice

December 2, 1918

Things moved quickly after Wesley's release from the stockade. Benton drove him to the business building where he could get at the books and cover up the commander's pilfering. Also he had worked out a system where the commander could pay back the Army what he had embezzled with no one being the wiser. With the job finished two hours later, he walked into the post store and bought a new toothbrush. Back at the barracks, he packed for the troop train and put the toothbrush he'd been using up to that day in the back pocket of the pants he wore. He set the new one in his shaving case next to his single-edged razor and shaving brush. Then he put his undershirts in the duffel bag and nestled the case in the midst of them. At the same time, he felt the nagging bristles of his old toothbrush at his backside like some unforgotten chore of yesterday.

He had permission to go to the mess hall and pick up any personal things he had left there while working as head cook. When he got to the kitchen, he found, in a long, narrow box, the special knife he had bought for cutting small pieces of fat and ribbons of gristle from officers' steaks and roast cuts. Brushing his thumb lightly over the sharp, thin blade, he remembered how he hated to spend the money for it when he could have all the knives he wanted for free. But it had made his day-to-day job much easier than any of the knives the Army issued. And it would come in handy for the big job he had to do that night.

Rummaging around in the storage closet, he found one of the old Army blankets used for soaking up spilled water, along with half a dozen pairs of coveralls the helpers wore when cleaning the big ovens. He chose one that fit him and ripped the blanket in half, returning one piece to the storage closet. He laid the other piece out on the floor, spreading the coveralls over it. He took the toothbrush out of his pocket and placed it and the knife box in the biggest coverall pocket. He rolled the blanket piece up with everything inside and set it on top of his regular blanket roll in his duffel bag and pulled the strings tight.

"Am I really doing this?" he asked himself. "Or is it just a damn dream?"

On the troop train, he put his duffel bag in the corner of the baggage car, somewhat aside from all the others and easy to retrieve, not overly conspicuous. He also made sure his fellow passengers knew he was on the train and could remember him, if questioned. Heads turned his way as he whistled and shouted out the train window to the send-off committee from Columbia, especially when he sang off-key along with the community band: "Over there! Over there!"

"Atta boy!" encouraged the young sergeant who replaced Denser. "Keep up the spirit, Trooper." Wesley chuckled and pointed to the name tag on his shirt. "Not Trooper, Sarg—Tooper." The sergeant patted him on the back. "I'll make a note of that, Tooper. I sure will."

Not wanting to take a seat and be lost in a flood of passengers, he stood in line with those who weren't settled yet. When he figured the train was a short distance from the little town of Ridgeway, he turned to a red-headed, freckled-faced private standing next to him and said, "I'm not feeling so good. I think I'll stick my nose out on the platform and get some air."

The boy nodded.

Back in the baggage car, he took the small blanket roll out of his duffel bag and put the coveralls on over his uniform. He slid his old toothbrush and knife box into the big side pocket on the right leg and put the watch Pa gave him in the little top pocket. Then he rolled up the blanket piece and stuffed it inside the coveralls over his chest. As the train slowed down for Ridgeway, he opened the train door.

Ready to jump, he whispered, "Now ease yourself off. As soon as you hit, roll over onto the grass. If you don't, you'll break your damn ankle."

Suddenly in Wesley's mind, Cleve and Benny appeared, giving him pointers, reminding him of what he had forgotten from the days of riding the rails in Bonfield when they were kids. Because of them, he landed without a scratch.

"Oh Boy, Oh Boy," he sing-songed between breaths, crossing four sets of tracks without stumbling once. He could have sworn he heard his brothers' whoops of encouragement behind him as he ran. But soon the whistle of the 7:15 to Columbia drowned out their imagined cheers, and the next thing he knew, the train was bearing down on him. Years had passed since he hopped a train, more years yet since he and Cleve taught Benny. Now he needed them to help bring back those skills so he could do what he must do.

"Don't rush it, you fool," Cleve rasped as they reached the other side of the track. "It'll swallow you up."

"Easy now," Benny cautioned as Wesley sprinted alongside the train.

"Grab it!" Cleve shouted. "Grab it, damn it!"

"I got it," Wesley announced triumphantly, "I got it, bro's."

"For Christ's sake, pull up!" Cleve hollered. "Pull yourself up!"

"You're okay now," Benny assured him. "You're on board. Head down now. Head down."

He had a smooth ride back to the outskirts of Columbia and rolled off the train easily. He was afraid someone would spot him on the tracks before he hit the woods, but he still had his brothers to help him. Everything he'd remembered, felt, and dreamed brought them back, not only in his mind but in his heart, clearer and more real than if they were actually beside him.

"You got these coveralls on," Benny reminded him. "If someone comes along, just pretend you're picking up trash or inspecting railroad ties like any workman would."

"Good idea," Wesley said under his breath, and soon he was crashing through the live oak trees and sycamores separating the train tracks from Camp Jackson. Reaching Gills River, he found a place where several large stones acted as a bridge. Jumping from one to the other, he stepped onto the opposite bank. A tall fence, fifty yards ahead, surrounded the Army post, but he knew he could scale it easily.

"Don't catch your damn crotch," Cleve nagged as he went over the top, "or that'll finish ya."

When he waited at the dark end of the long building where Denser always turned, he worried that someone else would come by this particular night instead of Denser. When he heard the door to the sergeant's building open and close, his tongue stuck to the roof of his mouth and he felt sweat creep down his back like a nervous spider.

"It's okay, Wes," Benny whispered. "The moon's out just enough to see it's him. Look how he walks! You could recognize him just by the sound of his steps because of his bully butt."

Wesley pulled out the blanket from inside his coveralls. As Denser's steps grew louder, he held the blanket out in front of him.

"No, not like that," Cleve snarled. "If he raises his arms, you won't get it all the way over him. You got to hit him in the stomach first. Knock his wind out."

"I can't. I've been doing office work too long."

"You gotta, Wes. You just gotta!"

Like a fairytale giant, Denser's shadow loomed up big enough to smother all three of them. Seconds later, the sergeant turned the corner and Wesley's fist shot out like a piston right into the soft part of Denser's belly. His captive made a sound like a tire deflating as he buckled at the knees, elbows bent and forearms limply pointing outward like a puppet on a string. Wesley's fist came out again, crumbling Denser completely. He flung the blanket over him and threw himself on top.

Denser gasped, then sputtered, lifting his feet off the ground in a futile attempt to move his body.

"Now, Wes," Benny insisted. "While his strength is gone."

Wesley eased Denser over on his side and wrapped the excess part of the blanket around the upper part of him so the sergeant's arms were entirely encased in it. Sitting on Denser's legs, he unbuckled the sergeant's belt, undid the buttons on his fly, and pulled his trousers down enough so he could see the crack of his rear end, the tops of his butt cheeks glowing in the moonlight.

"My money," Denser moaned. "Take my money. Not this. Please, not this."

Wesley took his knife out and held the point at the top of Denser's crack. "One noise, Gringo, and you will be dead foreverrrr."

In Wesley's mind, Cleve and Benny disappeared and left in their places two Mexican brothers who talked like the guard in the stockade. "Hold him down, Pancho," one said in a youthful voice like Benny's. "Go ahead stick him!" another said in a gnarled voice like Cleve's.

Denser squealed like the young pigs the Tooper kids used to catch in gunny sacks at the farm.

"Here, hold my knife, Carlos," Wesley said. "Keep him down, Pancho."

His brothers answered, "Right," and Wesley set the knife down and pulled the toothbrush out of his pocket.

"No worry, Gringo," he told Denser. "Just cleaning you up a bit."

He pushed the toothbrush into Denser's crack, moved it back and forth a couple of times and pulled it out. Denser jerked like he'd been hit with a lightning bolt, his voice turning on like a muted machine gun. Wesley picked up the knife again and cut an opening in the blanket, exposing Denser's face.

He reached into the blanket and grabbed Denser's hair. "We're going to brush your teeth just like you tried to do to one of us. Remember? Open your mouth now. Nice and wide."

Denser clamped his mouth down, breathing hoarsely through his teeth.

"Open," Wesley's younger Mexican brother ordered.

"Open, you bastarrrrd," said the other.

Wesley pushed down on the knife enough to draw a thin line of blood. Denser gasped, his mouth opening enough so Wesley could shove the toothbrush in his mouth, turning it around inside as much as he could.

"Now, to use your own words, Gringo, say 'yum yum, good, yum yum, good!'"

Wesley's mind flew back to a night years ago when he and Benny were hunting on Union Hill and heard a sound coming through the woods unlike any creature they had ever heard—low and haunting as if from some unknown time and place. Denser's voice, as he obeyed his captor, reminded Wesley of that sound.

Instead of feeling satisfied, triumphant in having Denser undergo the same humiliation the sergeant had brought upon the Mexican boy, Wesley wanted more—to ram the toothbrush further into Denser's mouth, so hard it would pierce his cheek. He wanted to make him suck everything out of it and swallow it all down. And then a shiver rushed through his body that almost caused him to release his hold. He was scared—not of Denser or what would happen to him if were caught, but of himself.

"Jeez, Wes!" Benny's voice returned. "You gonna keep at it 'til you cut him into little pieces and stomp him into the ground?"

"You did what you came here for." Cleve rasped. "Let the bastard go."

Wesley pulled the blanket off and got to his feet. Shaking his head to clear it, he directed his voice downward towards Denser. "You move in the next ten minutes, Gringo, and our knives fly into your back. You step on any of our boys again, and we'll get you— wherever you are."

Denser made no sound. His body shook all over, and for an instant, Wesley thought he might be crying but then doubted if the sergeant knew how. He kept walking backwards until he brushed against a garbage can and put the blanket and toothbrush inside, first wiping the handle of the toothbrush with the blanket.

Then he ran—ran like hell with Cleve and Benny right beside him again. He climbed the fence faster than a raccoon raiding Ma Tooper's chicken coop and stopped to catch his breath, taking his watch out of his top pocket.

"You don't even have ten minutes!" Cleve hissed.

"Go, Wes, go!" Benny urged.

How he got to the tracks and crossed them before the express train to Washington screamed alongside him, he didn't know. He felt his arm reach out, his fingers curl around the railing to the boxcar ladder, and his legs carry him to the second rung.

"You did it!" his brothers shouted through the steam. "You did it!"

"If only," Wesley said holding tightly now with both hands. "If only Denser doesn't talk and bring down the blame on every Mexican on the post. If that happens, I've made things worse."

"Aw hell," Cleve said. "Don't you know by now, bully bastards don't squeal after they get what's comin' to 'em. They know there's a hell of a lot of fellows out there waitin' for a chance to give him a dose of his own medicine, like you just did."

"Yeah," Benny confirmed. "And bully bastards are too flabby and soft to come after anyone themselves. You handled him like he was a baby doll, Wes."

"Thanks, bro's," Wesley said and climbed the ladder to the top of the car. He laid on his stomach, feeling the wind blow over and around him, drowning out the sound and smell of Denser, and finally the very thought of him. Cleve and Benny were no longer with him, but that was okay. They knew he could handle the rest by himself.

"Well-done, Wesley, well-done, Wesley," the train sang as it crossed into North Carolina. "Safe and sound now, safe and sound now," it chanted as it chugged toward the green, sweet-smelling hills of Virginia through counties called Essex, Caroline, Isle of Wight, and King and Queen, where the breeze brought the clouds closer and told an Illinois flatland boy stories he'd known only in dreams.

CHAPTER EIGHTEEN

The Goodbye Party

October 16, 1918

If he hadn't gotten mixed up in Occoquan, they wouldn't have nabbed him. The hobos told him the Carolinas were safe, not like Louisiana or Georgia where you could end up in the chain gang. So when he got through Greensboro and Durham, he rested easier. Virginia would give him no trouble, an old timer told him, so when he hit the small town of Independent Hill, he wasn't a bit anxious about getting off and catching the troop train before it got too close to D.C. By God, he couldn't have planned it better.

But the minute he grabbed a train at Occoquan, he knew he got it wrong. It picked up speed so fast he couldn't risk jumping off, and it didn't slow down until an even smaller town called Corton where he slid off into the outstretched arms of the county sheriff. The portly lawman removed his wide-brimmed hat and bowed, gesturing to a mustached deputy parked by a cross-gate in a very used Stutz Bearcat.

"We've been watchin' for you, Bo—since Occoquan. Got on the wrong train, didn't ya?"

"How … how did you know?"

"Oh, just from the temporary way you hung on to 'er. The way you looked around trying to find a place to lose 'er. Well, you don't have to worry where to stay anymore. We got a nice little room for you back at Occoquan—no charge at all. No Siree, no charge. Now stand up against this post here. Hands out in front for the handcuffs, if you please."

Wesley reached for the buttons on his coveralls to show his Army uniform. The sheriff's hand flashed to his side and came up with a pistol. The deputy in the car did the same.

"Hold it now," the sheriff ordered. "Don't reach for nothin'. We've got a bead on you. Don't be foolish."

Wesley held up his hands. "I … I just want you to see that under these coveralls, I'm a soldier. I've got to get on the troop train before it gets to Washington. We're goin' across to fight the Germans."

The sheriff thrust open the front of the coveralls and peered at the uniform inside. "Tooper, eh? Well, Mr. Tooper, you got any identification that matches the numbers here?"

A piercing whistle from the south reached Wesley's ears first and then climbed straight up his spine. How his bones ached to be on that train, to feel her clanking and banging beneath him—to watch her caboose tagging faithfully behind. He took his wallet from his pocket and pushed it towards the sheriff. "See? That's me. I gotta get on that train now!"

"How come you weren't on it all along? You don't sound like you're from around here."

The train whistle grew louder, flinging Wesley's hopes along the tracks like pieces of ragged newspaper.

"I'm … I'm from Illinois," he blurted desperately. "My mother … she died! She really did. I had to get home but … but there wasn't time to get a leave. I've been riding trains two nights and a day. I could make it yet. I just gotta get across. My … my brother's over there!"

The sheriff grabbed him by the coveralls and pulled him close. His face was round and soft like a bowl of pudding and his eyes clear and blue as marbles. He smelled like he'd been eating corn-on-the-cob, the second crop of it, just picked off the stalk and boiled fresh.

"Look at me, Tooper. Look at me and say, 'My mother's really dead!'"

Wesley looked into the blue eyes so intensely he could see specks of his own reflection. "My mother's really dead, Sir."

The sheriff released his grip. "By the good Lord, I believe you. I can tell when a man's lying about somethin' as sacred as his mother." He turned toward the man in the car. "Johnny, let's get a move on. This young fella's gotta catch a train!" He beckoned to Wesley to follow him. "We'll drive you down the road a spell where you can get on so smooth you won't even get your uniform dirty. You can shed those coveralls along the way."

Wesley got in the car and took the coveralls off. He felt he was abandoning a covering that had protected him through a long, crazy journey. His body shook when he got rid of it and he wished he could have kept it on. Hell, he might rub up against a mass of grease or the train might blow something foul all over his clothes, leaving him with a filthy uniform—a dead giveaway when he reached the troops.

The sheriff placed a gentle arm on his shoulder and pointed to the oncoming train. It charged over a viaduct ahead and then slowed down at the peak of a curve near the car.

"Go now, Son. There's steps there by that coach door. Quick!" He pulled Wesley to him in a severe hug, tears tumbling down his pudding cheeks. "Give 'em hell, Soldier. Go get 'em."

Wesley ran to the track and stepped up onto the train car as easy as walking up to a diner for a bite of lunch. The door opened and there—staring at him with his mouth open—stood the red-haired, freckled-faced kid he had talked to in the train going out of Jackson. "Tooper! What are you doing out here?"

"Oh, I like to step outside here every once in a while," Wesley said, realizing how silly he would have looked if he kept the coveralls on.

"I like to stand here and look out on these little towns and wave to the sheriffs while they search for bums getting free rides." He raised a hand of thanks to the two lawmen, diminishing in size as the train sped on, their farewell salutes frozen in the distance.

The kid followed Wesley's gaze down the track. "I wouldn't want to get caught by those fellas. They'd beat your head in."

"They sure would," Wesley said. "Say, I don't think I ever got your name."

The kid pointed to the name tag on his shirt, but the train car jiggled too much for Wesley to read it. "I don't like my first name," he said, "so everyone at home calls me Rusty." He reached a hand up and smoothed a cluster of red hairs standing in a stubborn cowlick. Then, wriggling his nose like a rabbit, he sniffed the air around him.

"Ya know, I think I smell corn on the cob. We just had dinner, and I don't see why we didn't have corn. In these southern states the warm weather lasts longer and they can get two crops of it. Do you know that, Tooper—two crops of corn?"

"Yes," Wesley said, trying to hold back a laugh. "Yes, Rusty, I sure did know that." Suddenly he became conscious of his empty stomach. He took a handkerchief out of his pocket and brushed it across his face, reluctantly wiping off the last airy traces of the hug from a trusting Virginia sheriff.

Rusty tugged at his shoulder. "Come on, we're supposed to get in line starting at car number four. They're gonna call roll."

Wesley took one last look out the window at the green, rolling hillside touched with nets of mist floating up from the Potomac. It seemed as though he should be telling someone goodbye. Instead he said, "Yeah, I'm coming, Rusty. Lead the way."

As he followed the others down the aisle, he felt soothed by the clacking rhythm of the train wheels and uplifted by the presence of the other men awaiting a new phase of their lives.

Suddenly Rusty stopped and turned, his eyes popping like they did when he saw Wesley standing outside the train car door. "Boy! I can hardly believe it. Pretty soon—off to battle we go. Guess if we ever need a guardian angel watching over us it'll be then."

"When I left for the Service," Wesley said, "my aunt told me my dead mother would be watching over me. I didn't believe that until just a little while ago. Now I think maybe she is."

Rusty looked relieved. "Hey, that's really something, Tooper. Tell her to watch over me too, will ya?"

Wesley ducked his head to look out one of the windows by the coach seats. He saw giant, dark trees with branches reaching in all directions, standing guard like sentinels over rows and rows of white crosses. Blinking his eyes to see through a murky, gray drizzle, he made out a sign that read, Arlington Cemetery. He shivered, not understanding why. He didn't know anyone buried at Arlington.

"I'll ask my mother, Rusty," he said. "I'll ask her to watch over both of us."

CHAPTER NINETEEN

Going Across

November 8-11, 1918

After the train pulled into Washington, Wesley rushed to a lunch counter and wolfed down a bowl of stew just in time to pick up his steel helmet and shaving kit with enough minutes to spare for catching another train. At Hoboken they filled out arrival cards to mail to their families when they reached France. He filled one out for Pa and Ma and another for Cleve and Mary, hoping Hazel wouldn't be mad at him for not sending her one. Lilly would tell her he arrived safely as soon as the folks got theirs. Then the troops marched in the early morning sunlight to the docks where they gulped lukewarm coffee, dry doughnuts, and soft apples from tables set out by the Red Cross.

"I think the guys who went over earlier in the War got all the fresh stuff," Wesley said, dunking his doughnut in the muddy coffee. "I haven't had a sinker this stale since I was a real little tyke. Had to get it down faster then."

Rusty craned his neck, trying to see everything, blinking his eyes as if to keep them from popping out. "Look! Those must be our ships over there. Five of them. All different sizes and colors. Why do you think that is?"

Wesley knew the answer from one of Benny's letters to Cleve. "That's to get the Germans in the subs all mixed up," he chuckled, "so they won't think we're a convoy of troopships and attack us. You think they'd catch on by now."

Rusty suddenly changed the subject. "Ya know, Tooper, that little click you make sometimes when you laugh? It reminds me of someone."

Wesley grinned. He'd been told about that now and then, particularly by some good-looking young ladies who thought it was cute.

"Can't put my finger on it," Rusty went on, taking off his hat and scratching the top of his head where the reddish-brown cowlick stood up straight as if at attention. "Oh, well, I'll remember it sooner or later."

When they marched up the gangplank, a brass band announced their departure. Although Wesley had never seen a band that big before, he didn't think it played with as much spirit as the small band at the Columbia train station. He hoped these musicians showed more heart when Ben went over. Everything was probably a lot newer then.

The next morning, after the troops were settled, the ship pulled out into the harbor. Wesley could easily separate the relatives of sons, brothers, and nephews waving from the docks from those patriots who came routinely out of duty to wave their flags and shout farewell. Most of them looked like they had something else on their minds. He felt privileged for the personal send-off he had from the sheriff and his deputy in Virginia.

He jumped with surprise when the fire boats saluted them with thunderous shots and rising columns of silvery water. South of Manhattan Island, the Statue of Liberty took his breath away. The sun blinded him until he shaded his eyes with his hand and gazed at her eternal torch held high over New York Bay. "I'm coming, Ben," he whispered. "Another Tooper across."

The next night, the men studied pamphlets and listened to lectures. "We are at war," a seasoned officer told them. "You have an enemy. To keep that enemy from destroying you, you'll have to destroy him."

Rusty grabbed Wesley by the shoulder. "Hey, I never heard it put like that. This is the…the real thing."

But it was nothing new to Wesley. Wasn't that how he made it past the tough parts of his life? When it came down to survival, you couldn't count on someone else or fate to let you slip through. You had to face the threat head-on. He knew he would be ready.

They were issued gas masks and put through drills on how to use them. When Wesley took off his mask, the smell of hay stored down in the holds wafted upwards, reminding him of the fields of Illinois. A private from Delaware told him this was feed for thousands of horses brought over on other ships.

Wesley wondered if there was such a thing as gas masks for horses. Poor animals.

"They didn't have enough feed last winter," the private went on," some of the horses ate their halters to stay alive. But the Army worked 'em so hard, they died of exhaustion anyway."

As the men played cards and rolled cigarettes, the talk of war went on.

"They call last winter a 'turnip winter'—that's all there was to eat over there. My cousin went three days without food."

"I heard it's against the law to feed pigeons bread crumbs in France or throw rice at weddings."

"We're gonna have Germans comin' at us with bayonets on the end of their rifles just like we have. If you can get past the front of his rifle, you've got him."

• • •

The Army put Wesley in charge of bookkeeping for the ship's supplies. His office was a small room above the ship's engines. Shelves filled with ledgers lined the walls, some of them dog-eared and out of order. He could have an assistant of his own choice to post figures and carry messages to and from the other departments, so he picked Rusty. The cheerful redhead did not have the handwriting of a clerk but learned fast, insisting on calling his boss "Mister" from then on.

"Say, Mr. Tooper," he said the first day of his new job. "Do you think you could order me a nice, big ring of rope from the supplies department?" He wrinkled his brow and looked down at his paper, trying to make it seem as though he were making a decision about the figures rather than just copying them down.

Wesley looked out the porthole. The dark gray sky made the choppy water seem blacker and colder than it probably was. "When it's on a ship, it's called a line, Rusty, not a rope. What do you want it for?"

"Well, I'm from North Dakota where there's not much water. My dad told me when I left home I should always have a roll of rope with me when I got on a ship and to know where all the winches and hooks are." He held his paper up to the light and glanced down at a sheet of Wesley's figures. He compared the two and shook his head in dissatisfaction.

"You attach that rope to something," he added, "and if you fall off, you can pull yourself back on. Otherwise, even if someone sees you go over, there's no way they could get you back."

"Didn't that make you want to get out of going overseas, Rusty, not being used to water?" Wesley squinted his eyes and searched the waves. Did he see something rising out of the water or just a flash of light? Rumors of German periscope sightings circulated throughout the ship almost every day.

Rusty placed his pencil over his right ear like Wesley often did. "No Siree! I've dreamed of fighting in a war all my life. I tried to lie about my age ever since June of last year, but they rejected me right away saying I looked about ten years old. So, the day I turned seventeen, I rushed right down there again, but this time with my birth certificate. They had to take me then. I don't know what I'd do if I couldn't get across."

Wesley checked the water again. A darkish object shot from the surface, becoming lighter in color the higher it went. Making a flip, it dove under again. Smiling, he resolved to write Lilly and tell her he mistook a dolphin for a German submarine. She liked to read about sea creatures.

He noticed Rusty watching his every move, suddenly looking like a light bulb went off in his head.

"I remember now, Mr. Tooper. That little click you make with your mouth? I worked with a guy on a farm near my hometown last summer. He made that same sound when he laughed. Jeez, he sure could work."

The ship rocked to one side, causing Wesley's hand to make a jagged line across his ledger. "Damn currents," he said. Inside he thought, don't get your hopes up. It could be anyone.

"This fella, Rusty, did ... did he look like me at all?"

Rusty took the flawed paper from Wesley and rubbed a square eraser back and forth across the unwanted mark. "Oh, a little, maybe —even darker than you, but then he was working in the sun all summer. He was taller and more ... more small-boned than you. His hands were smooth at first like he never did hard labor before. But, Jeez, could he work."

"Do you know his name, Rusty?" *Calm down now, don't get excited.*

Rusty squinted as if that would help him remember. "We never used first names but his last name was kinda short—a man's first name with an 's' on the end, like Jacobs or Franks."

"You know where he came from?"

Rusty blew tiny bits of eraser rubber off the paper. "I think he said his folks lived in Minnesota."

"Did he say how old he was?"

Rusty glanced up from his ledger sheet. "No, but he looked older than me, I think."

Wesley fought to hold back a smile. "Younger than me?"

"Than you? Gosh, yes."

Wesley laughed out loud. Everyone said he looked older than his years. Rusty probably thought he was as old as Abraham Lincoln.

Rusty hooted, pointing a teasing finger at Wesley. "There you go again with that click, just like that fella had!"

After Rusty calmed down and went on with his work, Wesley asked, "Did this Franks or Roberts or maybe Peters ever mention why he came to Dakota?"

"The guy with the click? He said he always wanted to work on a farm. And you know what? He had a chance to work in a bank that summer, but he had an inkling to work in the wheat fields."

Rusty pointed to the figures Wesley was writing. "Boy, if I had that neat little writing like you got and a head for figures, I'd throw my pitchfork in the Pipestone River. I would!"

Wesley liked the name Pipestone River. It brought to mind a deep blue stream, bubbling over shiny, colored pebbles in some faraway, mountain meadow. So different from the name Horse Creek. Whenever he grew sick of the city and scrambling to get somewhere, he yearned to have a farm of his own in some beautiful, peaceful valley. Maybe Willard, wherever he was, felt that way too.

"Rusty," he asked, "do you think he went into farming full time after you saw him?"

"Gosh no, Mr. Tooper. That summer was just a lark for him. He was gonna study to be a doctor."

"A doctor." No Tooper had even graduated from high school. "Are you sure?"

"With those delicate hands and that fancy, educated way of talking, what else could he do? But, no matter what he does, he's always gonna have that little click whenever he laughs."

Wesley looked at his own hands—short, stubby and gnarled from years of heavy, outdoor work. His memory flashed a picture of Willard's hands the last time he saw him, but all it could evoke were chubby, baby fingers on hands the size of cat's paws.

Drops of water appeared on the outside of the porthole. Wesley and Rusty looked out at the rain spreading over the ocean into the horizon.

"Rusty, you think you'd know the name and address of the farmer where this fella worked?"

Rusty frowned. "You see, we all worked at about six or seven different farms, according to who needed harvesters the most on a certain day. Course, I stayed with my folks. But this feller coulda been renting a room in Courtney. On the other hand, he mighta been getting his bed and board at the Sandersons' or with Iver Johnson or J. D Pickrow, or …"

"Pickrow," Wesley broke in, "you've got to be kidding. What a name for a farmer!"

"You think that's somethin'? Our other neighbor's name is Kickerbush." Rusty stood up and looked at Wesley. "Mr. Tooper, if you want to work on a farm after the War, I could find you all kinds of jobs at places besides Pickrow's."

"Thanks, Rusty." Wesley walked to his desk and made a note to himself to drop a letter for Pa in the ship's mailbag. He wanted to tell him about the young man Rusty worked with in the fields of North Dakota last summer, who laughed like his second oldest son and who looked a little like him too. But, in his heart, he knew he had to be careful not to give his father false hope. A Tooper in the medical profession? With delicate hands? It was too farfetched. Heaven knew there would be other things to occupy his mind when he got to France —a war to fight and a brother to find who he knew was real.

The next day, the sun brightened up the accounting room through the porthole. Sea gulls glided higher than the ship without moving their wings. Someone rapped on the door and shouted, "Bermuda! We're passing through the Bermuda Islands!"

Wesley reached for the atlas Uncle Napoleon sent him when he was stationed in Indiana. "Bermuda," he read out loud to Rusty. "A group of some three hundred small coral islands, twenty of which are inhabited, lying in the west Atlantic Ocean about 580 miles southeast of Cape Hatteras, North Carolina."

"North Carolina?" He threw the atlas on his desk. "I went to Cape Hatteras on a liberty once. Why did they have us take the train up north, get on a boat, and come all the way down again when we could have gone straight east in the first place?"

Rusty shrugged. "That's the Army for ya, I guess." He picked up the ring of line Wesley had requested for him, put his arm through it, and patted it fondly with his other hand. "Let's go topside and look around."

The breeze passing over the deck felt soft and light. The water was so clear they could see all the way to the bottom as deep as thirty to forty feet. Clusters of bulbous kelp and seaweed floated near the ship.

They passed between groups of islands that had nothing on them but rock and palm trees. Then up ahead, they spotted a large island with ships anchored off its shore. They passed sailboats with well-dressed passengers who waved and shouted to them.

"That must be the main island where all the boats are going," Wesley said, waving back. "That's where Hamilton, the capital, is."

Rusty tied his line to a nearby winch, unravelled it all the way and smiled approvingly at its extensive length. "I always heard Bermuda's the perfect place to go on your honeymoon. Do you think we'll stop there at all?"

Wesley was about to say he doubted it when he heard a noise louder than usual coming from the engines followed by three long whistles and a churning of water towards the stern.

Rusty dropped his line and ran to the railing. "The ship. The ship." His mouth curved downward and tears filled his eyes. "Mr.Tooper, it can't be. It's … it's turning around!"

Suddenly men were running all over the deck, hollering, waving, and jumping up and down.

"The War's over!" They shouted to Rusty and Wesley. "They signed the armistice!"

"Oh no." Rusty groaned, turning red and then almost purple. "All that trouble. All that training."

"Thank God," Wesley whispered. "Ben made it. He's safe."

He gathered up Rusty's line and walked toward the railing. "Take it easy, Rusty. It's all for the best. No more gassing. No more killing."

"They can't make me go back!" Rusty yelled, climbing up on the railing. "I've got to have my turn." He jumped over the side and tried to swim, arms reaching high out of the water, his skinny body bouncing on the blue-green waves like a fishing bobber.

"Ben's safe," Wesley told himself as he jerked his boots off. He put the end of Rusty's line in his mouth and stood on the railing. He had to cover as much water as he could with a broad dive. There wasn't time to reach the kid with just swim strokes. As soon as he hit the water, he breast-stroked forward instead of coming straight up. When he reached the surface, he put his head down, lay on top of the water, and swam faster than he ever had in his life—sea gulls squawking and swooping down, almost touching him, and darting up again.

Ma Tooper had always said she never saw a kid who could have as many things on his mind at one time. And she was right.

Ben's safe, he told himself, *Benny's safe, he's alright. Keep movin', Tooper. Stay streamlined. You gotta reach him before the ship stops turning. Before you get to the end of your damn rope. Benny made it. God, he made it! We'll find Willard next, and we'll all be fine. Jeez, Cleve. Look at me go. Even you couldn't catch me.*

Rusty's face had lost all its color except for his lips that had turned dark blue. Wesley grabbed him by the collar and felt the line to the ship go taut in his other hand. He tried to holler, but already a bunch of men were waving and whistling to him, pulling them in.

"Is he alright? What happened, Tooper? Did he fall over?"

"Yeah," Wesley gasped, trying to catch his breath and at the same time keep Rusty out of a desertion charge. "He … he was going so crazy over the War ending, he jumped too high and went overboard. Like a slippery fish."

They laid Rusty on deck and covered him with a blanket to prevent shock. His face was getting its normal color back, but Wesley saw tears mixing in with the freckles on his cheeks. "I'm sorry, Mr. Tooper," he sniffled. "I … I just wanted to be in the War—to do something special."

You did," Wesley said, pulling the blanket up to Rusty's chin. "You just did."

CHAPTER TWENTY

Waiting for Benny Again

November 16, 1918

Wesley couldn't believe his luck. After his ship landed in Hoboken, the Army sent him to Washington, D.C. to work on the preliminary closing of the books for the War. Right next door to the Quantico Marine Post. Almost every man in the Corps coming back from France ended up there. And Wesley vowed he'd be at his brother's barracks door to surprise him and take him out on the town. As Wesley walked the streets of Washington, he felt his brother was right beside him: Jeez, Bro, look at that monument! That girl's givin' us the eye, Wes. She's mine, little brother. You already got one.

He could have kicked himself for not getting Nelly's address from Ben the first time he mentioned her in his letters. If only he could find her, learn what she heard about her sweetheart's return, maybe swap stories about him. She must be going crazy waiting for her Marine to sweep her into his arms. Damn it, if he knew her last name, he might be able to find her. Then maybe he could take her out to dinner, even to a few dances. Hell, Ben wouldn't mind. He knew his brother would never act dishonorably around his girl. But all Wesley could do now was carry the picture of Nelly in his wallet. Whenever he saw someone who looked like her, he would take it out and compare the two. A couple of times he almost asked, "Excuse me, is your name Nelly?" But when he got closer, he saw a different girl. She didn't have the innocent face of the one in the picture or the soft glow to her hair.

The Army put the accountants up in boarding houses and gave them vouchers for meals in restaurants. They worked in offices set up in warehouses filled with crates of papers and shelf after shelf of ledgers. Except for wearing a uniform during the day, Wesley hardly felt he was in the Service. The men in his division could come and go as they pleased but worked long hours. The sooner they wrapped it all up and closed the preliminary books, the sooner they could go home, or like in Wesley's case, finish up their Service time close to home. Sometimes Wesley would work all night because he wanted to leave Washington by the time Benny got back from France. Having been in combat, he would probably get released right away and want Wesley to go back to Illinois with him. But on days that the accounting work was going faster than expected, he'd worry that he might finish before Benny's discharge. How awful to go back without him.

His operations officer was Captain Norling, a graduate from a fancy school in New Jersey called Princeton. He reminded Wesley a little of Cleve with hair graying around the temples before he was thirty years old and a mouth that wore a protective smile even around people he liked.

One day Norling asked, "Will you have a job when you're discharged from the Service in Chicago, Tooper?"

"Uh, no. Not really. I had a good job, but my boss was terribly sore when I enlisted. I wouldn't try to work there again anyway. The company did some things I didn't like."

"I'll write you a good letter of recommendation. You know a lot more than the university graduates I've come across—in or out of the Army."

"Thanks. I'd appreciate it."

Norling started to walk back to his desk but suddenly turned around, pulled a chair next to Wesley, and sat down. "You know,

Tooper, I honestly think you should go back to school. I'd hate to see guys who can't hold a candle to you walk into jobs you can't apply for because you don't have a degree. You'd cut through those business courses like a knife through butter."

Flattered, Wesley asked, "How long would it take me to get one of those degrees, Sir?"

"Well, a bachelor's degree takes about four years, but they might accept most of those courses you had at night school. You could maybe finish in three years."

Wesley felt as if someone had asked him to lay a million dollars on the table. "Three years at least? What would I live on during all that time? Where would I get money to send back to my folks or my brothers or sisters if they needed it?"

"Your folks? You mean they don't send you money?"

Wesley shook his head. Who in the world ever thought of such a thing?

Refusing to be discouraged, Norling pulled himself straighter in his chair and cleared his throat. "Well, then, let's not give up. Maybe we could find you a benefactor. You really are exceptional in your field, Tooper. How is your secondary school record?"

"Secondary?"

"Yes. A fellow with your brains must have done very well there."

"I … I don't think I've ever been to such a place."

"Come on, Tooper, get serious. We're just talking about high school, for heaven's sake. You must have whizzed through it with your eyes closed."

Wesley leaned towards his superior, checking his eyes for a reaction. "Sir, I've never been to one of those either."

Norling's body slouched—so low his chin rested on his chest, and he had to turn his head upward and look at Wesley out of the corner of his left eye. "You've … you've never been to high school! Does the Army know about this? They gave you the title of Purser on that ship you boarded."

Wesley shrugged. "When I enlisted, there was a line that said, 'last level of education completed,' and I put down LaSalle School of Business. Then later, when I got in, they had me write down all the courses I took there and all the jobs I had in business."

Norling was speechless, so Wesley continued.

"Sir, when I was twelve, I got so busy doing bookkeeping and accounting jobs, I quit school. Then I went back when I was fifteen and finished through the eighth grade so I could have a good education."

Norling squinted his eyes as if examining a creature that had just come down from a strange planet. "How did you learn accounting? Did someone teach you?"

"Well, I guess I kind of picked it up on my own. My mother got me started. I was adding and subtracting figures before I knew what it all meant."

"At what age?"

"Oh, about two. But, I wasn't balancing credits and debits until I was three or four."

Norling pushed back his chair and looked cautiously around the room. "Tooper," he said, drawing a deep breath and resting his hands on his knees. "Tooper, you might be a genius."

Wesley was not impressed. He had heard this before. His pa was a genius at inventing parts for the railroad that kept men from getting killed or injured. Cleve was a genius with motors. Benny was a genius the way he eased people into buying things they didn't even want. He would probably end up making the most money. "So," he said, trying not to be disrespectful, "what if I am a genius, Sir? Where has it got me?"

Norling threw up his hands. "There must be a way. A special examination you could take or something. I'm bound and determined to get you into a university."

Wesley stood up and patted Norling on the shoulder. "Don't worry about it, Sir. I wouldn't go to school now if I could. My brother's coming back any day from France. He was gassed in the trenches, but he made it through some battles they say were almost impossible to survive. I need to spend as much time with him as I can."

"Can't you visit with him a while and then go to school—go on with your own life?"

Wesley took his hand off Norling's shoulder. "The thing is, he is a big part of my life. I lost him when he was about two when we were in an orphanage. He and my youngest brother, Willard, were adopted out. We haven't found Willard and maybe never will, but we found Benny when he was about ten. We all loved having him back in our family, but I think I sort of took him for granted and was kind of tough on him sometimes. After he joined the Marines and went off to war, I realized what he meant to me. We're going to get an apartment together when we both get discharged. I'll never take him for granted again."

Norling turned his chair around and looked Wesley up and down. "You lost your brothers? You were an orphan? But, I've heard you mention your parents—about writing them and getting letters back. Why would you be in an orphanage?"

Wesley wanted to just say that it was a long story, but yet he didn't want this officer, his boss, to think he was feeding him a line of bull and not give him a good reference.

"Well, you see, my mother died when I was little, so our pa left our two sisters with relatives and put us four boys in an orphanage. They didn't feed us right at this place and beat the hell out of us a lot and signed Benny and Willard over to two other families for money. When my pa found this out, he roughed up the head priest, tore up his office, and took my older brother and me the hell away from there. We didn't want to live with relatives, so we just hopped trains and hoboed anywhere we could find work or food. Then our pa met the Illinois governor's cook and married her. They bought a little farm and put us on it—the four that were left. That's how I can talk about having two parents now."

Norling shook his head as if he were trying to clear it of cobwebs. "The governor's cook. That's the most fantastic part of the whole story."

"It would be even harder to believe if you tasted her cooking, though some of it was damn good."

For the first time since he'd known him, Wesley heard Norling laugh. "I think it wouldn't have been harder to believe even if you made it up. You know, Tooper, there are men in the Army whose specialty is tracking down missing people. Maybe I can get in touch with someone who could help you find more information about your youngest brother."

Wesley opened his mouth to thank him, but then Norling extended his hand and placed the other one on his shoulder. "I've got to tell you something, Tooper." He looked around as if to see if anyone was eavesdropping. Wesley thought the captain might be carrying something around inside him for a long while—something like he never went to bed with a woman yet. "Tooper, I swear, you are the first person I've known who … who hasn't gone to high school."

Wesley's mind plunged back in time trying to remember people he had known who had been to high school. Sister Stringy and the rest of the nuns at the orphanage must have had something like it at the convents. Father Fatso probably had the same kind of thing where he was trained. Marjory and old Charlie Kylie and his bosses from other accounting jobs—they all went to high school. Denser probably did too. Maybe that's why he could be a sergeant. Captain Benton, at Camp Jackson, seemed to treat people well enough, but under the table he was embezzling the Army's money.

Wesley could have gone on trying to remember others but felt he had to respond to Norling's confession. "Sir, you're the first person I've known who … who went to high school that I didn't have to worry about." He shook his officer's hand and they both went back to their desks.

Before Wesley left work that night, Norling called Quantico and tried to find out if Ben had been shipped back. He learned that some of the men from the 2nd Battalion of Company 96 came back the day before. More would be coming in a few days, but no names were available. Norling gave out the phone number at Wesley's boarding house in case someone at Quantico needed to reach him. Then he gave Wesley permission to use the office phone so he could call Aunt Jo and Uncle Ed. Maybe they had heard something from the folks about Benny. Pa and Ma didn't have a phone, and neither did Cleve and Mary. No one answered at Aunt Jo's.

When he got back to the boarding house his landlady said someone had called from Quantico and left a message for him.

"Quantico! Was it my brother?"

"He didn't have the same last name as yours." She shuffled through a pile of messages. "He said he was from your hometown though. Here it is."

It was from Marvin Heeler. He and Melvin Hixon were at Quantico. They wanted to meet him at a place called Shank of the Evening downtown at seven o'clock two nights later. The last line read, "Larry Kline didn't make it."

172 DARK BROWN is the RIVER

Wesley's disappointment that the phone call hadn't been from Ben faded when he started to read Marvin's message. How great it would be to see someone from home! Heeler and Hixon would know all about Ben and when he would get back. The stories they'd have to tell him! But then he thought about Larry Kline. Wesley had known a few other boys from Kankakee and Bonfield killed in the War, but this was Larry Kline who drove the milk wagon over the bridge at Horse Creek, who shouted names at him and Cleve. Then Heeler came along and took Kline's part and they all started to fight. Wesley hit Kline on the jaw so hard that Heeler had to drive the milk wagon back to the dairy for him. Benny had written Wesley about running into Heeler and Hixon in Virginia and how they reminisced about the fight. It all seemed so important when it happened, and now Kline was dead.

When he went to bed that night, Wesley kept thinking of all the things he would talk about with the boys from home—the War, Ben, and the old days when they were kids. But his mind kept wandering to Kline's family. How could they go on with their lives after the Germans killed Larry? What if it had been Pa in their shoes? Would it be worse for him to have a son killed in battle than it had been to lose his wife to sickness years ago?

The next day he dwelt mostly on meeting up with his old friends and seeing Ben in a few days. On his way to work, he still passed through gatherings of people singing victory songs and cheering whenever a man in uniform came by. He had stopped trying to tell them he hadn't been in the War. He let the women hug him and the men clap him on the back. At work he heard that President Wilson was going to Europe soon to bring about a final world peace—one that would last and prevent other wars from starting. And soon, he and Ben would go home together.

He felt so good that he bought a car during his lunch hour. He'd had his eye on it all week, but now couldn't believe he actually bought a Ford. He had been saving for something higher class, but there weren't too many other makes of cars manufactured in the last few years because of the War, and he could afford this one right now. And when would he ever get a chance again to drive his brother home from battle? Ben wouldn't turn up his nose at a 1917 Ford Touring Car, so black and shiny you felt nothing could ever hurt it. Not only that, it had a hard-shell radiator case and cushioned seats with a canvas roof that unrolled over the top when it rained. No, Ben wouldn't mind riding in it. He'd go nuts over it.

The salesman gave him a special deal because he was in the Service. He showed his bank book from the First National Bank of Chicago which showed how much he had saved since he'd been in the Army. The salesman said he just needed a reference, so Wesley had him call Norling. After the salesman hung up the phone, he told Wesley he could take the car that day before his money came from Chicago.

"If the United States Army will trust you to fight its wars, my boy, then I know darn well you'll get the balance to me before you leave town. If we can't trust our servicemen, who can we trust? Besides, the Army will always know where to find you."

Wesley wasn't as nervous as he thought he would be driving the car in Washington D. C. After all, he'd driven Marjorie's fancy sports car all over Chicago during the busiest of rush hours. He glanced at the big back seat. It looked so cushy it made you want to curl up and take a nap. He and Ben could take turns driving and sleeping—go straight through as soon as the Army and Marines let them go. They could take along some blankets and heavy robes, even a shovel and a bucket of sand. They would make it no matter the weather. Just as long as they went home together.

Then he remembered Christmas wasn't that far away. Maybe they could even make it home in time. He pictured Pa and Ma rushing out on the porch, he and Ben in their uniforms honking the horn, Lilly running down the steps with her arms open wide. Maybe Hazel, Dan, and little Danny would be waiting inside to surprise them, along with Uncle Napoleon and Aunt Annie, Uncle Ed and Aunt Jo—all standing by a big Christmas tree they had cut down near the quarry and lit up with gas lights. What a homecoming for Ben and the whole Tooper family!

When he drove up to the warehouse, all the clerks were waiting on the curb to see the car and congratulate him. They had been watching from the windows ever since Norling told them about the salesman calling for a reference. They kept slapping him on the back and exclaiming, "So grand! How slick! If you drive us around tonight, we'll pay for your dinner and all the drinks you want."

At quitting time, they piled into the car and rode around Washington—past the White House, the memorials, and government buildings. They tooted the horn and hollered at groups of girls going home from work. Often they'd shout back, "Hey, soldiers, where'd you get that car?" or "Nice car, nice car for you but any car, any car will do." The boys told Wesley to drive around the block again. But when they drove back to that same spot, the girls were gone.

They picked a restaurant for dinner at random. Older people, about Pa and Ma's age, filled most of the tables. They cheered when Wesley's bunch entered and told the waiters they would pay for any drinks the soldiers wanted. Some had sons already home from the War. Some, like Wesley, were waiting for a relative to get back. A few didn't come over and talk—they just waved from their tables, and Wesley figured they must have had sons they would never see again.

After dinner Wesley and his friends shook hands with the men and hugged their wives and piled into the car again. "Romeo's. On to Romeo's. It's time to dance!"

He saw her as soon as they entered. Her hair was so soft, he didn't see how it could hold the curls lacing around her forehead and bordering her rose-tinted cheeks. It picked up the colors surrounding her —pale-moon yellow when she passed under the lights, red-brown as she bent over the back tables delivering drinks, sandy-tan when she looked across the room at him. He pictured her wearing a nurse's hat with two starched, white wings coming to points on the ends, almost touching in the front but not quite. She walked through the noisy dance hall as if stepping into a place where wounds needed healing, where illness was losing ground. She carried drinks to the men with the air of bringing medicine or blankets, setting them down gently, looking into faces as if checking to see that they were getting better.

Wesley remembered a vision of an angel-like nurse as he lay in his orphanage bed years ago, his stomach cramping from bad food, his bones aching from strikes with a stick or belt. He knew in his heart his mother could never come back to him, but he believed she had sent such a nurse-like vision to comfort him, so he would not be alone.

Now the woman with the soft hair and a trace of rose in her cheeks looked across the room and sat down by an empty table. It was warm in the dance hall, but Wesley began to shiver.

"Hey Tooper," one of his companions said, nudging him in the side. "That girly over there's been giving you the eye. You better take your overcoat off and go sit by her."

Wesley didn't wait to take his overcoat off but walked to her table and sat down, still shivering.

She looked as if she were expecting him and put her hand on his arm. "Are you all right?"

"I thought I was Jim Dandy," he answered, trying to keep his voice from quavering. "But now I'm not so sure."

He searched her face, watching the way she held herself. So much concern, so much caring. It had to come from loving someone, watching over him, worrying about him. "Why, you're ... you're married aren't you?"

Her eyes answered yes.

"Was he in battle?"

She nodded. "His ship is coming in two days."

Her voice was soft like her hair. He was surprised that her unavailability relaxed him. He stopped shivering. "Don't worry. He'll make it back okay. My brother's coming in any day now too. You know, they could be on the same ship."

"I ... I don't know how to help him. He was blinded and lost a leg. He hasn't answered my letters. His friends tell me he can't bear the thought of being helpless, especially with me."

Wesley took her hands in both of his. "You'll help him. I know you will. He'll need you, and you'll be there. When my brother gets here, he'll be glad to talk to him. He has a way of perking people up —making them look on the brighter side."

She smiled and said, "My sister's young man was that way. He made you feel good just listening to him."

"You say 'was.' Did she lose him in the War?"

"She never knew he was killed. She came down with that ... that awful influenza. It must have been from working in hospitals for the wounded. She's been gone since September. I wrote to tell him about her but my letter came back marked, 'Verifiably Deceased.'"

He squeezed her hands. "That's terrible. I know you took good care of her. And maybe you'll feel better believing they're together somewhere a lot nicer than that War he fought in—someplace where there's no sickness. Who knows, eh?"

"Yes. Oh, yes. I think he would want that for them, if it were the only way he could be with Nelly again."

Wesley's heart did a seesaw and he held his hand over it to keep it from jumping up and down, up and down, right out of his chest. And the shivering started again. Nell, Nelly, a popular name. A common name. Just think of the song, *"Wait 'Til The Sun Shines, Nelly."* Then there's *"Nelly Bly"* and *"Seein' Nelly Home."* Everyone wants to name their daughters after songs. A common name, Nelly. A common name.

He leaned towards her, barely getting the words out. "Could you tell me his name, please? Her young man's."

His question brightened her somewhat. "Oh, we always called him Beeline. Whenever he could get to Washington, he'd make a beeline to our door. When Nelly went to see him at his post, he made a beeline to the train. You could always count on Beeline to be there."

He stood up. "No, I mean … I mean his other name. What was his other name?"

"His last name?"

"Yes—either that or his first name, his real …"

She interrupted him, answering her own question. "Oh, our family hardly ever tried to say it. We'd get it wrong if we did. We'd say Toaper or Trooper, something like that."

To Wesley, the room began to swim. *But a room can't swim. Not like we used to swim. The three of us—in Horse Creek.*

"It's not our real name," he said, trying to reach for his wallet in his pants pocket. If she could just see the picture of Benny's girl, she could tell him it wasn't her sister. "It's really Toupaunt. You say the 'aunt' part like when the doctor's looking down your throat and tells you to say 'ah.'"

His overcoat kept getting in the way. "But there's another … another bunch in New York. Tons of Toopers. Toopers from the start." The overcoat flopped down again. "Because they're English—not French. Beeline could be … could be one of theirs."

He struggled to take off his coat. The floor slanted upward—so much, it almost stood beside him.

She sat motionless, stiff and white, her hands pushing down on the table, her lips trembling.

"And besides," he said undoing the last button. "I've got lots of cousins. There's Clifford. Clifford Tooper. There's Chester Tooper too, and a bunch more. One of them might be him. Might be Beeline."

He crumpled to the floor, his coat half off.

She screamed, not because she thought he hurt himself or had suddenly gone crazy. She screamed because she could see his name on the pocket of his uniform—Tooper. She fell to her knees beside him.

"Oh no. Dear God, no! Which one are you? Are you Cleve?"

He tried to open his mouth to tell her who he was, but he couldn't. He just lay on the floor with half his overcoat on, looking up at the faces staring down, making a little imperfect circle around him.

Finally, one of the faces said, "He's Wesley. His name is Wesley."

She drew her hand up to her mouth and let out a sob. "Wes," she said to the faces. "Wes was his favorite."

Suddenly, the faces looking down on him began to spin faster and faster—so fast they became one pinkish-gray lump of moving color. But all at once, they tried to stop and spin the other way. They couldn't do it and came to a screeching halt, falling over each other. Then everything around him went black.

CHAPTER TWENTY-ONE

The Forgotten Night

November 22, 1918

When Wesley woke up the next morning, he discovered he didn't
have on any clothes. He started to panic but then spied his uniform
folded neatly over a chair next to the bed. Although relieved to see it,
he felt a wave of embarrassment creep over him like a rash of poison
ivy. He wished he were at least wearing the baggy Army-issued
underwear that went with the uniform. He had to wear it when he
lived in the barracks because the Army had inspections, but living in
a boarding house in Washington, no one knew or cared if he wore it
or not. He'd always hated wearing underwear; it was either so tight it
cut into him or too bulky, like a huge, flapping bandage.

How did his clothes get over on the chair? He looked around
him. A couch and a rocking chair stood off to the side. The freshly
scrubbed floor smelled clean and the windows looked so clear that
the sun shining through them hurt his eyes. He could hear splashing
and clattering sounds from somewhere behind him, taking him back to
years ago when he lay in bed listening to his sisters washing dishes.

"Agnes," he called, not knowing why. "Agnes!"

"It's all right, I'm coming," a voice answered, and he could tell it
was her—the girl from last night. How did he know her name? Did
she tell him, or did he remember it from Ben talking about Nelly's
sister in his letters. Ben. Oh, God! Ben.

She came carrying a cup of steaming coffee and set it on the table next to the bed. She wore a blue gingham housecoat and smelled of soap and lemon. She fluffed the pillows so he could sit up, and as if she were aware of his self-consciousness, pulled the covers higher around him.

He could hear babies crying in other apartments, and cars, and trollies somewhere far below.

"How ... how did I get here?"

"One of your friends drove us. Then he took your car to your place and left it there. He wasn't sure if you'd be able to drive it today."

He drew his hands up to his face. "I don't want to drive it—ever."

"Oh Wesley," she began, "you will again, soon."

He pulled his hands away from his face and clasped her by the shoulders. "You'll take it, won't you, Agnes? You'll need it to drive your husband around when he gets back."

The word, husband, alarmed him further. "Agnes, what happened last night? How did my clothes get over there? I wouldn't have folded them as neat as that. Who took them off me?"

"You did—with my help."

"You helped? You mean ... you mean we ... we .... Did we?"

She sat down on the edge of the bed. "Yes, we did."

"We did? Oh, Christ, Agnes! What kind of a rat am I?"

She put her arms around him and rocked him back and forth. "Don't blame yourself. I needed it and so did you. And we needed to cry."

"Cry! Did I cry in front of you?"

"Don't be ashamed, Wesley. We cried together. We cried for Ben and Nelly and my Tom and everyone hurt or killed by that terrible War."

"For God's sake, Agnes, what would I have done in battle? What if Ben had been shot down along side of me? I shouldn't have fallen apart like that. I should have been stronger."

She cupped a hand on each side of his face and said, "Believe me, Wesley. You would have been strong if Ben or any of the other men needed you. You would have been prepared for the worst. Last night everyone was celebrating. You thought he was safe and coming home."

After a while, her head resting on the pillows, she eased him beside her, and he knew she would not mind if time went by without words exchanged between them. The quilt covering him was peppered with hundreds of little red knots made of yarn, and he kept running his hand over them or twirling one round and round with his index finger.

"Agnes," he finally said. "When I woke up here this morning, I didn't know what in the world happened to me. But I felt like something was pulled out of me—some awful thing I'd been carrying around for weeks. Maybe I knew deep in my heart Ben was dead, ever since the War ended and I came to Washington. I'll never get over him getting killed. Maybe I fell apart last night because I knew I could. Because you were there."

"You were so full of pain," she said stroking his cheek. "But at the same time, you took my pain away from me. I think I can face Tom now, as soon as he's ready to let me help him."

"Oh, you will, Agnes. Please, won't you take the car? It could help you get around with him. And this place must be at least three stories up. How will you bring him all that way?"

"He'll be in a hospital here at first. Our families and our friends have chipped in to buy us a car and rent a bigger place with no stairs to climb."

He reached for her hand and brought it to his lips. Then suddenly he had an unexpected urge to smile. "I have to admit, Agnes, now that we've talked about it, maybe the thing I regret about what happened between us last night is that I can't remember it—I mean the good part."

She tilted her head back slightly and laughed. "Oh, Wesley, when you chuckled just now, you made a little click with your mouth, just like Ben did."

The mention of a trait he and his brother shared lifted his spirits. "Funny that you should say that. A kid on the ship told me it reminded him of someone he worked with in the fields somewhere in the Dakotas. This fella did the same thing when he laughed. For one crazy second, I thought maybe it might be …"

"Willard? Ben told us all about your family trying to find him. If he saw a fellow that looked like any of you, he wondered if it could be him."

"Yeah, I guess we all do that—even my sisters."

"Keep the car, Wesley. Take it home with you. And don't stop looking for Willard. Do it for Beeline."

"Okay," he said, resting his head on her breast. "Okay, I will. I sure as hell will."

CHAPTER TWENTY-TWO

A Toast to Beeline

December 10, 1918

The message said to meet them at a club called Shank of the Evening. As soon as Wesley walked in, Alva Heeler and Melvin Hixon waved him over to their table. They looked as if they had been Marines all their lives, like they had never worn a pair of overalls, or run down a pasture trail, never driven a milk wagon across a covered bridge, never swum carefree in a quiet stream.

After Wesley reached the table, there was an awkward silence. Then Wesley said, "I want to know how it happened. For God's sake, how in the hell did it happen?"

Melvin Hixon leaned forward, his arm in a sling, his face blotched with gas burns. "I got hit at the Hindenburg Line, September 27," he said almost apologetically. "That's where Larry Kline got it for good. I was in the hospital when Ben went down at Argonne, but Alv here, he saw it all."

Wesley turned to Heeler. "Tell me everything."

Alva Heeler had no cast on either of his arms or legs, no bandages on his body. He did not walk with a cane or crutch, but his eyes reflected invisible wounds, his chestnut hair dull and flecked with gray at age twenty-one. He cleared his throat and spoke as if watching the scene unfolding before his eyes.

"We were crossing this field through the fog on the edge of the Argonne. We started early, about 5:30, so we might catch them napping. We got within fifty yards of the German trenches and didn't hear a sound the whole time we moved forward. I kept telling myself, 'it's too quiet—too damn quiet.'" Suddenly a wall of machine-gun fire broke loose on us. I'd never seen anything like it. Bodies upon bodies, flashes of gunfire everywhere. And then … oh, Mel, help me tell it, will ya?"

Hixon, knowing what happened as well as if he'd been there himself, laid a hand on Heeler's shoulder and continued the story.

"These boys had one thought in their minds—get up there and destroy every last machine gun mowing them down and stopping their advance. They never faltered, Wes. They came on, wave after wave, climbing over their friends' dead bodies to get to those guns."

"And ahead of me," Heeler said, " down in the trenches with the Germans, stabbing like fury with his bayonet and flinging machine guns into the woods like little toys was … was …"

Wesley held up his hand. He could see it all so clearly—an arm guided by a fearless heart, rising and falling in the midst of smoke and fire. He could see the thrown weapons climbing in high arcs, their ammunition clips trailing behind like kite tails. He could hear the cries of dying men and the continuous, monotonous rapping of machine guns.

"Let me say it, Alv," he begged. "It couldn't be anyone else, could it? It had to be … it had to be … Beeline!"

He couldn't believe he said that name. He hadn't meant to. Why did he say it? Why didn't he say Ben or Bennie? Why not?

Hixon gasped. "That was his girl's pet name for him. How did you know it?"

"How … how," Wesley stammered, "did you know it?"

"I snatched her letter away from him once when he was reading it," Heeler broke in. "Just horsin' around. All I could see before he grabbed it back was 'My Dearest Beeline.' He said nobody else ever called him that, but he was Beeline to Mel and me from then on. How in the hell do you know that name, Wes? Ben said he never told anyone at home.

"Yeah," Hixon added. "He figured you'd all razz him about it the rest of his life."

Wesley didn't try to tell them what happened the night before. How could he say, "I ran into Nell's sister at Romeo's and she told me although she didn't know I was his brother? She took me home with her because I was such a wreck? Even though she's married, we slept together all night, but I don't remember it? And, by the way, Nell's dead too?"

Instead, he said, "I never told Ben this, but ever since he was a little feller, that's the way I thought about him. First thing in the morning, he would make a beeline for the barn and start milking. After breakfast he'd make a beeline for the field and start throwing hay in the wagon. When he got older and had something to sell, he'd make a beeline for the nearest house and start knocking on the door."

"That's how he was at the front," Heeler confirmed, "all through Argonne and St. Mihiel and at Aisne. He'd make a beeline for the German trenches and the guns. And we got through because of Ben and fellas like him."

Hixon reached for his glass. "Let's drink to Beeline."

Wesley and Heeler reached for theirs and all three joined in a toast. "Here's to Beeline!"

Heads turned at neighboring tables, and those sitting there raised their glasses and repeated, "Here's to Beeline. To Beeline!" Soon the toast spread to other parts of the room. Soldiers, sailors, pilots, businessmen, working men, their wives, and their girlfriends —glasses raised high over their heads, all chanting, "Here's to Beeline. To Beeline!"

Wesley thought his heart would thump out of his chest with pride and bewilderment. Everyone was celebrating the courage of his brother who was not there and never would be because of the very actions that made him a hero.

After the toasting subsided, Wesley set down his glass, and gradually, everyone in the room repeated the motion. He folded his arms on the table and leaned towards Heeler. "Tell me the rest, Alva. How did he die?"

Heeler met Wesley's eyes with his own. "That last machine gunner—he kept on firing, kept us from moving in. Ben went for him. There were two other Germans in the trench besides the gunner. One ran, but the other had a rifle. That's what got him, Wes. He never suffered."

"Thank God. I'll tell Pa and Ma."

Hixon reached for Wesley's wrist and shook it back and forth. "And Wes, ya gotta know this. Even though he went down, Ben threw that gunner off his stride just for a second—enough time for two of our men to get at him. Right, Alv?"

"That's right, Parker and Rose. When he saw them coming, the German who shot Ben turned and ran too. Then those two boys flew at the gunner. That left the rest of us free to push on. No one could stop us then. We swept through the woods and took over the whole village of Exermont."

"It's kinda like in the picture shows, isn't it? If I were there, I'd have probably tried to stop him from going near that trench. I would of told him, 'Christ, don't be crazy.'"

"No, Wes. You would of been right there beside him. If our fellow Marines didn't get those gunners, they'd get us all."

"That's what he told me in his letter, 'either you get them or they get you.' Do you think, if I'd been there, maybe I could of killed the German before he shot Ben?"

"Hell," Heeler said, "you could've been killed then too or before in some other battle. For God's sake, don't blame yourself."

"Look Wes," Hixon said rising to his feet. "We gotta get back to the post now. We just wanted you to know what happened and that Ben didn't feel no pain."

Wesley stood up and shook their hands. He wanted to say how grateful he felt to them for putting an end to any wondering, any endless dread he and his family would have to carry with them for years. He realized now that the wild tales Ben told the Tooper kids the day he met them maybe weren't so fantastic. If he had the chance, he could have helped Will Rogers in his shows, performed tricks on Will's horse, and danced to Will's favorite songs—just like he charged into that German trench, hurled heavy machine guns into the woods, and cleared the way for his buddies.

Wesley kept shaking his friends' hands, first Heeler, then Hixon, back to Heeler, then Hixon, until finally he managed some words. "Say fellers, I just bought a car. I've got a long Christmas furlough, then I'll be finishing up my Army time in Chicago working on the war books for Illinois. If you're getting out soon, you can hitch a ride home with me. I have lots of room—now."

Heeler shook his head. "I'd like to, Wes, but my folks are coming out in December. We're going to take the train together and spend Christmas with my aunt in New England."

"Sorry Wes," Hixon said, "When I was at Parris Island, I met this girl. She wants me to come down to South Carolina as soon as I get out."

Wesley managed a trace of a smile. "Oh, that's great. Have a good Christmas, both of you. I'll see you when we get home."

"That'll be swell," Hixon said. "Alv, are you gonna show Wes that button?"

Heeler reached into his pocket and came out with a small round knob with pieces of thread on it. "I wasn't even gonna show it to you, Wes. I found it in that trench—the one with the machine gunner and two other Germans. Those threads hanging on it could mean someone tore it off this Jerry's shirt."

Wesley's heart did a flip. "Someone like Ben?"

"That's right. My sergeant says this button is off a corporal's uniform. Our boys killed the machine gunner and he wasn't a corporal. The Jerry with the rifle ran away so fast no one could see his rank."

"So maybe this button is off the collar of the German who killed Ben."

"Unless the Jerry who owned it was in that trench on a different day and got it torn off him then. Who knows where he is now or if he's dead or alive."

"The bastard," Hixon said. "Whoever he is, corporal or not, he's a rotten bastard. All those Germans are rotten bastards."

Heeler was quiet for a moment and then turned to Hixon. "Mel, remember when word came about the armistice and we stopped fighting? We laid down our weapons, and those German fellas came over. Some of us shook hands."

"I didn't," Hixon snapped. "You did."

"Yeah, I did, and they were a lot like us. All those days, just trying to make it through, trying to stay alive. Maybe that's all this corporal was doing."

Heeler was silent for a moment and then turned to Wesley, the button in his open hand. "You wanna keep this?"

Wesley reached for it cautiously, as if he were about to pick up a poisonous insect. "It's not very heavy. It's got a picture of a lion on it."

"My sergeant thinks that stands for infantry. They stopped making buttons with gold and used steel instead. They paint them all black and add a different color according to rank, like red, gray, tan, or green."

"Come on Mel," urged Hixon, "or we'll be late. Wes, make sure you get together with us in Bonfield."

"I will. Stop by at the folks' place when you're in town."

Wesley watched the backs of his former schoolmates disappear out the door. Then he dropped the button into his overcoat pocket, sighed deeper than he had ever sighed before, and then headed back to his boarding house.

CHAPTER TWENTY-THREE

The Exchange

December 16, 1918

Wesley sat on a park bench above the Potomac River, his returned letter marked "Verified Deceased" in his hand, mailed October 4th. During the same moments he was writing it, Ben lay in a German trench, dead since dawn. While he battled back and forth with his conscience about that poor Mexican kid, stomped his feet like a lunatic on a toothbrush that had cleaned a toilet, lunged at Denser like a crazed animal, and gotten himself thrown into jail, Ben's body was turning cold, losing all warmth that life had given it.

His returned letter was delivered to the warehouse two days ago, but Norling didn't tell him about it until today. When the church bells started to ring across the city, Norling pulled the pencil out of Wesley's hand and said, "Tooper, you worked late last night and started early this morning. We've all been pushing hard so we can finish up and go on with our lives, but for God sakes, it's Sunday. I'm ordering you to get out of this building. Either go to church or take a walk by the river." Then he handed him the letter.

Well, he fulfilled his commanding officer's order. He had taken a walk by the river. Although he knew what was in the letter, he opened it, his eyes falling on the last words he had written to his brother: "I hope to meet and embrace you on some battlefield in France or Berlin." What a sap! He had no idea what a battlefield was and never would. Ben knew when he fell on top of it and his blood seeped into the dirt. He knew.

Wesley could hear the steady splashing of a huge paddle wheel as a steamboat rounded the bend parting the water in front of it. The river or the church. Maybe Norling thought either one could serve the same purpose.

Using his hands as a megaphone he steered his voice over the river and to the hills beyond. "If you're out there somewhere, and if you have so damn much power as they say you have, then … then bring him back to me. Just bring him back to me."

His answer came in a steamboat whistle so loud and sudden he almost fell off his bench.

What did that mean? Yes? No? Go to hell? Long ago, he prayed for his mother to come back to him and he got Ma. Well, that turned out fine in the long run, with the way miracles worked, if there were such things as miracles. If it have hadn't been for Ma Tooper and the farm, he and Cleve would've ended up in prison and for a lot more than a few days.

He closed his eyes and listened to the sound of the river. He'd gone through the whole gamut of thoughts in the last week. He blamed himself for throwing Ben in Horse Creek when they were kids, for not enlisting when he did, even for teaching him to play soldier when they were little. During fits of passion, he had imagined himself with his hands around the throat of the German who killed his brother and pounding him into the ground until nothing was left. When he calmed down, Wesley realized that the families of the soldiers who fell under Ben's bayonet could feel the same hatred towards him.

Now he was done with it all. Drained. His so-called prayer had said it all. He just plain missed his brother and wanted him back. His eyes cried out to see his face, his ears to hear his voice, his hands to grasp Ben's hands, to hold onto them. His arms ached to squeeze him in a big bear hug and his legs ached to walk down the street with him, matching him step for step.

As he watched a flotilla of canoes move off into the distance, he remembered when the young soldier, Rusty, jumped off the ship near Bermuda because his dream of fighting in the War was snatched from him. Now Wesley understood. He had dreamed of being with Ben for so long, and now when that dream was destroyed, he wanted to run to the edge of the hill and dive into the river and swim forever through the icy, cold water.

Suddenly he felt the pressure of a hand on his shoulder. Taking an unsteady breath, he glanced at it out of the corner of his eye. It was a younger man's hand. Not a large hand. Brown like … a French Canadian's? He sprang from the bench and turned around. Standing there was a shorter, darker Ben who didn't grin like him but smiled broadly with gleaming white teeth like popped corn. A Ben with blacker hair that glistened in the sun and curled into little waves.

"It's you!" he gasped, taking a step forward. "But your name— I never knew it. What in the hell is your name?"

"Hernandez."

"Hernandez!" Wesley cried, reaching out his arms. "Hernandez, am I ever glad to see you." He grabbed him by the waist, picked him up and twirled round and round, whooping, hollering, and shouting at the passengers taking the ferry across to Alexandria. "Hey, everybody. This is Hernandez. Do ya hear me? Hernandez!"

Hernandez spread out his arms, threw his head back and laughed. The more Wesley twirled them, the more he laughed. Then an impish look came over his face, and he threw his arms around Wesley and squeezed.

Wesley slowed down and squeezed back. "Think you can break my hold, eh? Sure are strong for such a skinny feller."

Finally, red-faced and tired, they relaxed their arms, stepped back, and looked at each other.

"Where did you come from?" Wesley asked, trying to catch his breath.

"Amigo," Hernandez wheezed. "I've been looking for you forever."

"Forever? Me? Why in the world ?"

Hernandez looked at him squarely. "Ever since that day at Camp Jackson I've tried to find you. You got yourself thrown in the stockade for me. You gave up your own freedom to stop my agony and shame."

Wesley shrugged. "All I did was shut the bastard up."

Hernandez grabbed Wesley's shoulders and shook him. "Listen! I know what you did. Some men never come out of that place once they get locked up. But that isn't all you did. I got transferred right away. They put me working with horses. It's been like heaven after what I went through at Camp Jackson. And Sergeant Denser? He's not bothering my people anymore, and I know you had something to do with it. Thank you, Amigo."

Wesley smiled. "I hear he's pushing papers around instead of people, bragging that he's been promoted. But you still haven't told me how you got here."

"The War ended before I could go across. They sent me here to help take care of the horses that didn't get shipped over. Those big barns outside of town? That's where I work."

"How did you find me?"

"Like I said, I was always looking for you. I couldn't believe it when I found out you were in Washington too. This morning I went to your job, and your boss said you'd be taking your lunch soon and that you might need someone to talk to. He told me why so I followed you here." Extending his hand to Wesley, he whispered, "I'm sorry, Amigo."

Wesley grasped his hand and shook it firmly. "Thanks for coming. I was feeling awfully low."

Then wanting to shed their talk of its heaviness, he thumped Hernandez on the arm and said, "Keep it to yourself, but you know what I heard? I heard Denser got what he deserved."

Hernandez's face lit up. "He did? How?"

"He got what he wanted to do to you. He had to clean the old choppers."

Hernandez's jaw dropped in amazement. "You telling me the truth? No joke? With what?"

Wesley tried to keep a straight face but failed. Laughter he couldn't stifle seeped into his answer. "With a dirty toothbrush. Dirt … dirt from his own bunghole!"

"B-B-Bunghole!" Hernandez choked as he grabbed his stomach. Wrapped in spasms, he pointed a finger at Wesley and wagged it back and forth. "You. It was you!"

Tears from laughter rolled down Wesley's cheeks. "Not me. I was far away on the troop train. But somebody told me the ol' sarge had this to say. He said, 'yum, yum good.' Ya hear that, Buddy? Yum, yum good!"

The kid's body shook with convulsions, and out of his mouth came rapid coughing with hardly any noise. He stamped his feet and almost bent over double. Then, straightening himself out in one tremendous jerk, he yelled at the top of his lungs, "Ya Hoo! Hallelujah!"

A mail-plane from the polo ground's makeshift field flew low over their heads. The pilot reached out and waved. Passengers on a ferry coming from Virginia thought he was welcoming them to Washington and hollered back, while another passing steamboat let loose its whistle. Then he and Wesley threw themselves down on the bench and laughed past the point where they had no voice left within them—only "huu, huu, huu," sounds coming out of their throats.

CHAPTER TWENTY-FOUR

Christmas Miracle

December 15, 1918

Shortly before dusk on Christmas, Wesley guided the Ford Touring car through Chicago. Hernandez helped him follow directions a mechanic gave them in Crown Point, Indiana.

"Ya know," Wesley said, trying to see through the steam on the windshield, "my brother, Cleve, got married in Crown Point. After he got out of the Army, they eloped. Didn't tell a damn soul about it."

"Cleve? Isn't he the one who tried to help General Pershing catch Pancho Villa?"

Wesley chuckled. "I think ol' Cleve really wanted him to go free. Anyway, Pershing never even got close to finding the rascal."

Hernandez wiped a rag across Wesley's side of the windshield. "Some of my people believe Pancho is alive. In Ohio."

"No kidding? Cleve said if he met up with him that's where he'd tell him to go."

Hernandez let out a laugh and grabbed the steering wheel to keep them from running into the gutter. "Easy, Amigo. We're in Chicago now."

"Jeez! I better watch what I'm doing. I hope a tire doesn't decide to blow in the middle of the city. We put the last spare on in South Bend."

Hernandez smiled. "Don't worry. We made it this far, didn't we?"

Wesley thought back to their trip. They had been through freezing rain and blinding snow. His car bounced over roads with holes a foot deep and crawled up hills standing like giant walls threatening to block their way.

After Wesley almost fell asleep going over the Blue Ridge Mountains, Hernandez took over the wheel and taught himself to drive something besides a horse. Thanks to the blankets he brought from his Army job, they kept from freezing. He also brought feed sacks that they spread under the tires for traction on icy spots.

Along the way, they picked up servicemen trying to get home for Christmas. They exchanged stories, laughed a lot, and sang into the night. When the car got stuck in mud or snow, everyone put a shoulder to it, making it seem more like fun than a chore.

In each state, country-folk and townspeople helped the boys get home for Christmas. A farmer near Cumberland, Maryland, pulled them out of a steep embankment with his biggest bull. An Amish man from Lancaster, Pennsylvania, rode his horse to the nearest town to bring them a can of gasoline even though he said the auto was an invention of the devil. Families urged them into their houses to share a meal and to take a warm coat, scarf, or pair of gloves belonging to their sons, some who would never come home. A widow in Ohio heated buckets of water on her stove so they could bathe and shave. A couple with six children and one bedroom in West Virginia offered them a mattress to put on the floor. "You're welcome to sleep 'mongst' us," the husband had said.

Now, they made their way "mongst" an army of other cars on Chicago's Outer Drive. Wesley's Ford Touring Car, splashed with mud and peppered with scratches and dents, had become a veteran itself. Like the men who rode in it, bringing with them physical and emotional injuries, it would need repairing and cleaning up.

"I wonder if my mother's here yet," Hernandez said, straining his eyes for a last glimpse of Lake Michigan.

His mother had traveled by train from Brownsville, Texas with her two younger boys several days ago. His sister had moved from San Antonio the year before with her children to an apartment on the north side. Now the whole family would spend the holidays together.

Even though Wesley had grown accustomed to this city before he went into the Army, driving in Chicago now seemed like wandering around in a huge spider web. Hernandez gave directions whenever a decision had to be made. Sometimes they made the wrong turn and had to drive back until they found where they made their mistake. But, all in all, the driving went easier than Wesley expected. When he turned off the main thoroughfares, he found less traffic than on a holiday in Washington.

"I think this is the street," Hernandez said. "Look, there's the place. Two doors down on the right side—2134."

Wesley pulled in front of a red brick apartment house, and Hernandez got his duffel bag from the back seat. Wesley could hear someone playing Christmas carols on a guitar and children's voices singing along in Spanish.

"Won't you come in, Amigo?" Hernandez asked. "Meet my family and have Christmas dinner with us."

"Sounds terrific," Wesley said, wishing he could. "But I've got to go straight to my aunt's and find out how my folks are. And I've got to check on my brother, Cleve. His wife is having a baby any time now."

Hernandez reached for Wesley's hand. "My prayers go with you. Thank you for everything." He walked up the steps to the apartment door and knocked.

"Hey," Wesley called after him, "I never got your first name."

Hernandez turned. "Ralph. It's Ralph. Merry Christmas, Amigo."

A little boy opened the door. He threw his arms around Hernandez's legs as cheering and joyous weeping swelled from inside the apartment. Hernandez lifted the boy into his arms and disappeared inside.

"Ralph," Wesley said to the closed door. "What in the hell kind of Mexican name is Ralph?"

Half an hour later, he pulled in front of Aunt Jo's house on the west side. She ran out to meet him immediately, as if she'd been waiting by her window the whole time he'd been away. As he got out of the car, she charged into his arms, almost knocking him down. "Oh, Wesley, thank God you're here!"

Wesley remembered how the Tooper and St. John kids always made fun of Aunt Jo because she cried, laughed, shrieked, or squealed at the drop of a hat. But it felt so good now to be cherished by someone who didn't hide her feelings, who was caring and loyal.

"How are Ma and Pa, Aunt Jo? Has the holiday season been rough for them?"

"It's been hard, Wesley. We got back from Kankakee an hour ago after spending all day with them. The Whitehouses are staying there tonight. Benny was their son too, you know. That little Lilly is such a comfort to your pa and Kate, and Hazel's always coming over with food."

"Have you seen Cleve and Mary? How is she?"

Aunt Jo clamped her hand over her mouth as thin puffs of breath, turned white by the cold, seeped out between her fingers. "Oh, my God! Get back in the car. Get back in the car right away!"

"Why, Aunt Joe? What in the world's happened?"

She put one hand on her forehead and grabbed a lapel of Wesley's coat with the other. "As close as Mary is, they insisted on coming with us to Kankakee. On the way back she thought she started labor. We dropped them off at the hospital. Go there now. Cleve needs you."

Wesley pulled open the car door and flung himself behind the wheel. "Which one?"

"Oh, I can't remember. Yes, I can. St. Lukes. That's what it is— St. Luke's Hospital on Racine Avenue. I should've gone with them but I wanted to watch for you. I knew you were coming, Wesley, I just knew it."

The traffic increased with folks coming home after visiting friends and families for Christmas or going to night services. To make things worse, the streets were becoming slippery as the temperature dropped.

If I slide into something or that tire blows, I'll just leave the car here and run to the hospital. That's what I'll do.

Aunt Jo said Cleve needed him. That was a switch. He'd needed Cleve ever since he could remember, and Cleve always took care of him, solved so many of his problems, no matter how impossible they seemed.

He drove around the hospital twice before finding a place to park at the back of the building. He tried the closest door and then two side doors. Locked. He didn't want to go back in the car, so he ran all the way to the front. When he opened the entrance door, he saw Cleve standing in the lobby with his hands in his pockets, a dazed look on his face. Cleve walked towards his brother, hands still in his pockets. Reaching him, he leaned forward, resting his head on Wesley's shoulder, his body swaying.

"Easy, Bro," Wesley said, "it's okay. Everything's okay."

Cleve stepped back and opened his eyes wide. "Okay? Why shouldn't it be okay? I'm a father—a goddamn father!"

"Already? How's Mary? Did she make it all right?"

"Mary? What that little, scrawny thing handled I couldn't have stood for a second. She took it like a Trooper. A Tooper Trooper. How'd ya like that? A Tooper Trooper."

Wesley laughed. "That's funny, Cleve. Real funny. But what in the hell did you have?"

"Me? I didn't have anything. Mary did."

"For God's sake! Did she have a boy or a girl?"

Cleve turned, walked to the counter, and picked up a piece of paper. He walked back to Wesley and held it in front of him. They stood and read the birth certificate together, silently, each holding a side with one hand. Towards the bottom, Wesley saw the name, Edward, after their father. The boy's middle name was Benjamin.

Without looking up, Cleve said, "You know what, Wes? He remembered."

"Remembered what? Who remembered?"

"Benny. He wrote me right after the St. Mihiel battle. He didn't know where to reach you, so told me to pass it on. Some kinda explosion hit him hard—knocked him out cold for a while. When he came to, he remembered the book."

"What book, Cleve? A diary? A book from the Bible?"

"No, no. That book I used to read to both of you at Father Fatso's place. The book I wrote his name in. The one I got in Ohio. He always said he didn't remember anything before the Whitehouse's got him —Pa, us kids, that damn orphanage … nothin'."

"*A Boy's Ocean Adventure,*" Wesley murmured.

"Yeah," Cleve said. "He wrote me that he remembered the part where Ocean Boy escapes from the jaws of a whale by jumpin' on the back of a sea turtle. I never told him about the whale or the turtle after he came back to us. I just read it to you little fellers when you was three and he was two. I know the little bugger never read it himself, so he must of remembered it the second he fell from that explosion at Saint Mihiel."

"Maybe at Argonne," Wesley said, "when … when he went down for good, he remembered it all—the orchard at Sheldon, Mama, even Willard."

"Yeah," agreed Cleve, the usual roughness gone from his voice, "when everything was swell."

SECTION III

Three Years Later

CHAPTER TWENTY-FIVE

Shattered

January 15, 1921

Wesley followed the smartly-dressed, young man across the dimly-lit floor of the speak-easy towards the men's toilet. To the rest of the Tooper family, eating their meal at a long table set with coffee cups filled with illegal alcohol, the man's name was Mitchell. But, right before the waiter in a black tuxedo with tails brought their dinners out on a tray as big as a tractor tire, Wesley heard him called something else. In a voice, almost as low as a whisper, the hostess addressed his prospective brother-in-law as "Sparky." That's when his suspicions of the last few months came to a head, and instantly he decided on his plan of action.

Each hair on his wavy-blond head meticulously styled, trouser pleats razor-sharp, Sparky walked with steps springy and self-assured, swinging his arms confidently back and forth as if in time to a military march or college song. What light there was in the room picked up the shine of his jewel-studded cuff links, bouncing their gaudy brilliance off the polished glass of French doors and shimmering mirrors.

Wesley grimaced, hating to think of what he had to do. Nevertheless, he couldn't give up. He had to be there when the man stood over the urinal—when he undid his pants. He had to see it to be satisfied. The thought of what would happen in the next ten or fifteen minutes made him sick to his stomach.

He looked back on how fine things had gone today. Mitchell had driven Lilly, the folks, and Hazel and Dan up to Chicago from Kankakee in his new Stutz Bearcat. They stopped at Wesley's apartment and invited him to spend the day with them, and to invite his girlfriend, Esther, as well as Cleve, Mary, and little Edward. Wesley, in his Ford with Esther, and Cleve with wife and son packed into his one-seater coupe, followed Mitchell to Jackson Park where the group went swimming in Lake Michigan. Even Pa and Ma walked in water up to their knees and tossed a ball with the rest of the family.

Later, Cleve and Mary dropped little Edward off at Aunt Jo's, and the rest came over to Alfonso's for dinner and drinks—at Mitchell's expense. Lilly, her usual chatter today delightful as birdsong, bubbled with pride at her gentleman's unselfish extravagance. Cleve and Mary, seldom without their little boy, tonight became lovers on a date, unable to get enough of each other. Pa and Ma smiled and laughed more than they had since Benny's death.

Wesley quickened his pace. He wanted to give Mitchell time to get settled in front of the urinal, but he wanted to get there before he finished. Ever since he was out of the Service and working in private business again, he managed to keep the rakes and the riffraff away from his sister. When she started going with Mitchell, it seemed to the rest of the family that she found a decent man who would love her and take care of her the rest of her life. Most of the time, Wesley felt that way too and tried to smother doubts about Lilly's perfect boyfriend. Now, he wanted it all to be over. During the meal, he noticed Mitchell getting up and going towards the restroom but saw other men headed towards it so he didn't follow him then. Now he hoped, almost prayed, he could be alone with this dandy his sister was so crazy over.

When he opened the men's room door, a combination of stale and acrid smells, the glare of white, diamond-shaped floor tiles, and monotonous dripping of sink faucets deepened his already-low spirits. He spied Mitchell standing before a urinal, the room otherwise empty. Wesley chose an adjoining urinal, his hands almost shaking. Glancing over, he couldn't get a clear picture. He had to have a close look—see it fully. He must.

Mitchell took his arrival in stride. "Hi there, Wes. Having a good time?"

"I always do ... Sparky."

Surprised, the man turned quickly, dribbling on himself and the floor.

Then Wesley saw it—red and inflamed, bumpy, and sore. Instantly, he buttoned himself up and grabbed Mitchell by the collar. "You sick son of a bitch. Take that rotten thing out of here. If you ever see my sister again, I'll kill you!"

"Hey!" Mitchell croaked as the pressure on his throat increased. "What in the hell's wrong?"

"Wrong?" Wesley hissed through his teeth. "It's that infected thing between your legs. That's what's wrong!"

Mitchell's attempted laugh came out as a gurgle. "Oh, you mean Junior here? Too much workout with the chickies. Nothin' serious."

"You ... you bastard!" Wesley increased his grip.

"R-r-relax, Wes. By the time I marry your sister, it'll be all calmed down."

At the sound of the word *marry*, Wesley saw nothing but red. Before he knew it, he had flung Mitchell across the room. The man's outstretched hands made a painful, blackboard screech as they slid over the tiled floor. Wesley threw himself upon him.

"Marry?" His voice bounced off the tiles and porcelain furnishings of the lavatory. "You're not gonna be within a hundred miles of her! You make sure you go out the back door in the next minute, or you'll never walk again. Hear?"

His face pushed into the floor, Mitchell groaned.

Wesley let him go, making sure he left the bathroom before he broke the man's neck.

As he walked into the dining room, Wesley knew Lilly expected Mitchell to be right behind him. "What did you do, Big Brother—run off my sweetheart?"

Wesley placed his hands on her shoulders. "Mitchell had to go away suddenly. I'll tell you more about it later."

Immediately suspicious, his sister sprung from her chair and took enough steps toward him so that their faces almost touched. "I don't believe you for a minute. He would never leave me like this. Something's wrong!"

Wesley tried to ease her back into her seat. "I found out he was bad, through and through. He'd ruin your life, Lilly—yours and any kids you might have."

Lilly kicked him in the shins and pounded on his chest. "You skunk. You dirty skunk!"

He felt Cleve's hand on his shoulder. "Jeez, Bro, what'd the guy do? He's a bookie and a bootlegger, but, hell, who isn't these days?"

Wesley pulled Cleve aside and whispered what he saw in the men's room. Cleve took a surprised step backwards, walked over to Dan and Hazel, and spoke to them in tones so low no one else could hear. Hazel gasped. Dan Palmer's face filled with relief because, for once, so much fuss had nothing to do with him. He walked over to Pa and whispered in his ear.

Hitting his fist on the table, Pa shouted, "Goddamn it!" Then he leaned over and whispered in Ma Tooper's ear.

Ma shrieked, ran over to Lilly, gathered her in her arms, and whispered in her ear, afterward pouring out comforting phrases as she held her close. "There, there, Honey. Wesley done what he had to. Pa woulda thrashed him good if he shirked his duty."

Wesley shook his head in amazement and sat down next to Esther. "Ma hardly ever takes my part," he told her, blinking his eyes in an attempt to grasp the situation. "Hardly ever in my whole life. And, Pa ... Pa couldn't thrash any of us now if he tried."

Esther looked around the table as if in a dream.

Mary, sitting across from her, shrugged her shoulders at her as if to say, "This kind of thing happens all the time in the Tooper family."

"Oh," Lilly sobbed. "What am I going to do? What will I do?"

"You'll do like the rest of us are gonna do," Pa told her. "You'll go to the bathroom and wash your hands. Wash 'em real good."

Wesley paid the bill and asked Cleve to take Esther home so he could drive their parents and Lilly back to Kankakee.

Cleve scratched his head. "Yeah, we'll figure out a way to fit her in. She'll probably have to sit on Mary's lap. But what I want to know is what in the hell gave you such a damned notion about the son of a bitch—enough to make you look at him like you did?"

"Something about his skin, I guess—so scrubbed and sweet smelling. From the first time I saw him, I pictured him all infected underneath. Besides, I learned to watch for those things in the Army."

Cleve reached for Wesley's hand and shook it. "My hat's off to you, Little Bro. You sure know your way around these days."

Lilly cried quietly during the drive back home and Pa grumbled on through the darkness.

"That big supper bill. All that money you paid out, Wesley. You'll never get enough to buy a Studebaker now."

"Don't worry, Pa. I've been looking around. I'll have a better job soon."

"Prices rising, wages, lagging. Railroad won't buy my inventions. Fella can't make it anymore."

"It'll be all right, Pa. There's other things going big, like cosmetics."

"Politics. It's all politics."

When he got back to Chicago, Wesley figured Esther would be in bed, so he waited until the next day after work to see her. They met in front of the Opera House like they did every weekday evening.

"Well, you had some unexpected commotion to deal with yesterday," she said as casually as someone talking about the weather. "But your family has always kept you hopping, hasn't it?" She did not look at him but kept staring at her fingertips as if checking for a hangnail or chip. "You're either protecting Lilly, smoothing things over between Dan and Hazel, helping Cleve and Mary make ends meet, or trying to cheer up your folks."

He opened his mouth to say something, but she silenced him by patting him on the shoulder and winking. "So, since you've got your hands full, Wesley Boy, I think the time has come for me to step out."

He knew from the light-hearted way she talked, it would be useless to try and change her mind. As they walked in different directions down Dearborn Avenue, they turned and waved goodbye.

On the way home, he bought a newspaper. "Record Broken in Flagpole Sitting," the headlines read. The story explained how Alvin "Shipwreck" Kelly, "steadied by discs and stirrups," had been sitting on a flagpole for twenty-three days and seven hours.

"That's just fine," Wesley said out loud to his mother's picture when he got back to his apartment. "Some joker sits on a flagpole for over three weeks, Esther says she's through with me, wages are down, prices are up, and where in the world is Willard tonight?"

CHAPTER TWENTY-SIX

A Case Reopened

March 12, 1921

The next weekend Wesley drove to Kankakee and rummaged through his father's rolltop desk.

"Pa, I'm looking for a letter. I sent you one from the ship on my way to France. My helper, Rusty, told me about a kid he worked with one summer in the wheat fields of Dakota. Said he made a funny sound when he laughed—just like I do. Rusty mentioned his last name, and I wrote it down on a balance sheet I had in front of me. I think I copied it and slipped it in with a letter I sent you. Did you get anything like that?"

Pa rocked in his chair and sucked on his pipe. "I dunno. I got so many things in the mail from offices in Washington, some from the Marines."

"My God, that's right. When … when I wrote that name down, the Marines might have been loading Ben's body in some ship along with hundreds of others. You probably got word of it just a short time after I wrote that note."

"I dunno just when I got it. Hardly paid attention to the mail after a while. All kinds of flim-flam—high-blown condolences, fake sympathy. Politics. All politics."

"Aw, I hate to bring this up now. But, you always told us to never let anything go by that could be the slightest clue to finding Willard or Ben. Remember?"

Pa stopped rocking and stared into space. "And just think of poor little Benny. We followed every clue we could think of after Cleve came home from Ohio with that book. And find him, we did, only to lose him for good. What good did all that searching do?"

"Don't talk like that, Pa. Oh, why didn't I write down a copy of that stuff for myself? I guess I thought I'd be at war and wouldn't need it over there."

"Maybe it's all for the best, Wesley. Maybe if we never found Benny, he wouldn't be dead now."

Wesley slammed one desk drawer closed and opened another. "That's crazy, Pa. If we didn't find him, we wouldn't have had the time with him that we did. Besides, I've been all through that: maybe I shouldn't have taught Benny to play soldier; maybe I shouldn't have fought with him when we were kids. If I hadn't, maybe he wouldn't have joined the Marines. That gets you nowhere. Only nowhere."

"Let it go, Wesley. Stop looking."

"Damn, what was that kid's last name, anyway? Pretty simple—like a man's first name with a 's' on the end of it—like Williams or Richards or … or Michaels. And the guy he worked for—a name you'd make up for a farmer just to be funny. Like Plowfield or Beanrow."

Pa knocked the ashes out of his pipe into a spittoon. "What in the world's got you started on this anyway?"

"Maybe I thought we were getting over Ben enough to start thinking about the other boy—the one we hardly knew. Maybe it's got something to do with with a promise I made to a young woman in D.C. who wanted the best for me. But maybe you're right, Pa. Maybe I should give it up. I not only can't remember that kid's last name, I can't even remember Rusty's last name or where he lived."

"That's right, Wesley. Let it go."

The next six months moved by quickly for Wesley. He landed a job as head accountant in the purchasing department for a cosmetic company. He bought the Studebaker he had dreamed about and found a new girl friend named Madeline. He went to Kankakee often for the folks' sake, trying to help Hazel with her problems about Dan and keeping the rakes and dandies away from Lilly.

Pa's grief slowly lessened. The railroad awarded him a monthly payment because of a coupling he invented for train cars and a leg injury he had received years before. "How do you like that?" He grumbled. "They wouldn't give me any money for getting hurt on their car joiners until I came up with one that works like it should. I always told 'em those knuckle couplers of Major Janney's needed improving. There were too many of us brakemen getting killed or injured that didn't have to be."

Recognition for his efforts softened his outlook. Retired at the house on Schuyler Avenue, he spent his time raising vegetables, working on geometry problems and his favorite science and mechanical projects. Then a letter came in the mail with another check. It came from the lawyers representing the church connected with the orphanage that didn't exist anymore. Father Farellsi, the director, had long passed away, as well as the nun in charge.

The lawyer Pa had hired years ago came to see him. "They say they're sorry," he said regarding the church officials. "So many men back then had wives die and leave them with kids to raise. Some fathers were relieved if the orphanage found another family to take their children. Not many looked for them like you did, Edward."

Pa took the money and hired a detective from Chicago. He even started writing a few letters, referring to the addresses on the crumpled piece of paper the orphanage gardener slipped him years ago as he fled the institution with his two remaining boys. "I gave no permission for any of my sons to be adopted," he wrote. "No permission whatsoever."

Since Pa started writing letters again, Wesley wrote to Norling, his former Army boss in Washington who had offered to help him find Willard. Norling replied saying he would request a government man from the federal records office to contact Pa's detective. After weeks of digging, the combined efforts of the two men came up with something significant.

"It's a certificate of adoption issued in Benton County, Indiana," Pa's man reported. "It reads, 'Tooper infant to John W. and Marie Flowers, April 9, 1901.'"

"There's 133 John Flowers in the United States," the detective told Wesley. "Sixteen of them are John W. Flowers."

A month later, he located the right one, a postal worker in Hannibal, Missouri, husband of Marie Flowers, deceased.

After much pleading, Wesley persuaded Cleve to accompany him and the detective to Hannibal. "When you see Willard, you might remember something I wouldn't," Wesley told him on the train.

"If that's him," Cleve said.

John Flowers stood waiting for them at the station platform and drove them to his home. "I'd be glad to tell you all I can about the adoption," he said after providing each visitor with a chair and a cup of coffee.

"We'd appreciate that," Wesley said. "As you know, we have reason to believe the child you and your wife adopted in 1902 is our brother."

Flowers looked stunned. "No! That's impossible."

"I told ya," Cleve rasped at Wesley. "Just from lookin' at us he knows it ain't a match. Probably some blond with snow-white skin."

"You're so right," Flowers said. "But that's not the point."

The detective grabbed Flower's arm. "But we talked about so many things fitting together. How can you be sure until we look into all the evidence?"

John Flowers opened a large envelope he'd been carrying under his arm, took out a photograph, and thrust it towards the three men. "This is all the evidence you'll need."

Wesley and the detective sucked in their breaths.

Cleve groaned. "It's a girl—a goddamn girl!"

CHAPTER TWENTY-SEVEN

On the Trail

March 14, 1921

"Hey, what's goin' on?" the detective cried, his arms locked behind
him in Cleve's firm hold, the view of the countryside speeding by
through the open train door. "I thought we were going for a smoke."

"You'll go for a smoke, all right," Cleve growled, "in the great
outdoors."

"You can't blame me. The guy in Washington should've checked
on the kid's sex."

Wesley grabbed the detective by the shirt front. "He did his part
by telling you where to find the records. I checked with Flowers while
you and Cleve got our tickets back to Chicago. His document says
July 7, not July 9 like the one you found, and it says Toops infant,
not Tooper."

"That's crazy. There's no such name as Toops."

"It's a lot more common name than ours, you cheap floorwalker.
Your fingers itched so bad for our pa's money, you saw what you
wanted to see and didn't check for anything else. We didn't pay you
to play horseshoes."

Cleve increased his hold and raised his voice to overcome the
rattle and clank of the train cars. "That's right. Close ain't good enough.
Stand aside, Wes, I'm throwin' him out."

Wesley saw the terror in the detective's face as he looked down
at the flashing wheels, felt the powerful draft that could sweep him

underneath. "No—please don't! My wallet's in my back pocket. Take it."

"You bet your life we will!" Wesley shouted. "And you'll give back everything our pa paid you or out you go."

"I'll even pay for your trips out here. Take it!"

Cleve edged him further through the doorway. "Say please, pretty please."

Wesley heard a prolonged plea rising higher at the end than the hoot of the train whistle six cars ahead: "Please take my money. Pretty pleeeese!"

The two brothers hauled the detective in and at the Illinois Central station in Chicago, let him disappear into the crowd. An hour later, they were in Kankakee.

"The lame-brained gumshoe," Pa grumbled. "He should've made sure the two certificates were alike before he dragged you all the way down there on my money."

"As it turned out, Pa," Wesley said, laying down the wad of bills the detective begged him to take. "We went down there on his money, and there's enough here to pay back everything you gave him."

Pa, unable to hold back a grin, stared at the money. "Well, well. Looks like I taught you boys a thing or two after all."

With Wesley's urging, Pa hired another detective, this time from Indianapolis with Norling's recommendation. Although Flower's adopted child was a girl, the new man thought it wise to try to find the woman who gave birth to the Toops infant. "It could lead to information about what happened to your son," he told Pa.

After two weeks of tracing, he found that the mother had been a sixteen-year old girl named Margaret Toops, who gave birth out of wedlock but drowned in a boating accident in Lake Michigan off the Indiana Sand Dunes in 1913. The detective located her brother who said his sister received payment for the child from a bank in Terre Haute but didn't know the name.

"You know," Wesley said. "Every company I've been with uses the same bank for transactions of one kind then another one for transactions of a different kind. If this bank handled payment for the Flowers adoption, it might have handled payment for other adoptions."

Pa looked at the new detective. "I think you should go to Terre Haute and check out the banks there."

The detective came back with a skimpy report—no statements or records as to who had paid for the Toops child or anything else that seemed significant. Instead, he produced a scrap of paper with the words, "Malenday transaction complete."

"It was in a desk drawer in the back room of the Indiana National," he explained. "The bank had some old records they let me browse through, and this was in the corner of one of the drawers."

"And this is all you bring me?" Pa said, rubbing the scrap between his thumb and forefinger.

"Don't throw it away," Wesley said. "You never know."

Wesley wrote Norling in Washington who wired back, "Check hotel records near orphanage when brother was taken."

Some of the hotels were closed for years. Some were remodeled and their names changed. Some, like the orphanage, had burned down. According to the detective's report, he poured through name after name on registration lists in hotels within thirty miles of where the orphanage once stood on both the Illinois and Indiana sides. None of them had a connection to any of the information the family had gathered, so he pushed a little farther east to Rensselaer, Indiana. The main hotel in town had guest books going back to the late 1800's stored in its basement. One name flashed out to the detective—Dr. L. E. Malenday—the same last name on the note in the corner

of a drawer at the Indiana National Bank. Dr. Malenday had stayed
at the hotel the nights of July 7th through the 9th in the year 1902.
Willard was taken from the orphanage on July 8th.

There weren't as many Malendays in the country as Flowers, but
there were five Dr. Malendays, three whose first names started with
the letter "L." There was a Dr. Lee Malenday in San Diego, a dentist,
and two medical doctors—one in Worcester, Massachusetts, with
the first name of Leander, and a Dr. Leland Malenday in Chicago.
The proximity of Dr. Leland Malenday made things convenient, so
the detective checked him out first. His office was near the University of
Chicago where he taught medical courses. He received his medical
degree from the University of Minnesota 25 years ago and practiced
in St. Paul for nine years before moving to Chicago.

"Minnesota," Wesley mused when the detective brought his
findings. "Remember, Pa, I told you about that kid who worked with
Rusty in the wheat fields, the one who laughed with a click, like I
have sometimes? I'd swear Rusty said he came from Minneapolis or
St. Paul. But his name didn't sound like Malenday. More common
than that."

"A similar chuckle is not much to go on," the detective said.

"Let's not just charge in," Pa said. "First, find out if he has a son
Willard's age."

Dr. Leland Malenday had no children, and the detective found no
record of a death or adoption. The dentist in San Diego had three sons
all under the age of fifteen. The doctor in Worcester, Massachusetts,
had a set of twins—a boy and a girl twelve years old.

His money running out, Pa had the detective finish the job by
phoning Leland Malenday at his office in Chicago. The detective,
posing as a reporter doing a story on Indiana landmarks, said he
was interviewing guests who at one time or another stayed at the

Rensselaer Hotel. He would appreciate Dr. Malenday offering his impressions of that hotel when he stayed there in July of 1902.

Dr. Malenday remained silent for a while and then said he was sorry, but he remembered very little about it.

"Do you remember if you were there on a long trip, Doctor," the detective asked, "visiting people in the area or on business? We're also collecting reasons why guests stayed there over the years."

Malenday sounded irritated. It was unrealistic, he said, to expect him to remember what he was doing that long ago. "I may have been coming back from a medical meeting at Purdue University and became too tired to go on to Chicago. Who knows after all that time?"

The detective checked with Purdue's records of medical conferences and found a meeting concerning the causes of cholera held around the time of the doctor's stay at the Rensselaer Hotel.

"Why in hell's name didn't he just come out and ask Malenday if he knew anything about an adoption in Benton County?" Cleve asked after hearing about the phone call.

"He did ask why he was staying in that part of the country," Wesley reasoned. "Malenday had his chance to talk about it. He either doesn't know or he's holding back."

"Let's forget about this whole Malenday thing," Pa said. "I'm tired of dead ends."

At night Wesley kept slipping in and out of dreams, unable to distinguish between fancies of sleep and chains of disrupted thoughts. He saw himself back at the orphanage and he could see Willard. Was it before or after they took Benny away, when Sister Stringy put Wesley in Farellsi's room full of papers? Yes, it was Baby Willard. Baby Willard smiling and waving in and out of rooms, down hallways. Baby Willard's laughter in rising, thrusting peals like the chattering of a red squirrel.

Through the mist of dreams, Wesley could make out grownups carrying Willard. Father Fatso, the nuns, some of the workers dressing him up, showing him off. "How sweet-tempered, so good looking. So well-behaved."

A man with a soft-flowing mustache and a stethoscope around his neck walked the hallways, heels clicking on the tiles. Father Fatso bowed to him, his robes spilling onto the floor like pools of blood. "Thank you, Doctor. This way, Doctor. Bring the little fellow in this room, Doctor. So healthy. Yes, very healthy."

Other forms lurked in the background—slow, deliberate strides of a man in baggy pants—a flash of a flowered dress, stiff curls and nervous smile of a woman too old to have a boy just learning to talk. In later dreams she reached for Willard, his toddler-voice hollering out, "Eeeeve, Eeeve."

Wesley would wake up shaking, his sheets dampened with sweat, his body throbbing as if pierced by a sword. A sword as thin as Willard's baby-shrieks calling out for Cleve, the closest person he had to a parent in such a parentless place.

As a way of becoming too tired to dream, Wesley threw himself into work. When his company asked for an accountant willing to travel throughout the Midwest that fall, he agreed to do it. One clear September afternoon on his way back from Dayton, Ohio, he looked up from his newspaper to see where the train stopped. The sign on the depot said "Rensselaer."

"Is this Rensselaer, Indiana?" he asked the conductor.

"Yes. We'll be here fifteen minutes. If you want to stay longer than that, another train for Chicago will be along in two hours."

Without thinking, Wesley pulled his suitcase from the shelf above the seat and walked off the train.

"Where is the Rensselaer Hotel?" he asked the brakeman.

"You can see it right down on the next block. It's the biggest building on the street."

As he walked, he felt like he did when he had followed Lilly's boyfriend, Sparky, to the men's room of the speakeasy. Nothing could stop him from doing what must be done, but this time he didn't know what that could be. He had no plan. Entering the hotel, he walked across the seemingly-endless lobby to where a clerk stood behind the desk.

"Would you like a room, Sir?"

"No, what I want is … "

"Yes, Sir?"

"I want to see the registration records for 1902, specifically for July."

The clerk sighed. "They're way down in the basement. Someone came here last spring looking for the same thing."

"I know that. My father sent him."

The clerk frowned. "I really can't spare the time to go rummaging around down there now, Sir."

Wesley took a five-dollar bill out of his wallet and held it in front of him.

The clerk disappeared into a backroom and came out, grinning sheepishly and carrying a large, thick book. "Guess I never put it back downstairs after the other gentleman looked at it."

Wesley paged through the early July pages. There he saw written Dr. Leland Malenday of Evanston, Illinois, like the detective said. He traced his finger above the doctor's name to occupants of neighboring rooms: Mr. and Mrs. Marshal Greenfield and two children of Louisville, Kentucky; Mr. Albert Dawson and son of Livingston, Ohio; Mr. and Mrs. Thomas Fullson of South Bend, Indiana.

"Nothing rings a bell here," Wesley said half to himself and half to the rest of the world. "I could spend the whole day here and wind up in another dead end."

Weary and disgusted, he moved his finger over the lines below Malenday's name. Staying in Room 213 next to the doctor's were Mr. & Mrs. J. J. Edwards of St. Paul, Minnesota.

A sound echoed through Wesley's head like tumblers of a lock falling into place. "That's it," he said to the clerk. "Edwards—the name of the kid with the click."

"Click, Sir?"

"Sure! The kid that worked with Rusty in the wheat fields. The guy who had a last name like a first name with the letter 's' on the end."

Letter 's' Sir?"

"And … and the old guy with baggy pants and the woman with stiff curls. The Edwards. Maybe they're the ones who took Willard. And that Dr. Malenday in the next room—he'd be in on it too."

The clerk blinked his eyes and jerked his head back as Wesley handed him the five dollar bill. "That's good, Sir. If you say so. Very good, Sir."

CHAPTER TWENTY-EIGHT

Getting Close

March 12, 1921

When he didn't have to keep his mind on his job, Wesley kept trying to reach Rusty, often postponing dates with his new girlfriend, Madeline. He felt so compelled to find out about the hired hand named Edwards that he wasn't sure if he made plans for a certain evening with her or not. He did feel sure, though, that contact with the red-haired, freckled-faced friend he had in the Service could take him closer to finding his brother.

Two men he met on the ship during the War lived near Chicago —one in Harvey and one in LaGrange. He made arrangements to meet with them on different nights and ask them questions about Rusty. As it turned out, neither one could even remember his first name. They just thought of him as the lame-brained soldier who jumped off the ship at Bermuda.

Disappointed, Wesley drove over to Cleve's to tell him the bad news.

Cleve was in his garage working on his car. "You're one hell of a detective," he said, after Wesley told him about what little progress he made. "The Army can find that character a lot faster than you can."

"I wrote the Army but they don't have enough to go on. I couldn't give them the kid's last name because I never paid attention to it. I just knew him as Rusty and they didn't have a record of anyone with that first name. It must have been his nickname."

"Wasn't he your assistant for workin' on the books?"

"Yeah, but …."

"Well, they'd have a record of that, wouldn't they?"

"They didn't," Wesley answered, becoming more discouraged than ever. "Things were more lax on the ship than they were on the base. I think they just sent him over to me when I needed someone."

"Well, damn it, get in touch with that boss you had in Washington. He helped us before, he could probably help us now."

"How dumb do you think I am? I thought about doing that but I don't have anything more to give him than when I wrote the Army in the first place."

Cleve touched Wesley on the shoulder, leaving a black hand-mark on his brother's white shirt. "Listen, Bro, those bigwigs got ways me and you don't even dream about."

So Wesley wrote to Norling with the company number he had before his assignment in Washington and the name of his ship. When he was at the point of losing hope, he received a short note and telephone number of the post office in Winesocket, South Dakota. In the note, Norling said to call that number at 6 p.m. the following Wednesday.

Aunt Jo and Uncle Ed had a telephone, so Wesley left work early and drove to their house. On the first two tries, a loud, buzzing noise came over the line. Then everything went dead and he had to ask the operator to reconnect him. Finally, he heard a distant voice—thin and laced with static. "Mr. Tooper. Mr. Tooper?"

"Yes. Who is this?"

"It's me, Mr. Tooper, Rusty."

"My God, Rusty, what are you doing in the post office? Are you the postmaster?"

"Oh no, that's Bud Stamper. He has the only phone around here so he lets us all use it."

As their conversation continued, the interference over the line lessened, but Rusty kept talking loudly—so much that Wesley had to hold the receiver away from his ear.

"I'm buyin' my dad's farm now, and Maisy and I have two of the cutest little boys ya ever saw! Gee whiz, why didn't ya tell me that kid with the click might be your brother? Maybe I coulda told you more about him right then and there."

"We thought we were off to war, Rusty. Remember? Maybe never coming back."

"Well, thanks to you for hauling me back to the ship, I'm right where I belong. Married to the girl I loved since the sixth grade. I'll get Mr. Pickrow to send you that Edwards feller's first name. Okay?"

"Pickrow? I thought his name was Pickbush."

"No, that's our other neighbor—Kickerbush. Now don't forget. If you and your brother ever want a job working in the wheat fields, I'll hire you any time. Then I'll get to hear two clicks instead of one."

"I'll remember that. I sure will. And if you and your wife ever want to take a second honeymoon and come to Chicago, I'll be glad to show you around."

"That'd be fine, Mr. Tooper. We never had our first honeymoon yet. I better say goodbye now. Two of my neighbors are in line to use the phone."

"Goodbye, Rusty—and thanks."

Wesley felt so good after hearing Rusty's voice, he drove over to Madeline's to see if she wanted to go dancing as a way of celebrating.

Her mother told him she left with someone else over an hour ago. "When you didn't show up last week, she accepted an invitation from a gentleman in her singing group. She's at the pictures with him tonight and doesn't want you to call on her anymore. That's probably a good idea, Wesley."

He hadn't expected such an abrupt rejection. When he got back to his car, he decided not to drive right away. Instead, he chose to stroll around the block. As he walked, his mind wandered briefly to his work, the news he might receive about the Edwards boy, a pretty girl on the other side of the street, but not once to Madeline. His attention focused on the colors of the houses, the types of cars passing by, a father walking hand-in hand with his son.

He returned to his car and drove to a dance hall where he took Madeline several times. He danced the first three dances in a row, each with a different lady. Madeline never liked to dance as much as he did. If she were with him now, he would have to sit out half the numbers making small talk and bringing her refreshments.

The touch of relief he felt in being alone bothered him. His brothers and sisters had all fallen head-over-heels in love and stayed that way. Cleve never had any other sweetheart except for Mary, and Dan had always been Hazel's one and only no matter what he did. Bennie and Nelly had truly loved each other and would have stayed together forever if they had been lucky enough to stay alive. And Lilly had turned down all her fancy men now for a homespun, hard-working boy named Herman. Maybe he didn't make as much money as some of her former boyfriends, but he would always love Lilly and stand by her through thick or thin.

And what about Wesley? Would he find someone who would stay with him for the rest of his life, or would he just go on losing girl friends and getting new ones? He never had trouble finding them, and now, since he owned such a grand auto, he had all the dates he wanted. Every time he began to hope he found the right girl, the romance would fizzle.

His thoughts were interrupted by the piano player walking out to the middle of the dance floor with a large megaphone in his hand.

"Ladies and gentlemen," his voice boomed, "we're going to do something different tonight. The ladies, not the men, will choose their partners for the next dance."

A chorus of feminine squeals floated over the room, and the men tried to hide their embarrassment with overdone smiles or laughter.

"Come on, now, don't be shy," the piano player coaxed. "They do it in New York, so why can't we do it here in Chicago? Now ladies, grab your favorite gentleman and bring him out on the floor."

The dance hall became silent. Stunned, Wesley realized that Ma Tooper's prophecy, on the day women got the right to vote, had come true. "The world was going to smithereens," she concluded, and before you knew it, "women would be asking men to dance." The family still laughed about it, as if she had predicted something as ridiculous as a man walking on the moon.

The piano player walked back on stage, and the band started up with "Indian Love Call" played to a foxtrot beat. A few couples, obviously married or engaged, started dancing. The men standing on the edges of the dance floor began adjusting their ties, checking their cufflinks, or suddenly became occupied in a conversation which appeared to take all their attention. Wesley didn't have anyone to talk to, so he sat in a chair and gazed at his feet. A few seconds seemed like hours. What if he would be the only man in the room without a partner? Now he knew how ladies felt waiting for someone to ask them to dance.

Suddenly he heard a tapping sound in front of him. As he looked up, his eyes focused on two little, round garter buttons staring at him without blinking—each attached to a pair of flesh-colored stockings covering slender but shapely legs. Her dress was as high above her knees as she could wear it without getting arrested. As her right leg moved up and down to the music, he caught a glimpse of a ruffled piece of green slip peeking out from under the creamy white dress, retreating and returning as if on a dare. He had seen a few girls wearing such dresses before, but he was always too shy to ask one to dance. It would have been like walking in on her before she finished dressing.

The tapping went on as he looked upward to her face. Now he saw firsthand why his company could pay him what it did. His boss was right when he said the cosmetic industry would be netting a hundred and fifty million dollars a year by 1925. Wesley saw the truth of this in the face in front of him.

All the mascara he recorded on his accounting sheets during his present job seemed brushed into this one pair of eyelashes, magically extending and thickening them. Like gates to a mansion, penciled lines of arched eyebrows proclaimed the boundaries of her blue-gray eyes. Soft but sculptured curls rounded two rouged cheeks, pointing like picture-show ushers to a pair of rosebud lips, painted daintily but amply with bright red lipstick.

She stood with hands on hips, extending one leg forward and tapping it in time to the music, the look of a mischievous imp on her face. Her arms were adorned with simple gold-colored bracelets, some at her wrists, some reaching almost to her elbows. The top of her dress had no sleeves or shoulders, just straps reaching up and over. He tilted his head and looked down one of the sides of this dress. It was open from a place below her underarms and almost down to her waist. How easy it would be to slip his hand inside, like reaching into a briefcase for papers. The urge frightened him, and he wanted to run from a danger threatening to suffocate him. Yet, he would pay everything he had in the world to stay.

She threw back her head and laughed, a high, abandoned nicker that turned heads. Leaning forward, she teased an index finger back and forth, daring him to come ahead.

The next thing he knew they were dancing. She stayed with him at every turn, every stop, every dip, more one with him than his shadow. So light on her feet, she almost caused him to wonder if he were dancing by himself if not for the invisible force flowing from her, steering him, sending silent messages of what to do next. As they danced, this lightness made him unaware of their proximity, and it was not until she suggested they pause for a cigarette that he became aware of it.

As they left the dance floor, one of the copy boys from work tapped him on the shoulder. "Cheek-to-cheek, loin to loin," he said admiringly. "Snazzy, Mr. Tooper. Snazzy."

She made no attempt to conceal that she liked him and admitted she asked the band leader to announce a lady's choice dance.

"I was at a dance in New York with my cousin when they did the same thing," she said, pursing her lips and blowing out a thin cloud of smoke slithering into the air like a curious serpent. There was no gent here I cared to dance with tonight until I spotted you, so I decided to request it."

Still transfixed by her eyes, he held an ashtray out for her. "Didn't you think I would ask you to dance myself?"

"Maybe. But I don't like to take chances."

"What's your name, Miss Requester of Dances?"

"Lillian Mae Hogan. And no one better dare call me Lilly."

His look of amazement when she announced her name caused her to thrust out her lips into a childish pout. "Oh," she whined in a baby-like falsetto, "you don't wike my name. Bye, bye." And in tiny steps imitative of a three-year-old, she began to walk away.

Stepping forward, he grabbed her arm and pulled her back. "Don't be silly. It's just that your name is the same as my little sister's. But we call her Lilly. You're Lillian Mae. I won't get you two mixed up—ever. Come on, let's dance." They tripped the light fantastic to "What'll I do?" from the *Music Box Revue* to George Gershwin's "Fascinating Rhythm," and Ray Henderson's "Button Up Your Overcoat."

After the band played "Good Night Ladies," she told him that Paul Whiteman was playing for a tea dance the next weekend on the south side. "And he's not going to play with Bix Beiderbecke this time. He's bringing the Rhythm Boys with that hotsy-totsy new singer, Bing Crosby. I'm mad about him, I really am."

"We'll go see him. Should I pick you up at your place?"

"Whatever you say. He's sharp, that one—almost as wild as Harold Lloyd. You know his new picture, *Safety Last*? It's held over at the Capital for two more days. He actually hangs twelve stories above the street. They say he got a dislocated shoulder from doing it. Can you believe that?"

"Go with me tomorrow night and see if I believe it. Find out when it starts."

"Whatever you say."

CHAPTER TWENTY-NINE

A Change in Course

March 26, 1922

During the next two weeks, Wesley and Lillian Mae Hogan became as close as a couple would be after many months of dating. She seemed to like wherever he took her and she loved his car. She let him kiss her on their second date and did not care what people might say if he came to her apartment when her roommate was gone.

She would even talk to him from the bedroom while he waited for her to change clothes.

"Wesley, did you know that the Marx brothers are coming to town next Saturday? They're going to do the same acts they did in the old Vaudeville days. You know that one with the curly hair? What's his name—Harpo? He only spoke once in all the shows they ever did. Just three little lines. Can you believe it?"

She didn't let them part without making sure they had a date set up for the next evening or the one after that. He didn't mind. Flattered and exalted by the whirlwind she was leading him through, he acted as though he were the leader, not she.

After they were dating about a month—dancing, going to theaters and the latest picture shows, enjoying dinners in the Loop, cruising in his car Sunday afternoons—something came to Wesley's attention. And for the first time since he met her, he stopped thinking about the most exciting, appealing woman who ever came into his life.

He had come home to his apartment from work, in a hurry to change clothes and drive to Lillian Mae's, when he found a letter in his mailbox. The return address bore the name J. D. Pickrow, Rusty's neighbor in North Dakota. He did not open it right away but brought it inside, laid it on his kitchen table, and looked at it. *Calm down, calm down. It's probably just another dead end.* Then he tore it open.

Mr. Pickrow began the letter by apologizing for not writing sooner as he was in the middle of planting time. The next line said about five years ago, he hired a boy named Edwards to work in his fields. The only job the kid had before was as a clerk at a St. Paul bank, but he turned into a darn-good field hand. He went by the first name of Bill.

My God, Bill—a nickname for William or … or Willard?

Mr. Pickrow wrote that he might have Bill's address buried away somewhere, but it wouldn't do Wesley any good. Wanting to hire the kid again the next year, he explained, he wrote to him at the address Bill gave him when hired on. In about two weeks, he got the letter back with no forwarding address. He said Bill talked of going to college and medical school in Minneapolis, so he might be in one of those places or at a bank in the Twin Cities. Mr. Pickrow ended the letter by apologizing for not helping Wesley more.

Damn it, Tooper, don't just sit there! Get on the night train to St. Paul as soon as you can. Stop at all the banks. Ask questions. Go to colleges and the University of Minnesota. Find Willard. Bring him down to Kankakee and give Pa and Ma the surprise of their lives.

Then reason set in. It wouldn't be that easy. It could take weeks, probably months. And what if this guy turned out to be someone else—not Willard? No Tooper ever thought of becoming a doctor. He, Wesley Tooper, had gone to LaSalle Business College at night for years and Cleve Tooper to South Chicago Machinery School for six weeks, but a university medical student was a completely different kind of human being.

Wesley felt a wave of emotion rush through him, a familiar sensation that in the past came solely from the hope of finding Willard. Now it was accompanied with the pressing demand to be with Lillian Mae, the desire to relive the thrill he had the first time he saw her as ripe as a summer berry. She might understand if he told her about Willard, that he had to look for his brother. Madeline and the others hadn't understood, but Lillian seemed to care for him more than any girl he had before. Should he risk it?

He decided not to tell Lillian the truth yet. Instead, he told her he received word that his stepmother was sick. He would have to drive to Kankakee that night and break their date. He eased her disappointment with a promise to bring her with him as soon as Ma got better. He wanted her to meet his family, he said, the only part that wasn't a lie. Then he got in his car and headed for Kankakee —not to visit an ill stepmother, but to tell Pa about the letter from Mr. Pickrow. And, most important, to tell him something else.

Later, he sat with Pa in the Schuyler Avenue house. They faced each other in big, oak chairs backed with hard, black leather, their feet on a common hassock. Ma's wispy figure, as she brought dandelion wine, promising cherry pie and coffee, drifted in and out of their pipe smoke.

Pa sucked seriously on his pipe as Wesley read Mr. Pickrow's letter to him. Ma shrieked, "Praise the Lord," from the kitchen. The traffic on the avenue swooshed by at irregular intervals, a renegade night breeze gently flapping the white brocade curtains against night-black window panes.

Pa said, "We're close, Wesley. So damn close. So many tie-ins. Write some letters, make some phone calls, take some trips to Minnesota, and you'd have it."

Wesley knocked the ashes out of his pipe and set it back in the stand where his father kept it for him. Ma silently carried their desserts in blue and white dishes and set them on a little table next to Pa's chair. Wesley remembered the dishes, decorated with tiny figures of children skating on a country pond, from the farm in Bonfield years ago.

"I can't do it, Pa," he said, standing up and taking a step toward the closet for his coat. "There's so much going on in my life now. I can't let it all go. Some of the others will have to help this time."

"Others. Who? Cleve can't write worth a damn. Neither can Hazel. Lilly not near as good as you."

Wesley snorted, "You know there's plenty around to help you— Uncle Napoleon, Clifford, Chester, and who knows how many others. You write better than any of us, including me. You've been talking for ages about taking Ma to that Mayo Clinic in Rochester and having her bones looked at. I'll help with the money. For the first time in my life, Pa, I have a girl who can't be with me enough. Look at the rest of us kids. They've all got someone permanent. I can't let this slip through my fingers."

Ma carried his pie over to him. He ate it standing up.

Pa set down his coffee cup. "My little boy," he murmured.

Wesley could tell from Ma's sigh that she thought Pa meant Willard, but he knew differently. Misty bits of memory floated through the crack of open window replacing the fading pipe smoke. Time wore away like water over creek rock. He heard Pa's words to him twenty years ago. "Both little boys are gone, Wesley. We've got a big brother, a big sister and a little sister. We need a little brother. You're my little boy again."

Pa stood up, his hand on his game leg. "You've done plenty, Wesley. Go ahead and court your girl. Your Uncle Napoleon and me—we'll handle it."

"Thanks, Pa. Just give me half a year."

"Surely. Just bring your sweetheart here so we can meet her."

"I will. Can I tell her about Willard—how we lost him, and what we're doing to find him? She knows how important brothers are. She has two older ones who would always help her, if she ever needed them."

Pa hesitated. "Maybe you better wait a while. We don't want this to get out and spoil any plans we make. See how things go with you two and what we can find out on this end. Can we ask your advice now and then?"

"Why not? As long as you don't ask me to write any letters for you, make phone calls, or take any trips."

"Done. You have my word."

Searching for Willard

CHAPTER THIRTY

Telephone Calls

August 16, 1922

1082 N. Schuyler Ave.

Kankakee, Il

Dear Son Wesley:

Your special letter was received just a little before the double one, and your instructions were followed accordingly. I see by your letter you want to can your sweetheart because she loves you too much.. That is not a reasonable pretext. I imagine you do not love her as you pretended to her and she is beginning to find it out. Well, anyway I hope your attitude towards her is not the result of any advice I might have given in my last letter. You must assume her religious sincerity in this matter. She is not intellectually capable of adopting your ideas all of a sudden. You must expect that it will take time and patience.

In regard to the matter of approaching the Malendays in view of locating Willard. By the way of posting you, the J. J. Edwards, August 15, 1915 were living at 409 Bates Avenue. Willard worked in the First National Bank of St. Paul in the latter part of 1917. He then resigned and worked in the Stock Yards in South St. Paul until July, 1918. In June he was working on a farm near Courtney, North Dakota. At that time the Edwards were living at

244 DARK BROWN *is the* RIVER

306 Cleveland Avenue, St. Paul. The dates may be of use to you in making up a plausible story.

I would suggest that you go to the Malendays and announce yourself as Mr. Allpine. That you formed an acquaintance with Willard a few years ago while working together in the Bank or Stock Yards and that your friendship had become very mutual, that you had written him a number of times while he was in Courtney and since then you had written him at the Cleveland Avenue address, but the letter was returned with a notation—"not at that address." And right here you might state that Willard had made mention of them on several occasions and now being in Chicago you had looked them up in the City Directory and if they would be so kind to give you his address.

Of course, this is only giving you an idea and you can perhaps improve on it. Have a talk with your Uncle Ed and he may be able to help you. It is possible that this plan would work over the telephone with less embarrassment. In this case, I think your Uncle Ed could do it better as he is more experienced and would not be so apt to get nervous as you might. I have great confidence in playing the game on these lines and I wish you would try it. If it fails, I cannot think of anything that would be any better. So try it.

Hoping you are well as also your Uncle Ed and family and Cleves. Tender our best regards to all not omitting yourself.

Affectionately, your Father, Mother and Sister
Edward Tooper

As Wesley pondered his father's letter, a constriction in his throat threatened to suffocate him. The stockyards. When he first came to Chicago as a boy, he worked at such a place. What inkling made him search for Willard there? The lowing and bellowing of cattle, the grainy rankness whenever he took a breath, and the bits of straw and ground-in dung beneath his feet sent him a message that he scratched off as imagination. He was right. The time and place were wrong. Willard Edward's jobs at a bank, a farm, and the stockyards all added up. He and Wesley Tooper might share the same blood.

In his mind, Wesley consciously emphasized the word "might." The name on the records at the bank, the stockyards, and the wheat fields was William Edwards, not Willard Tooper. Because of the chain of events he uncovered, Pa assumed they were one and the same. But hadn't he learned by now that coincidences, similarities, mix-ups, and false conclusions were a part of life? Didn't he realize that truth, whether uplifting or disappointing, could be more fantastic and shocking than any chain of reasoning might suggest?

Wesley's eyes focused on his mother's picture hanging on the wall. Her look was one of concentration like when she worked on figures, just as he did most of his life, as Willard most likely did at the bank in St. Paul in 1917.

My God, he was just seventeen then like the last two numbers of the year. A year and a half younger than Benny and Benny still alive then.

He called Uncle Ed and read Pa's letter to him over the phone.

Uncle Ed immediately jumped right into it. "Come right over, Wesley. I better make the call. That way, if it doesn't work out, they won't hear your voice and you can still try something else. I better not give my name as Allpine. You can use it later if you need to."

Wesley hurried to his car. He was ready to start looking for Willard again, and to his amazement, Pa knew it.

As he drove along, he wondered how Pa figured out what was going on with Lillian Mae. In a recent letter to his father, he wrote that she was a strict Catholic and how he was afraid, if they ever got married, she would have one baby after another. He didn't mention his fear of something awful happening during one of the births and her dying like his mother did. Could he raise the children without farming them out like Pa had to do? Neither did he mention the change that had come over his one and only the last several months —how much more discreet she had become in her way of dressing and how dependent on him for her happiness. Sometimes she let her emotions run away to a point where he became alarmed by her fragility, but then she would catch herself and everything would go back to normal.

Sure, he felt smothered sometimes but didn't want to "can" her, as Pa put it. He was actually flattered at her need to be with him, proud of the way she turned heads when they walked into a room together. But true, never-ending love—why wasn't he sure?

When he drove up in front of Uncle Ed's house, Aunt Jo came running out and almost knocked him down as he got out of the car. "Isn't it wonderful, Wesley? Just like the verse your mother and I repeated in church when we were little. 'Straight is the gate and narrow is the way.'"

He reached out to steady her and walked her to the house. "What does that have to do with us, Aunt Jo?"

"The gate … the gate is the same as Dr. Malenday. He was a true, straight clue but we didn't know it at first. Many of the other clues were crooked and didn't fit into the narrow way, but because you began with a straight clue, you, little by little, found the right ones. Like your Pa and Napoleon learning that J. J. Edwards saved Dr. Malenday's life in the Spanish American War, so Dr. Malenday helped the Edwards couple find a healthy little boy to adopt and paid the adoption fee. He became like a second father to Willard, helping him get into college and doctor school."

She took a deep breath as if she had been running to catch a train. "So you see, Wesley, the way was narrow but the gate was straight."

Wesley didn't see but felt eased by Aunt Jo's demeanor. What he saw was an affectionate, passionate woman who could became overly emotional to the point that you thought she was on the verge of going out of her head. He felt this way about Lillian sometimes. He reminded himself that Aunt Jo had the most generous heart of any-one he had known since his mother died. When someone needed her, all her faculties came to the fore and she did whatever needed to be done to help. He never sensed any danger in her presence and, consequently, neither did he suspect it in Lillian Mae's.

As they entered the house, Uncle Ed sat by the phone writing down what he would say when he called. "Here, Wesley," he told him, "get up close to the receiver so we both can hear the voice at the other end."

Mrs. Malenday answered the phone when Uncle Ed called.

He told her his name was Warren Twain (after President Warren Harding and Uncle Ed's favorite writer, Mark Twain). "I'm a friend of Willard Edwards, Ma'am. We worked together at the St. Paul Stock Yards five years ago. I'd been writing to him when he worked in North Dakota."

Mrs. Malenday said nothing.

"You see," Uncle Ed went on, "Willard gave me his parents' address on Cleveland Avenue in St. Paul, and when I wrote him there, my letter was sent back with 'not at this address' stamped on the envelope."

Before he could say anything more, Mrs. Malenday demanded, "What do you want? There's no one called Willard here. How did you get our number?"

Uncle Ed started to say he looked it up in the city directory when a man's voice came on the phone.

"This is Dr. Malenday. Why are you calling here?"

Uncle Ed coughed a few times and said, "Well, Willard talked about you so many times, I thought you might be so kind as to give me his present address."

Dr. Malenday hung up the phone.

The next day during his lunch hour, Wesley sat in Lillian Mae's apartment, suppressing the urge to laugh at himself. Here he was with a beautiful girl in his arms and that girl says, "Wesley, what can I do to make you happier?" And what does he answer? "Well, sweetheart, you could make me a doctor's appointment."

"A doctor's appointment?" She took in her breath sharply and pulled away from him. "That would make you happier than anything else?"

"Yes it could help me with something that's caused ... that's caused a lot of suffering."

Her exasperation turned to concern and then to fear. She threw her arms around him and cried, "Oh, Wesley! Are you ill?"

"Well, you might say I am, and then ... and then you might say I'm not. That's why I need to see a doctor."

"Are you in pain?"

"Yes. Ah ... yes, I am. As a matter of fact, I'm in considerable pain right now."

"Where?"

"In ... in my joints. My hands. In my knuckles. I can hardly hold a pencil sometimes."

She took her arms from around his shoulders and picked up his hands, moving the fingers back and forth.

"And my legs," he continued. "My knees hurt when I walk."

She dropped his hands and stroked his legs.

"I have a great aunt who had rheumatism at my age. She can't walk at all now. Everyone carries her around."

Wesley figured he wasn't lying completely. He told the truth when he talked about Aunt Pearl being all crippled up. The Toopers had a history of rheumatism and arthritis. And for a fellow of twenty-five, he had more aches and pains than you'd expect. So did Hazel and Cleve—maybe because they had to work so hard when they were young. Bennie never talked about such things, but he hadn't done hard labor as early as six or seven years old for ten to twelve hours a day. Wesley wondered if Willard felt any pain of that kind.

"Wesley," Lillian Mae said, interrupting his thoughts. "I'd stay with you even if you became crippled like your aunt. I swear I would. I'd always take care of you."

Oh, there she went again, talking about the future and them still being together. He ought to be grateful. Isn't that what he wanted—someone to be with him always and forever?

"Wesley," she said, holding him tighter, "would you stay with me even if I were crippled and couldn't dance ever again?"

Cripes, why did she have to ask such questions? "Sure. Sure I would. Once we were together, that's where we'd always be, no matter what happened." Saying those words made him experience the same kind of delight as on the night she'd picked him out of a whole roomful of men and asked him to dance. He knew he would stay with her once he made that decision. And the name Lillian Mae made him think of springtime with the smell of lilacs everywhere. But how ... how would he know if she was right for him?

"Listen, Lillian Mae, forget about making this appointment. It was a selfish thing to ask. Let's plan on the pictures tonight. Lon Chaney's playing in *Shadows*. He takes the part of this old Chinaman. It got best picture for the whole year."

She walked to her writing table. "But, I want to do this for you. I really do. Now what doctor is it? Do you have his number?"

He pulled a folded piece of paper from his pocket, straightened it out, and gave it to her. "Dr. L. E. Malenday," she read. "And what's this name underneath his telephone number—Clarence Allpine?"

"That's who you make the appointment for—Clarence Allpine."

She looked puzzled. "But I thought the appointment was for you?"

"It is."

"Then who is this Clarence Allpine guy?"

"That's me, it's really me." Oh, damn it, he was handling it all wrong. She was starting to get upset—making little breathy sounds and rubbing her feet together. Where in hell did Pa get that damn name, Allpine? Whenever he wrote to investors to get backing for one of his inventions, he introduced the inventor as Edward Tooper but signed his name Stephen R. Allpine. Once Hazel hired a man to follow Dan so she would know if he were stepping out with other women, and Pa said she should tell the sleuth her name was Gladys Allpine. Cleve used to say that when judgment day came and St. Peter with his record book asked their father for his name, Pa would say Noah Allpine.

"Listen, Lillian Mae, I can't give my real name to this doctor. I can't."

"Why not?"

That was a tough one. If she gave his name as Tooper, everything would go to hell. He couldn't make the appointment himself because, if his voice resembled Willard's, the doctor might get suspicious. "Lillian," he said solemnly, "some people in my family use this doctor. And I'm afraid maybe if I gave my real name, someone in the office might let it slip out, if … if he … "

She finished his sentence for him, her eyes filling with tears. "If he should have bad news for you?"

"Yes, if he should have bad news for me."

She sniffled, dabbed at her eyes with a handkerchief, and reached for the phone. "Of course I'll do this for you. Just think, here I was so worried when I asked you what I could do to make you happier, you might think I meant something improper. You didn't, did you?"

"Oh God." He reached for her hand like a man in a desert crawling toward a half-buried canteen of water. "Of course not," he groaned, covering her wrist with kisses. "Not now or ever."

CHAPTER THIRTY-ONE

The Appointment

August 27, 1922

Dr. L. E. Malenday sat on his stool, legs apart, hands on knees, as though he were overseeing the transactions of the world. His walrus mustache, Benjamin Franklin bifocals, and dominant presence made Wesley think the physician might remain there long after the pyramids and Taj Mahal turned to dust.

The doctor examined Wesley's ears and nose, held his tongue down with a cold, flat instrument, peered into his eyes behind a yellow, cone light, took his blood pressure, and listened to his heart without rising from his sitting place. With skilled fingers, he felt along Wesley's neck for swellings, checked the flexibility of his joints and reactions of muscles, and counted his pulse without once moving his feet from their fixed position.

Wesley, stripped down to a pair of baggy, army-green shorts left over from his Service days, answered the doctor's questions the best he could regarding his made-up symptoms. He felt as if he were watching himself in a movie but he wasn't Wesley Tooper, he was Groucho Marx. He wanted to laugh at the movie or at least chuckle but restrained himself for fear he might make that dratted clicking sound Rusty heard from a field hand in North Dakota. If the young man he thought might be Willard had that same habit, the doctor might put two and two together. But how could he, this early in the game?

Sometimes Wesley forgot which leg was supposed to be hurting or going numb. But then he would say, "Come to think of it, the other just started doing the same thing." He resisted the urge to knock ashes out of an imaginary cigar while moving his eyebrows up and down like Groucho or reach over and take off Doctor Malenday's mustache and put it under his own nose.

"Walk back and forth in front of me," the doctor requested. "Several times, please."

The long-stored underwear began to scratch and chafe, making Wesley wonder if Ma Tooper hadn't starched them after he got back from the Army. How in the world did other fellows wear these things everyday? His walking stint completed, he watched as Dr. Malenday produced a long, thin stick like the kind teachers used to strike pupils at Bonfield school and touched Wesley on a place halfway between his knee and hip. The cold rubber tip on the end of the stick created a tiny circle of discomfort.

"Do you feel pressure there?"

Wesley nodded. How could he not feel pressure when some damn fool was poking a stick in his leg?

"Move your left leg up and down if you can," ordered the doctor. He pressed again with the pointer. "Does movement hurt there?"

Wesley nodded. He felt so hot from wearing the Army shorts that he wished Malenday would lift the hem of the underwear a bit with the pointer and let a little air in.

"Swing your arm back and forth for me. Now stop." The pointer poked again, this time below the elbow. "Does that hurt?"

Wesley nodded, not sure if he was still playing a part or if he actually felt pain.

The doctor placed the tip of his pointer on a spot below Wesley's left knee. "Is it sore there?"

His Groucho character now banished forever, Wesley became a diagram of a skeleton on the wall. The skeleton nodded.

"Can you hold your arm out in front of you for an extended time without losing strength?"

Wesley was certain he could, but after several minutes his arm quivered as if it could not make up its mind what to do.

The doctor, after mysteriously making the pointer disappear, leaned forward and rested his hands on his knees as he had at the beginning of the examination. He sat silent for a while, and Wesley wondered how late he would have to stay at the office to finish the work he started in the morning.

Finally, Malenday spoke. "Mr. Allpine, did you ever live in an orphanage?"

Wesley was prepared for all sorts of questions, but this. "No," he lied. "Why would you think that?"

"Because, after feeling your joints and observing certain movements, I have reason to suspect that as a child you were afflicted with pellagra."

"Never heard of such a thing," Wesley said, thinking that this Dr. Malenday might not be so smart after all.

"Pellagra," Dr. Malenday explained with authority, "is a condition that affects the skin and nervous system in early years but later on causes symptoms similar to that of arthritis or rheumatism. Did you spend much time out in the sun when you were young? Do you remember having redness of the skin or blisters accompanied with an upset stomach?"

Wesley's opinion of the doctor's ability changed immediately. He forgot all about his fear of being discovered and began to remember. He remembered the nausea and vomiting at the orphanage, the itching and burning on his face and hands. He remembered the days he and

Cleve spent on the road under a hot sun before Pa brought them to the farm in Bonfield. And he remembered the solace he found there in the huge, sheltering oaks.

"Yes," he answered. "Yes, I did, but why would that make you think I lived at an orphanage?" He didn't like the way the doctor looked at him as though seeing right through him. But he couldn't stop himself from pushing on, finding out what Malenday was driving at.

"You see, Mr. Allpine, there's been considerable research about pellagra recently by Joseph Goldberger, a doctor with the Public Health Service. He found that a high percentage of children with symptoms of this disease spent at least some of their early years in an orphanage. At first, he thought the disease was caused by poisonous or infected food, but later discovered it came from a lack of fresh milk, eggs, and meats—food with protein and nicotinic acid."

Wesley's mind plunged back to the place he lived after his mother died. *I got news for you, Malenday. Your Mr. Goldberger had it right both times. We did get poisoned. We were poisoned with rotten food and served a big, damn lack of anything that was good for us. Fresh milk, eggs, meat—we never saw any. They gave it all to the priests.*

"Doctor," he said, trying to pull himself together. "There were a few years when my parents had it pretty rough. We didn't have much to eat. My older brother ate what I did. How come he didn't get this pellagra thing?"

"If your brother were old enough, maybe he already went through the crucial growth stage so wasn't affected as much by an unhealthy diet as you were. Are there any children in your family younger than you?"

"No," Wesley lied. "I'm the youngest." My God, he thought. Benny and Willard. Did they get it? Were they even sicker than he had been? Willard was chubby the last time he saw him. And Benny.

He was always a good eater at home but skinny as a jack rabbit no matter what he ate. He never even got sick when the rest of the family came down with something. If he hadn't had good food when he was little, he couldn't have been so healthy when he got older. Maybe Farellsi and his rats kept them both fed right, so the orphanage could adopt them out easier, just like they didn't hit them because they wanted them looking good.

Reality hit Wesley as hard as a sledge hammer. What a trickster life was! What if his little brothers, by being stolen, were saved from the disease that struck him? Maybe if they stayed at the orphanage long enough, they would have gotten pellagra too.

He noticed Dr. Malenday watching him closely, one eyebrow raised. "How old did you say you were, Mr. Allpine?"

"Twenty-five," Wesley answered, relieved he could answer one question honestly.

The doctor looked skeptical. "From the stiffness I detected in your joints and the calcification in some of your muscles, I would have guessed you to be in your early forties."

Wesley flushed with anger. Here he had been giving this doctor a line of bull during the whole examination, and when he finally told him the truth, the damn sawbones didn't believe him. Sure he looked older for his age but not that damn old.

"I was in the Army during the War," he said. "When it ended I was twenty-two. My ship never made it across before the armistice, so I never saw battle. I had a physical when I joined and another when I finished up. No one there ever said anything about this pellagra."

Malenday seemed not to hear him. "Your hands look like you've done some hard physical work. Yet, from the way you are dressed and manicured—just the way you carry yourself, you seem to have left that life behind you."

"I've been going to night school ever since I got out of eighth grade."

"What kind of school?"

"Business school. I started out in bookkeeping and went right on through higher accounting."

"Where?"

Oh, no you don't. I'm not having you go over to LaSalle and not find anyone named Allpine on the records and find Tooper instead.

"In Omaha, Nebraska. At the Randall Institute "of Business."

That'll put it so far away you probably won't bother to look. And if you do, the name of the school is different now—Faraday Financial Academy. You'll find it so confusing, Doc, you might even fall off your stool.

Dr. Malenday looked at his watch. "Well, that's all the time we have today. I'm going to give you something for pain. It should help you through those rough bouts and make you sleep better. I'll give you a more thorough exam next time. Stop at the desk before you leave and make a longer appointment."

"Thank you, I'll do that."

As he dressed, Wesley felt like the drab gray rug in Malenday's office had been pulled from under him. He came here to find out about Willard and didn't accomplish a thing. Instead, the doctor found out a lot about him.

But as he walked out of the room, everything changed. In the alcove between the doctor's chambers and the reception room, he stopped and leaned against a wall, trying to clear his head.

His gaze rested on a picture. It was of the doctor, looking younger than he did now and a woman, probably his wife. Between them stood a boy about nine or ten years old.

Good Lord! It's Benny. No, you fool, it can't be. He couldn't have been with the Malendays. He was with us by then.

Wesley looked closer at the boy's features. They seemed more delicate than Benny's, the smile not quite so open. Oh God, Willard! Thin like Benny—not like himself, or Cleve, or Hazel, or Lilly. All big-boned like Pa. No matter how much weight they lost, they could never become as slight as the boy in the picture.

Wesley collapsed to his knees and for the first time in his adult life, wept tears for his brother. Not for the boy in the photograph, who could be the brother he hadn't seen in more than twenty years, but for the one who, in his mind's eye, still lay on a battlefield stained with blood. Benny, who didn't know his brother almost a year older never reached him because the War ended too soon, who never knew that his sweetheart didn't mourn for him, couldn't mourn for him because she died first from some damnable curse called the plague.

Wesley wiped tears from his eyes, his cheeks, his throat, the top of his shirt as wet as his handkerchief. He sniffled. Benny was the real loser in this. Benny would never know Willard—the infant he used to point at and try to say "baby"—the boy only eleven months younger than him, almost his twin. Maybe if they'd grown up together, Benny wouldn't have been so set on running off to war. This Willard looked studious. Maybe he would have gotten Benny interested in something that didn't rob him of his life.

Wesley heard a phone ring inside Dr. Malenday's office. He walked closer to the door and listened. He heard no scuffling of feet or sound of footsteps but a releasing of the phone receiver.

Evidently the doctor could reach it without rising from his eternal stool.

"Dr. Malenday here." A pause and then, "Oh, yes," the words suddenly full of energy and anticipation. "So good to hear your voice, Bill. Did you get those books and graphs I sent? Wonderful! Glad to hear the job's going well and Rae's keeping you happy. You coming next Tuesday? No, don't wait until I'm done here. We'll have lunch and then you can see my patients with me. Maybe we'll both learn something. Thanks for calling, Bill. Goodbye."

Wesley straightened his tie, smoothed his shirt, and walked through the alcove to the receptionist's desk. Glancing at his reddened eyes and sodden collar, the girl smiled at him sympathetically, possibly assuming he received bad news from the doctor. Without comment, she told him what he owed. He took out his money and paid her.

"Did the doctor want to see you again, Mr. Allpine?" Her voice reminded him of Christmas tree ornaments breaking into pieces.

"Yes, he does. Next week. The only time I can come is early Tuesday afternoon."

"There's an opening at 1:30."

"Fine, perfectly fine," he said, taking a deep breath, not realizing until then that he'd been holding it.

CHAPTER THIRTY-TWO

The Week Between

September 3, 1922

Wesley is amazed. How much time must he endure before his next appointment with Dr. Malenday? A whole week—seven days, seven nights. Waking up, going to bed, falling asleep (if he can sleep), going to work, eating lunch, working at his job, thinking about Willard, not thinking about Willard, walking to the trolleys, walking from the trolleys.

Maybe I should drive, even though taking the trolleys is cheaper than taking my car. It's not just the gasoline, but the parking—too scarce, too expensive. If someone nicks me on the way to the office or I nick him, then it costs more in the long run. But, on the other hand, if I drive, I'll have to concentrate more. Won't think so much about Willard.

Willard. Wesley wonders if he's really found his brother. It has to be him—names fit, picture fits, except the boy looks so damn thin and delicate. Wesley figures he shouldn't tell anyone yet, especially Pa. The kid might not even come to Malenday's office Tuesday. He might get sick, might not be reliable, might have too much to do. He's a university student studying things like biology and chemistry, not easy stuff like business and accounting.

Wesley remembers what Malenday said over the telephone. "Glad to hear the job's going well and Rae's keeping you happy." My God, he thinks, my baby brother has a job and a girlfriend along with classes and homework. How can the kid get anywhere on time? Jeez—168 hours to go yet. Too long, too long. But look back to when they stole him. How many hours had to go by then? Call it 20 years. That's 14,500 hours a year, times 20 equals 175,200 plus extra hours for leap-years.

I lived through it then, resigned myself to it. But this is different. This is possible. But maybe he won't like me, won't want to meet the rest of us. Maybe he'll disown us, disown us all for good. Maybe he'll be a snooty bastard, a wise guy son of a bitch. Maybe, after all this searching, we find he belongs in the garbage. But, if he knew us once, loved us once, why wouldn't he feel something towards us now?

"Paper, Mister?" A crisp, newsboy question cuts through frantic brain chatter. The weighty *Tribune* with its pulpy coolness brings him back to real things, away from hopeless speculation. Headline: "Shipwreck Kelly Does It Again." That flagpole sitter, a Baltimore boy, a while back atop Old Glory's standard, ten minutes, ten hours, ten days. The mayor then, with open arms, cried out "Kelly—the pioneer spirit of early America."

Wesley asks himself if he remembers that news article. He does, but wonders why it caused Willard to come back to mind after so many years. What made the search start again, pushed back so long after Bennie died? Now Shipwreck Kelly, this time publicizing National Donut Week, hangs upside down on a plank atop a skyscraper eating thirteen sinkers. Thank God for Shipwreck Kelly, the luckiest fool alive!

"Hey, Bub, wanta buy a password? Membership card just costs a little more." The huckster's eyes are greedy, his counterfeit smile sporting two gold teeth. He motions Wesley into a doorway. "Seriously, my friend, hooch hounds are closin' in. You need new addresses? I got 'em. High class juice. Girls gettin' squiffy, spifficated, fried to the hat." He winks, nudges Wesley with an elbow.

Wesley nudges back. "I got my own squiffy chick. What can your party places do for me?"

Mr. Huckster, covering his gold teeth with a thin upper lip, presses an index finger against a spitty bottom one. "Ummm. Ummm." His face lights up like a cartoon character with a bulb over his head—a light bulb with yellow lines shooting out all around it to show an idea is generating. "I'll tell you what they'll do for you, Bub," he says, "they'll make the time pass by faster."

"Time pass by faster," Wesley repeats, then reaches into his pocket. "You know what, Hawker? You might turn out to be my savior. You got horn blowers? Piano pounders, string plunkers?"

Mr. Huckster rolls his eyes and nods.

Wesley goes on. "You got the Turkey Trot, the Grizzly Bear, Kangaroo Dip, Bunny Hug?"

The hawker snickers, holds out his hand for the money. "Natch, natch. That much'll bring ya a password and a card for two different places."

Wesley steps into the street, greeted by a breeze laced with cinder, gum wrappers, and a whiff of the drainage canal.

"A buck more'll give ya a recipe for 'bathtub,'" the hawker calls out. "Real safe."

"Think I'm stupid?" Wesley barks over his shoulder. "I'm not going blind."

As the week goes on, he sees how Lillian Mae loves the new speakeasies and Rudolph Valentino movies. "Sheiki," she calls Wesley, her once-upon-a-time farm boy from Kankakee. She adores Clara Bow pictures—scenes of petting parties in purple dawn. Loves his new on-the-go state of mind. Tells him, "That's because you're fine now. Right?"

He squeezes her hand. "You bet your life I'm fine."

After dinner in the Loop, she eases him up to a jewelry store window—diamonds, mostly engagement rings. He doesn't balk. Doesn't try to draw her attention to something else. His joints are old, he reasons. Lillian Mae loves him, she'll take care of him. She's fun, knows how to make time go faster.

"Yes," he tells her, "that's a swell ring. We'll come back when the place is open. Find out more about it. See how it looks on your finger." Staring at the gold band with its weighty sparkler, he remembers buying one like it before. Did I buy it for Maggie, Eleanor, Gladys, or what's-her-name?

Whoever, she sure chucked it at me—with the force of a pitcher's windup. Made a funny ping noise when it hit my chest. Helped buy the Studebaker though. Seems I bought another one somewhere down the line for somebody. Can't remember. Must've been a cheap one.

When he can't sleep, he studies cost accounting. He figures that's where the better jobs are. He'll need one to save money for if he's laid up. Besides, it's fun—production and distribution. Makes sense or cents, ha ha. He assures himself he's not going to be laid up. Hell, he outdoes the young ones, still wet behind the ears.

He buys magazines to read on the trollies. Makes the week go by faster. Paging through one, he spies Anne Harriet Fish cartoons poking fun at divorce, a new fad among the rich. "The mating game ends and begins at the altar. No sooner have vows been made than new alliances form and partners switch." The girls are dressed like Lillian Mae—the kewpie-doll hairdo capped with showy headbands. Bored, they loll on stripped, hard furniture smoking cigarettes, their backs long and droopy, their poses blasé. Their smoke, like a lazy serpent, wafts upward in the direction of two plaques. "God Bless Our Home," says one. "For Three Years," says the other.

He remembers Ma Tooper coming to the farm with Pa after being married to him for two hours—wind sneaking through cracks in walls, rags piled in corners, and scruffy children materializing out of empty cold rooms. Like the women in the Harriot Fish cartoons, did she too become bored? Bored with scrubbing floors until her knuckles bled, with cooking on a stove that didn't work without wood, with leaning over a scrub board, washing clothes until her back could no longer support her for very long? Did she become bored with the Tooper outbursts, with the endless needs of another woman's children, and disgusted with having to do so much with so little?

Wesley looks at the next cartoon. The women wait at the train station for the Reno Special to chug them off to the land of short-order divorce. Snuggled in warmth, they luxuriate in soft muffs, high, furry collars, wrap-around blanket coats. Their cast-off husbands, resentful but helpless, bid farewell. How many women like these, he wonders, looked down their noses at his father on the trains, wiping their valise handles if he happened to touch their baggage? Or, worse yet, didn't notice him at all? How many lives like theirs had he saved—this maintainer of tracks, this dedicated brakeman, this inventor of safer train parts?

Wesley looks at the next cartoon and reads. "The vicious cycle starts over again. The same pampered women off for happy honeymoons with new husbands."

"Not my type," he concludes.

CHAPTER THIRTY-THREE

The Last Appointment

September 10, 1922

Wesley couldn't believe it. All week he didn't think he'd make it through—counting the days, hours, and minutes until his appointment with Dr. Malenday, wondering if he could stand up to setting eyes on a missing piece of his life's puzzle. All week he drove himself crazy thinking maybe this fellow Bill wouldn't be Willard after all. Or maybe Malenday became suspicious and made sure he wouldn't show up. Or that he, Wesley, would fall apart at the doctor's office, reduced to rolling on the floor, shaking, crying, slobbering, finally giving up to whatever would befall him.

Now like an ordinary patient, he lay quietly on an examining table allowing a young medical student to move his limbs back and forth and firmly, yet gently, feel his muscles and joints.

How thin he is—how delicate. A thinking man. A calm man, unfamiliar with the unleashed feelings of a Tooper—a foreigner to shouting, to punching, to crying, to wailing, to giving in to rage.

Bill Edwards, hands cupped around Wesley's right knee joint, turned towards Dr. Malenday. "I agree, Uncle Lee. There are definite signs that Mr. Allpine here was inflicted with pellagra when he was a little boy."

Dr. Malenday, sitting on his stool as Wesley saw him a week ago, beamed.

"But," Bill continued, "you say he can't be classified as one of Dr. Goldberg's orphanage children because he didn't live in one of those places?"

"That's right," Wesley echoed from the examining table, so caught up in his role that he almost believed it himself. "I never did."

"What would you say of his present condition, Uncle Lee? Did this childhood disease make him a sitting duck for arthritis."

Dr. Malenday chuckled. "What would you say, Dr. Edwards?"

"Well," Bill pondered, running his hand through his dark Tooper-like hair. "I'd say arthritis has been present for some years."

"Very good. Now would you take a stab at his age, judging from the progress of his arthritis?"

Wesley stiffened. *What the hell is this all about. I wrote my age down on the office form. Why put the kid on the spot?*

"That's hard to say, Uncle Lee. I read a study done at Johns Hopkins suggesting that not everyone who has arthritis acquired it at an older age. And someone who had it for years could be at a stage of stasis and the condition might not have noticeably intensified."

Somehow Wesley managed to keep a straight face. *That's a boy, Billy, get him at his own game!*

"We have to be careful with new studies, Bill," Dr. Malenday cautioned. "We shouldn't accept them until they're proven conclusive."

"I'm sure you're right. But I do think this patient's symptoms come and go—that he enjoys lengths of time with no pain or stiffness, and suddenly it all returns for a while and then goes away as quickly as it came. Am I close to the truth, Mr. Allpine?"

Wesley was astounded. The kid really knew his stuff! Maybe there was going to be a doctor in the family—a full-blown university-educated doctor. Suddenly he refused to contribute to the solemnity of the hour. After all, regardless of what kind of upbringing Bill

Edwards had, he might be a Tooper. When Toopers talked to each other, no matter how mad or sad or full of pain they were, they didn't let much time pass without making fun, without cracking a joke, without lightening things up.

"You know, Doc," he quipped, sitting up and addressing the skilled medical student. "Sometimes I'm so achy I can hardly drag myself to work. But when night comes and the city lights go on, I can't wait to go out and give the chickies a whirl."

He followed his remark with a wink and a "you-know-what-I'm-talking-about" look. He was so relieved from allowing some kidding to take over that he let a chuckle slip out. He touched his hand to his mouth to stifle it, but it was too late to stop the clicks that followed.

Before they escaped, Bill was already reacting, revealing perfectly aligned Tooper-type teeth, drawing back his lips in a modest grin. "Now, Mr. Allpine," he quipped back, "that's what I would call a non-persistent pain." Then he folded his arms and clucked like a shy but tickled hen, unconsciously matching Wesley click for click. The twin sounds floated through the medicinal-smelling air and hung suspended like confessions in a courtroom.

Wesley glanced over at Malenday. The doctor's mouth dropped open, the action almost knocking off his spectacles. He leaned forward, scrunching his head down between his shoulders as if preparing to roll off his stool like an oversized ball.

The incident had no effect on Bill. He picked up the sheet of notes he made during the examination and looked them over, moving his lips like Pa Tooper did when he read something important.

Dr. Malenday straightened his back, dusted imaginary lint off his trousers, and cleared his throat. "Uh, Bill, would you do me a favor and take those slides on the instrument table over to Dr. George? I borrowed them last week, and his nurse called and said he needed them."

The young man reacted like Benny would have—eager to please, to fulfill a request of someone he admired. "Sure. I'll probably be back before you leave, Mr. Allpine." He disappeared out the back door, footsteps banging down the outside staircase.

Wesley and Dr. Malenday stared at each other. Water dripped in a sink by the window. From below came the whine of trolley cars, the scolding honk of a taxi, the sing-song chant of a peddler. Slowly, Dr. Malenday stood up, took off his spectacles, and laid them on his desk.

"Get dressed," he commanded.

Wesley knew the jig was up. He stepped out of the boxer shorts, threw them into a waste basket, and reached for his trousers. "I never could stand those things," he said, tucking in his shirt. "Never wore them except in the Army."

"You were never in the Army," Malenday spat out. "I checked all the way back to the Civil War. There never was a Clarence Allpine in any of the armed services. When I examined you last week, I could tell from the condition of your body, that you were too old to have served in the last War. What's more, the Randall School of Business in St. Louis has been closed for years. You're a fraud, Mr. Allpine."

"My name is Tooper," Wesley said. "Like Cooper only with a 't' as in Tom."

"I don't care what your name is. I do know there's something fishy going on. You're not who you say you are."

"You figured that out, did you? Well, you just tell me what else you think you know."

"I'll tell you what I don't know—how a man could desert the woman he got with child and drop his infant son off at an orphanage like he were a piece of mail."

Wesley stepped back and took a breath. "What? Who in the hell are you talking about?"

"You!" Malenday shouted, almost poking a finger into Wesley's chest. "You, Mr. Trooper or Toppet or Toaper or …."

"Tooper. My name is Tooper and so might be his."

"What do you want from us? He's going to medical school. He has a fine girl he plans to marry. Why are you coming into your boy's life now?"

"My God, you think I'm his father, don't you?"

"How can you even say the word father? You gave him up and left his mother in such a terrible state of health that she died. How can you live with yourself?"

Wesley reached for his wallet and took out his armed services card and thrust it toward the doctor. "I've got news for you, Malenday. The only thing you got right is that I lived in an orphanage. I was there when you and those Edwards bought him. I'm his brother. He has another one right here in Chicago who never forgave himself because he couldn't stop that crooked priest from selling Willard. He's got two sisters who've been worried sick about him. He has another brother lying in Arlington Cemetery he'll never get to know, never get to see how alike they were."

Obviously shaken, Dr. Malenday looked at Wesley's card. "According to this, you're only three years older than he is. So you're telling me you were one of the orphanage children when we saw Bill for the first time? That this card is really yours?"

"You're damn right it is."

Dr. Malenday closed his eyes and placed a hand to the side of his head. "I remember a boy there that day—a boy hollering at the top of his lungs, thrashing out at the priest, fighting off the nuns. They said he was having a spell, that he went out of his head. Was that you?"

"No. They locked me in a back room. That was probably my brother, Cleve, you heard trying to keep Willard with us. The next day some people by the name of Whitehouse took our brother, Ben. They thought everything was legal and his parents were dead."

"But why did your parents give them up? Why did they put the four of you in that place?"

"My pa would never give up his kids. He did everything he could to get his boys back. He found Benny when he was ten, and he never stopped looking for Willard."

Dr. Malenday stammered. "But … but the Edwards—they have a paper. They have a paper showing that the boy's father signed him over to the orphanage for adoption. We made sure there was such a thing."

"Sure you did. Like my pa thought sure we were safe in that rotten place. That paper was forged—everything was forged. What you saw had the name Chalmers on it, didn't it?"

The doctor nodded. "That was fake," Wesley went on. "That name has nothing to do with our family. The Edwards changed his last name, so why did they keep his first name, Bill, short for Willard or William? You'd think they'd want to change everything. Start from scratch."

"He was already responding to that name at the orphanage— Willard or Will. We wanted him to keep what he was familiar with. Gradually it turned into Bill. Willard is on his birth certificate."

"Will," Wesley repeated. "Little Will. That's what our mother called her youngest son. She died and left our father with six kids. His relatives could only take the two girls. He worked on the railroad, so he had to put us boys somewhere for a while, until he could get a home together for us. The only wrong thing Edward Tooper did was believing what those bastards told him, that none of his kids would be adopted out."

Dr. Malenday stared at the floor. "And what do you want to do now? Confuse him—rip his life apart? Throw him off his stride so he doesn't finish school?"

"Good God! You mean he thinks he was born an Edwards?"

"He was always so smart—so intuitive. Like he knew the truth all along even though no one ever mentioned it."

"You keep saying "we." What's your stake in this?"

"I wouldn't have gotten off San Juan Hill if not for J. J. Edwards. He wasn't well enough to work steadily after that. I paid the adoption fee and helped the boy with school. He had such a mind for the sciences. Even when he was very little, he wanted to know about my work, about diseases, about the human body."

"Maybe he inherited that from his real father."

Malenday winced at the word *real*. "Is your father still alive?"

Wesley's mind lept to a story his Uncle Napoleon told him about the family's journey from Quebec. Little Edward Tooper, six years old, fell from the ship into the St. Lawrence River. Because of the current, the boat could not get close enough for someone to rescue him. His mother and all the sisters were screaming and Grampa Louis and the uncles tried to jump overboard and swim after him, but the crewmen held them back. The captain proclaimed the boy a goner, but Edward managed to keep his head above water for six miles and over seven rapids. He was about to go over the highest falls when a fishermen from the other side of the river reached out a pole and snatched him from the water.

Wesley wanted to tell this to Dr. Malenday, how his father faced whatever life dished out to him and never gave up. He opened his mouth to tell the story, then, in the next second, felt sure it would be lost on the man standing before him. "Yes," he said. "He's alive."

Before the doctor could respond, the sound of glass breaking, of metal clanking on metal came from across the room near the back door. They turned and saw Bill, half leaning, half falling into a table full of instruments and flasks. Trying to hold himself up, he pushed one hand down flat on the table, his face white, as if all his blood had drained into the containers beneath him, his eyes half sunk into his head.

"Dr. George wasn't in," he said, weakly, "I came right back." He held up the bleeding hand that had kept him from falling, looking at it curiously, as if it belonged to someone else. Smiling weakly, he turned to Malenday. "You know what's funny, Uncle Lee? All this time I thought it was you. I thought you were my real father."

CHAPTER THIRTY-FOUR

Facing the Unfaceable

September 10, 1922

The next moment froze for Wesley—Bill with sun streaming down through an unshaded window on his black hair, stiffened a little with hair tonic, himself—blurred and undefined, Malenday between them, around them white-washed walls glaring with starkness.

Who am I with these two men? Who am I if I'm not looking for him, Little Will, the lost prize? If this isn't him, then who for God's sake am I?

The moment passed. Bill shivered, causing the glass under his feet to make little tinkling sounds. Trembling, he pulled himself to a standing position and moved forward.

He's going towards Malenday. Will he wrap his arms around him for helping him all these years or will he pound him to a pulp for his betrayal? Despite what's happened, he has a bounce to his walk, sort of a lope. I don't lope. Cleve doesn't lope. We shuffle, we trudge, we plod. Benny loped, loped to the recruiting office, loped up the steps on the ship taking him for his one-way ride alive across the pond. Cleve's boy lopes, lopes after garter snakes, frogs, lacy butterflies. If I have a son, maybe he'll lope too.

Now what's going on? Willard's picking up a roll of gauze off a tray and winding it around his hand. Malenday reaches out to help him, but the kid's passing him by. He's coming this way. Must be heading for the door. Maybe I'll never see him again. Maybe nobody will.

But Willard, holding onto his wrapped hand, came to a halt in front of Wesley. "Tooper," he said slowly and clearly. "Is that how you pronounce it?"

I can't talk to him. My lips won't move. I'll turn to solid rock forever.

"Perfect," he heard himself say. "For years it was Toopah, but Pa's father, Louis, changed it to Tooper when they came down from Quebec so people would think they were English and he could get a better job on the railroad."

"Is that French?"

"Yeah. Changing it didn't help. People have just as much trouble saying Tooper as Toopah. I don't know why. They can say Cooper or Hooper as easy as pie."

"Uncle Lee," Bill said, turning to Malenday. "Can he … can he be from my real family?"

Dismayed, Wesley cursed himself for telling Willard what he did. *He doesn't want to be French Canadian. He doesn't want to belong to a lowly railroad family.*

"I don't know, Bill," Malenday answered. "We don't even know if he's telling the truth."

Bill's eyes met Wesley's. "If you're my brother, why wouldn't I have felt something when I first saw you? You just seemed like any regular fellow to me—kind of easy-going, not hard to talk to."

"Thanks. That's how I always wanted people to think of me. But Dr. Malenday here likes to think I'm a liar about everything I've said today. Tell me, great doctor, why in the hell would I lie about Bill here being my brother? Where would it get me?"

Dr. Malenday seemed prepared for answering that question.

"In not too many years, this young man is going to do quite well. And here is someone who claims to be his true flesh and blood, right there with his hand out."

Angered and frustrated, Wesley looked around the room. He saw a bowl on the table that Bill had almost tipped over earlier. By the window he saw a sink. He rushed to the table, grabbed the bowl, and filled it with water. He set the bowl on the doctor's desk, and reached into his pants pocket for his handkerchief. Then he spread it out next to the bowl of water. Dr. Malenday looked at him as though this man, who first claimed to be Clarence Allpine, and now said his last name was Tooper, had gone completely mad.

"Watch me," Wesley said to the young medical student. "Don't think anything. Just watch me." He dipped his hand into the water, making it into a little cup like his mother taught him. He spread his fingers so the water could drip through and sprinkled the handkerchief evenly.

"That's enough of this craziness," Malenday said. "Bill, let's go somewhere and have a cup of coffee. Let your head clear. This Mr. Toppett, or whoever he is, can stay here or leave."

Bill backed away from the table and eased himself down on the floor. "I used to dream about a hand doing that—a hand dribbling water over and over on a piece of cloth. But it was a little hand. Very little."

"That's because I was very little then." Wesley said. "My mother had me sprinkle clothes for her before she ironed them. My youngest brother, Willard, wasn't even walking yet but he loved to watch me. He didn't miss a thing."

"Be careful son," Dr. Malenday warned Bill. "The power of suggestion can be awfully strong."

"I don't know, Uncle Lee. I just don't know."

Wesley took a pencil from his vest pocket and a tablet from Dr. Malenday's desktop. He walked over to Bill and got down on the floor next to him. Both young men sat cross-legged, their noses straight, nearly aquiline, their black hair combed up from the forehead—one man slightly stocky yet muscular, the other taller, almost ascetic looking.

The tablet on his lap, Wesley started writing columns of figures. It was automatic for him. He could do it with his eyes closed.

Malenday sighed impatiently. Wesley kept writing. The sound of pencil on paper continued—the scratching of dashes, the scraping of circles, double circles and half-circles, connected and rapid like the gnawings of a mouse. Wesley started another page, another set of figures, another column, another one next to it.

Bill shuddered. "I wrote just like that when I tried out for a job at the bank. It … it was like someone taught me already. They said I was a natural."

"You watched me do that too," Wesley said. "It's from my mother. Thanks to her I make a decent living."

"Figuring always came so easy for me," Bill said." Everyone at the bank told me I should go on with it. But science and mathematics stuck with me more."

Wesley laid down his pencil. "My pa is always dabbling in experiments and inventions. Tired as he was from working on the trains, he'd stay up late sweating over a geometry problem."

Bill smiled. "I like geometry."

"Similar skills and talents don't always prove blood lines," Malenday said, "but say you are his brother, Allpine. Say it really was a mistake he was adopted out. What are you going to do?"

"It wasn't a mistake, Malenday. It was a crime, but probably not yours. I don't want anything from you folks and neither does my pa.

We just wanted to know if he was alive and okay. Well, he's more than just okay, so I'll stop looking now." Dr. Malenday cautiously offered his hand.

Just as cautiously, Wesley took it. Bill did not get up from the floor, his hands now covering his face. Wesley touched him on the shoulder. "You're an honest, straight-forward fellow. You'll know what to do when the time comes."

CHAPTER THIRTY-FIVE

Will I Bring My Brother Home?

337 Ramsey Street

St. Paul, Mn.

April 6, 1923

My dear brother Wesley:

Your letter came to hand several days ago and I was SO glad to hear from you. I guess after all we are pretty much alike, Wes, for I have the same feeling of longing that you do. I would give much to be able to see you once in a while.

Yes, Wesley, it sure does help a lot to have a good girl like Rae is. A girl thinks pretty much of a fellow when she is willing to marry him, keep on working and also go to live with his parents. We are going to have an up-hill climb for several years, but we both have so much love and confidence in each other that I know we will come out alright. I hope, Wesley, that your girl will be one who would do that much for you, for after all, true love finds expression in giving up things and making self-demands for one who should be dearer than life itself. You deserve that kind of girl, dear brother, and it is my sincere wish that you will find one like that.

We have all been feeling bum for the last month. We have all had the grippe, and it sure takes a long time getting over it.

Do you know, Wes, I have been just about breaking my head to think of some way whereby we could all be nearer each other. I feel just as you do about this matter, and I thought if we could find suitable living quarters and also get suitable work, I would be tempted to come down there. I am afraid I would not be able to get a job like the one I have now, one which allows me a little time to study. Well, I am in hopes that I will be able to be with you permanently in a couple of years, anyway.

Had nice letters from Dad and Lilly. I wonder how Lilly will like housekeeping.

I have run out of interesting material, so will stop writing now. Rae sends her love and best wishes. The folks also join us in sending best wishes. Love from your bro.

Willard

• • •

Caught in the middle of a traffic jam on Wabash Avenue, Wesley rested Willard's letter on the steering wheel of his slightly used Packard. Despite horn's honking, drivers shouting and shaking their fists, he could not only read the heartfelt message but could ponder it.

"I hope, Wesley, your girl will be the one … for, after all, true love finds expression in giving up things and making sacrifices for one who should be dearer than life itself."

"Damn it, Willard," he wished out loud, "if only she could be."

He wondered why something good hardly ever worked out with Lillian Mae lately. Something besides dancing. Dancing gave him hope and they entered every marathon they could. Each time he wondered if he could hold up, even though he was only twenty-six and strong as a horse, regardless of that pellagra Dr. Malenday said he had as a child. A few days ago in Houston, a twenty-year-old male contestant collapsed on the dance floor, so marathon officials rushed him to a Turkish bath down the street. He and his girlfriend had danced for forty-five hours, the world's record for a twosome.

Lillian Mae could go on forever. They won small purses here and there in Chicago and Indiana, even taking the ferry over to Michigan. He always gave her the prize money so she would lay off him for a while for not taking her to church or stop hinting about setting a wedding date. She was ecstatic when they'd win a marathon, but if more than two weeks went by without seeing a contest advertised in the newspapers, she would become bored and restless, dwelling on upsetting happenings and working herself up terribly.

When Sarah Bernhardt died, Lillian Mae kept reliving Bernhardt's death scenes, her skin becoming as cold as the stones in the bottom of the Kankakee quarry. Or when Bessie Smith came out of nowhere singing that new type of jazz called the blues, she kept insisting Smith wasn't good enough to become such a star. When they went to a party or riding with friends, she'd start singing, "Taint Nobody's Bizzness if I Do" more than slightly off-key. The other women would exchange glances and start talking among themselves while the men came out with rounds of "Row, Row, Row Your Boat."

It seemed romance couldn't turn into what he wanted for the entire course of his life, with no looking backward. Benny had a true love before he went across the pond to die and, today, so did his brothers and his sisters. Maybe it didn't matter if Hazel's Dan wandered a bit, if Lillian and her Herman had to struggle sometimes to make ends meet like many young couples, if Mary henpecked Cleve more than she should and he never got to be an airplane pilot or mechanic. He was happy with his garden and his motorcycles.

And Willard, hopefully his new-found brother, had a wife who looked upon him "dearer than life itself."

And what would Wesley be doing in the days ahead with his love life? Trying to get the courage to tell Lillian Mae that most of the dance contests in the country were canceled. In Baltimore the winning girl's ankles had swollen to twice their size, and right over in Gary, Indiana, the weight of the young lady who wore out five partners went down from 113 to 89 pounds. Parents raised an outcry. Some lawyers branded dance marathons illegal, and dance hall owners worried they might be sued.

Wesley took a long, slow breath through his nose, detecting, besides the smell of car exhaust, a sourness in the air—a sourness coupled with the odor of human perspiration. He looked out his side window and saw a man, apparently standing on the car's running board, pointing a short, black pistol at him. He had a homemade bowl haircut, and his skin reminded Wesley of milk standing in the barn too long. A front tooth stood out broken and jagged, the rest the color of licorice.

"L-l-listen, Mac," he said, "Put your wallet on the s-s-seat next to you and g-g-get out of the car. Just w-w-walk away and I'll let you l-l-live."

Wesley thought of when the cows would get into the corn back on the farm in Bonfield. He had felt sorry for their need but knew he had to stop them. Now, grabbing the door handle in his left hand, he pushed as hard as he could. The man flew backwards, still staring at Wesley, the gun now pointing upwards. A few seconds later, his body hit the pavement, turning over and over, rolling down the avenue as if following the silvery luster of the trolley tracks.

Wesley saw the driver in front of him lean forward and heard his engine start up again. He did the same, and the traffic began to move forward.

By God, I'm free. Free! If I can stop a thief with a gun pointed at
my head from killing me, from stealing a car I worked day and night
for, I sure as hell can handle a girl whose only crime might be loving
me too much.

Tonight he would write Willard and urge him to come to Chicago
as soon as he could. Then he would have Cleve and his sisters meet
at Pa's house on that same date. After that was arranged, he would
tell Lillian Mae about the dance contests closing. He would tell her
about Willard and how he had been trying to find him for so long.
And he would tell her why he asked her to make the appointment
for him with Dr. Malenday. After all, she did that for him out of love.
He probably had only himself to blame for her edginess and mood
changes because she sensed he was keeping something from her.

If she accepted what he told her and forgave him, then he would
ask her to come with him to meet Willard and Rae at Union Station.
Then they could all go to Kankakee together. Maybe Lillian Mae
would even be wearing his engagement ring by then and they would
have a date set. Maybe, after all, she would turn out to be the girl
Willard spoke of when he said, "You deserve that kind of a girl, dear
brother ...."

Deserve, Deserve, Deserve.

• • •

May 9, 1923
Dear Wesley
We read your letter some time ago, but we have been so
busy moving and getting located that neither one of us
had time.

We are living with my sister and like it quite well. You
know, Wesley, Willard's Mother and Dad are really too
old for a young boy like Willard, and we both make quite

a bit of extra work for them. They are a lovely old couple, but they have their faults like the rest of us, but it's hard for Willard, when he's going to school and working to listen to it. He is inclined to be nervous anyway, which is only natural when he has so many things on his mind. He's such a sweet kid, one couldn't help loving him to pieces. I love him a lot and try to be good to him.

It's so nice to be married when you get a good husband like mine. I know your girl would think the world of you too.

We sold our Ford, so we will have to take the train, and I'm glad because we won't have anything to worry about. We are leaving the 8th of June on the 8:30 train, so we will arrive in Chicago sometime Sunday morning around 8 a.m. I see where Wesley will have to take me to church. Willard can hardly wait until he sees all you folks. I'm in hopes we will be able to locate there, if we could find suitable work for both of us.

How is your girl? I'm sorry she's Irish because they don't amount to much. What do you think? I'm only kidding, so don't take that too seriously.

I expected to see you coming to St. Paul on your honeymoon this spring, but it seems you aren't married yet. We would like to have you here alright. I just know that we will have such a good time when we come to see you all, we won't want to come back home. I wish we wouldn't have to come back.

Well Wesley, it's time for us to go home, so will have to run along, and you be sure and write to us before we leave.

Lovingly, Rae and Willard

• • •

May 10, 1923

Dear Brother:

I started with pencil but could not write so changed to ink. Well, "old dearie" why don't you write once and a while? If I had not went home I would not ever heard from you. I read the letter you wrote to the folks. Maybe you think I owe you which may be true because of your letter to them, but I don't know. How are you and how is every little thing coming these days?

I have our home all straightened now. Our living room set is here now, and everything is all fixed up. I certainly like the living room set. I imagine you will too. It makes that little room so cozy. Daddy don't like it very well. I suppose because he cannot put his feet on it. Ha! Although he thinks it's pretty but not comfortable. Well, I know you will think so, and I want you to bring Lillian along with you sometime when you come, and then you can spoon all you want on the Davenport. Ha!

But it would be a fine time to bring Lillian here when Willard comes, the reason being that you know the folks will put themselves to a lot of work for his sake as they are fixing the house up and doing lots of things and mother will be in a humor to treat Lillian as would be best. And, of course, I hope you are not ashamed to bring her to our flat as there is nothing in the least wrong with it I am sure. Outside of not having a Victrola and piano, our furniture is as up to date as her folks, so I see no reason why she could say anything. and our place is very respectable.

Well, I must close. Write us soon and let us know
how you are once in a while. Come whenever you can.

With love and affection. I am your sister, Lilly

• • •

1082 N. Schuyler Ave.

Kankakee, Il.

May 27, 1923

Dear Son,

Your kind and welcome letter received a little over a week
ago. I received a letter from Willard yesterday and he
says they will leave for Chicago June 9th. They figure that
you will meet them at the depot and probably drive them
straight through to Kankakee. He alluded to this as some
arrangements that you had suggested to them in one of
your letters.

Well, that would be very nice and besides I hope it
will be convenient to arrange your vacation so you can be
here with them and we then can take them out to see the
country. I will only be too glad to pay for the gas. I would
like to take him to Sheldon, to see the cottage where he
was born. Perhaps you would like to refresh your memory
too. Also we might go over to your Uncle Charley.

Lilly and Herman are well and Herman is working
quite steady. Lilly quit her job yesterday. She is beginning
to feel miserable and clumsy, you know.

I wonder if Cleves will be able to come when Willard
is here. I sure hope they can.

Tomorrow I will try and send them some radishes, onions and lettuce. So if you want a taste of my garden, you had better go over for supper Tuesday night.

> With love and sincere affections,
> I remain your father,
> Edward Tooper.

• • •

St. Paul, Minn.

June 1, 1923

Dear Bro. Wes:

Your letter came today just after Rae had written to you, so I am writing a short answer.

We will not be able to leave until Saturday night, June 9. I tried to arrange it so we could leave so as to be able to arrive at Chicago Saturday noon, but it was impossible as both Rae and I have to work. However, we will get to Chicago at 8 a.m. via C. B. & Q. Railroad on Sunday, June 10. I think the C. and B. comes into the union station.

Gee Wes, the damn days are getting to be weeks until I see you. Don't worry about taking us to Kankakee and laying off from work Monday. If you are not able to take us there, we can go on the train and then see you later in Chicago. (Hope to hell you can come though). I am just like a big kid waiting for Xmas to come.

Well Wes, this will be all until I see you. By the way, Rae would like to go to church Sunday when she gets to Chicago, so if you know of a good Catholic church where they don't preach too long, we would like to go to it. Rae is a good kid. She never misses church if she can possibly help it.

Love to Cleve and all the rest including
yourself from your kid brother.
Willard

. . .

By God, Lillian Mae slapped him. She talked to him so sweetly until he told her about the dance marathons closing. After he finished his explanation, she slapped him right across the front of his face—nose, mouth, cheeks—the works.

"You … you have the nerve to come over here," she hollered so loud her voice went hoarse, "and you tell me a lie only an idiot would believe! That's what you think of me. You think I'm an ID-DI-OT!"

He held his hand across his face to keep it from throbbing but that didn't help. It wasn't like a hit on the face was brand new to him. When he was a child hobo, railroad dicks punched him there whenever they caught him hopping trains. Guys in the Army too, if they got in the first swing. He remembered Ma Tooper backhanding him if he reached across the table for more mashed potatoes without asking, but this hurt the most. It meant no forgiveness, no taking her to Kankakee to bring Willard home, no true love from one "who should be dearer than life itself."

"For Christ sake, Lillian Mae," he pleaded. "It's true. Just look in the papers."

She had her voice down to a whisper now. "Don't you dare take the name of the Lord in vain with me. You just want to go to the contest with some whore. Well, you just go ahead. Go ahead!"

As the door slammed behind him the dampness of a late spring rain crept over his face, cooling the place where she slapped him. A mild breeze, fragrant with cherry blossoms from the yard next door, promised to soothe the wound inflicted on his feelings. But what about the rest of his life? Even if she apologized to him all over the place he couldn't bring her to Kankakee with Willard and Rae. The same thing could happen again and ruin Willard's homecoming. He should tell Willard he couldn't get off work and let them go to Kankakee on the train without him. Feeling a tug on his heart, he realized what a big part Lillian Mae played when he dreamed about bringing his brother home—if that was his brother.

CHAPTER THIRTY-SIX

An Interval

June 8, 1923

The next Tuesday, Wesley went to Cleve's and Mary's for supper like Pa said—to get a taste of the early summer vegetables he sent from Kankakee. Wesley showed them Pa's letter, the real reason he came. He read out loud the part where Pa wrote, "I wonder if Cleves will be able to come when Willard is here. I sure hope they can." They didn't discuss the letter, mostly talked about the weather, until, at supper, as Mary set a plate of the lettuce, radishes, and onions on the table, she said, "You know, Wesley," Cleve and I aren't sure about this Willard."

Later Cleve brought Wesley out to his shed to show him the Harley-Davidson he was putting together from parts. "Damn it, Wes," he said, "it's awful shifty how all of a sudden, he wants to get close with us. First, he doesn't know if we're his family, then he does, then he doesn't, and then he comes out with this brotherly love crap gushin' all over the place. Then out of the blue, he tells everyone his name's Willard and signs his letters that way. Even that fancy, new wife calls him Willard like it's been that all his life."

"It has been his name all his life, Cleve, but he didn't know it until now. I sprung it on him awfully fast. It took time for him to piece it all together. Once he did, his feelings for us rushed out like a stream when the dam is pulled out."

Cleve picked up a gear off the floor looking at it like an old friend. "Maybe all that's gettin' pulled out is Pa's wallet. Maybe this guy is going along with things you told him to get money outa Pa. I saw Pa slip a fiver into a letter he was mailing to him last week. Pa never gave us a damn thing."

"Oh, don't start on that, Cleve. What's a measly fiver anyway? If you saw him you'd know he's our brother. He looks like your son. Talks like him too—all about science."

Cleve seemed glad the subject turned to his son. He gave the Harley's rear tire a gentle kick and chuckled. "That damn little guy comes up with stuff I never knew about and never will."

"Maybe if I ever have a son," Wesley said wistfully, "he'll have a knack for science too, instead of figures like his old man."

"Speaking of having kids, Bro, how's Lillian Mae doing these days?"

Wesley could have made something up or just said she was fine or at least okay, but he didn't. He told the whole story—the slapping, the accusations, and the strange way she'd been acting during the past year.

Cleve nodded his head like he'd been expecting it. "Well, you sure can't take her to Kankakee if she's acting crazy. And what are you gonna tell this guy, Willard? I can't bring my girl along because she's loonier than hell these days? You'd be better off forgetting about going to Pa's. Just tell this Willard you can't get off work, and you can see him and his wife later here in Chicago."

Wesley took a deep breath of relief from knowing the person closest to him in the whole world had the same way of handling a problem he did. "That's what I've been thinking, Bro. That's just what I've been thinking."

• • •

Pacing next to Track 8 at Union Station waiting for Willard and Ray's C B & Q to come in, Wesley thought how easier it would be if Rae hadn't had her heart set on going to church. As soon as they got off the train, he could tell them he had to work, drive them to the Illinois Central Station, and put them on the train to Kankakee. But how could he just drop them at the church and let them find their own way to the right station? Yet, it would be a lot harder going with them, letting them get used to him being there and then telling them he wasn't going on to Pa's house. Still, if he told them right away before they went to church, it would put a damper on the time they would have together before Willard and Rae had to catch their other train.

Although absorbed in his problem, as soon as he saw the man with a megaphone coming around announcing arrivals, Wesley got the same rush of excitement he had as a little boy. The train still seemed like a monstrous dragon bursting in from off the cornfields, shooting white steam, brakes screeching, like a giant running its fingernails across a gargantuan chalkboard. He loved the mood of the station—children squealing, jumping up and down and clapping their hands, redcaps pushing luggage carts asking, "Take your baggage, Sir? Watch your step, Ma'am."

They were the first ones off the train—Rae, chic, every hair in place, Willard serious, yet overflowing with pride like when they met in Omaha two months before when Wesley was on a business trip, the young couple on a two-night honeymoon.

Because their train was fifteen minutes late, he had to rush them on to Van Buren Street and didn't have time to tell them he would be staying in Chicago. One of the girls at work had told him about a church where the service didn't last too long. If you sat on the left, you could slip out through an alcove without waiting for the whole congregation to give their compliments to the priest at the door. Wesley found plenty of seating on that side, the three of them tiptoeing in fresh from their reunion at the station, Willard and Rae trying to restrain their giddiness in anticipation of the days ahead.

Halfway through the service, Wesley saw her. *It can't be her. By God, it is! No one else knelt as if she'd been poured like concrete; ivory-white hands making a little tent for prayer, back straight like a nun's. She had her eyes closed lightly, matching the pious seal of her lips—her whole profile sending the message: "I've done nothing wrong. Not once."*

Wesley ushered Willard and Rae towards the alcove upon the first notes of the organ's recessional. "I'll run ahead," he whispered, "and bring the car around to the side door." But when he rounded the corner in the hallway, she was waiting, arms crossed, tapping one foot on the floor like she did the first time he ever saw her.

Before he could say anything, she flew at him. "You bastard. Won't go to church with me, but you'll take that bitch."

He gasped, trying to push her away. "For God's sake, that's my brother's wife!"

Bengal-tiger nails flashed towards his face. "You think I'm stupid? I know Cleve's wife. This is the whore you've been cheating with. I knew it!"

He dodged the flailing nails, reaching out his hands so they wouldn't touch his face. "No, not Cleve! My brother, Willard. That's his wife. Stop it, Lillian Mae. Stop it!"

She aimed the nails at his eyes. He saved his face but they dug into his wrist, tearing his shirt and drawing blood. "Liar. You've only got one brother!"

Wesley didn't see Willard until he heard his voice—firm and solid like his hands seizing her by the elbows. "Miss, I'm Wesley's brother, and this is my wife, Rae. My family's been searching for me for years."

He backed her out the door, Lillian shadow-kicking, turning her head and hissing at Wesley, "Rat. Won't take me to church but you take them at a drop of a hat!"

When the door shut behind them, Rae rummaged through her purse for a handkerchief, murmuring, "Drop of a hat? Not one of us is wearing a hat." Her mouth forecasting a grin, she blotted the blood on Wesley's wrist, keeping it from running down his arm. "In some queer way, she might have been flattering me, you know."

For her sake, Wesley managed a smile. He knew she said that only to take the terrible tension away from what happened.

Soon Willard came back and led them out to the car. He guided Rae into the seat next to the driver's, motioning for Wesley to sit on her right. Walking around the car, he slid behind the steering wheel, leaned across Rae and said, "I'm driving, Wes. I don't want you to move your arm."

In a daze, Wesley nodded.

"I have some disinfectant in my valise," Willard went on. "Is there some place on the way where we can wash off the blood?"

"Sure, but I wasn't … I thought I'd … I'd …"

"Rae," Willard broke in," do you have your little sewing kit along so you can mend the tear in Wesley's shirt?"

"Yes, I do, in my satchel. Good Heavens, Wesley, did you forget your suitcase? I don't see one anywhere in the car. You'll need to shave and change clothes while we're there."

Trying to slow the blood flow by holding up his arm, he replied, "Oh, I always leave extra clothes and shaving things at Pa's, in case I go down there on … on the spur of the moment."

CHAPTER THIRTY-SEVEN

House of Dreams

June 12, 1923

They stopped at a picnic spot near Oak Lawn where Wesley, years ago, had discovered a wellspring. Willard cleaned and dressed his wounds while Rae mended his shirt sleeve and rinsed off the blood. When Wesley asked Willard what had become of Lillian Mae, the young medical student answered, "I turned her over to a fellow who said he was her brother."

"That would be either Jack or Michael," said Wesley. To himself he uttered, "Thank God for older brothers everywhere."

Back on the road, Wesley held his shirt out the window, hoping the current from the car's movement and sun's heat would dry it by the time they got to Kankakee, and he could put it on before they got to Pa's. During the rest of the ride, they took in the soft colors and fragrances of spring flowers along the road, as well as the green of the fields, promising knee-high corn by the fourth of July.

As they pulled up to the house on Schuyler Avenue, the family was waiting. Pa forgot about his bad leg, taking strides as long as a conductor's. "Just look at you. My God, look at you!"

He kept pumping Willard's arm so hard and fast Wesley could feel it in his own shoulder. "Careful, Pa, not so hard, not so hard."

Lilly and Hazel threw themselves on Willard, Hazel crying, "I named my son after you," Lilly proclaiming, "it's like I knew you all my life!" Ma, perhaps afraid he would search for a wisp of his mother's memory in her, stepped back, Rae next to her, looking pleased for everyone, and Wesley, his chest bursting inside, knowing he had brought them to this moment.

Later, Lilly carried out an armload of photo albums, showing Willard and Rae pictures of the family: Pa and their mother with little Clarence who died; Wesley with bare feet and a big bow around his neck; Wesley, Cleve, Hazel, and Lilly united after Pa brought them to the Bonfield farm; Benny in a three-piece suit before he joined the Marines; Cleve in his uniform ready for Mexico; dozens of aunts and uncles, cousins, and more cousins.

"Now we'll take pictures of this wonderful day," Hazel exclaimed. Lilly had a new camera Uncle Napoleon gave her for a wedding present. They snapped pictures of Pa and his children, Lilly and Hazel with Willard, Willard and Rae by Ma's rose trellis, Willard and Wesley by Wesley's new car, Pa and Ma on the top step of the front porch.

Afterward, Willard took Ma's hand and kissed it, saying, "Thank you, Mother Tooper, for being here all these years." If Cleve had been there, Wesley thought, his older brother would have whispered sarcastically in his ear, "Now isn't that the perfect thing for a true brother to say?"

The next day they went to Sheldon to see the cottage where the Tooper kids were born. They found the house locked but the front porch no longer had a door. "Here's where Mama had a short table for me to stand over when I sprinkled clothes," Wesley told Willard, "and you would sit in your high chair and watch me."

He noticed the three steps going up to the porch were now slanted and shaky. "This must be where we set the bowls of milk for the cats."

"Did they come?" Willard asked.

"Like grease lightning. Like grease lightning."

Hazel came running up from the orchard breathless like she did in Bonfield when the cows got through the fence. "Wesley! The trees are gone."

"Not all of them, Hazel," he said, after she dragged him down to see it all. The unpruned branches of the surviving trees had grown crooked and twisted as if trying to crowd out each other. Here and there, he would find a tall tree that had died, right in the middle of a cluster of smaller, living ones. Stopping by one that had survived time and neglect, Wesley wondered if that was the tree he sat under long ago, cuddled in his mother's arms with his baby brothers. Then going on to others, he'd ask, "or that one? Or that one?"

He'd been hesitant to go to the orchard, knowing he'd feel his mother's warm touch, hear her voice as she read, "Boats of mine a-boating, where will all come home?" But mostly he feared the breeze carrying with it Benny's voice crying, "Carge! Carge!" A tiny Teddy Roosevelt—one who never came back from battle.

From there they went to see their mother's brother, Uncle Charley, at Onarga. Their aunts and cousins had brought food for "dinner on the ground," even though Uncle Charlie now had a porch all around his house where they could have their picnic. Willard kept eating as fast as he could, but the women kept putting more food on his plate. "You sure skinny'd down over the years," they said, "you used to be so chubby."

Wesley remembered Willard's fat little legs when he was a baby. His mother had said all her children were like that when they were little. Now, Wesley noticed, as grown-ups they were all a little stocky or on the plump side—himself, Hazel especially, Lilly, Benny, when he was last home on furlough, and Cleve—all except Willard. Willard.

Uncle Charley, peering over his wired-framed spectacles at all the family members, asked, "By the way, where in the hell's Cleve?"

Wesley was about to make up some kind of an excuse when he heard a sound like echoing thunder coming up the lane, then a rumbling like a garbled, "potato, potato."

"It's ol' Cleveland Grover," cousin Chester declared. And he was right on the money—Cleve with goggles and leather helmet with flaps covering his ears, straps fastened under his chin.

"What the hell are you all doin'?" he shouted over the roar of his Harley.

"We're eatin'," hollered Basil St. John, the cousin with the loudest voice. "What the hell are you doin'?"

"I'm lookin' for Toopers. Now give me some food."

Wesley let the St. Johns gather around Cleve and Willard and went off to the back of the porch with his dinner. Even though he remained stricken by the terrible way things ended with Lillian Mae, a thread of joy ran through him as he listened to the cheerful chatter and laughter around him, to his relatives enjoying themselves and each other. After a while, he noticed Uncle Charley sitting beside him eating, as if he'd been there all along.

"Many thanks, Wessie Boy," he said, managing to shovel a fork filled with spring peas into his mouth without spilling them.

Just then Wesley felt something cold against his leg—an open, brown bottle of beer, most likely from the St. Johns' latest batch. He picked it up, took a long swallow, and sighed. "What would you be thanking me for, Uncle Charley?"

Charley took a gulp from an identical bottle. "For bringing our little boy back, that's what. Your mother, my little sister, is smiling down on you with pride."

"I'm sorry it took so long," Wesley said. "We ran into a lot of dead ends."

"Sure you did. And though it was hard on everyone not having him with us all that time, it's been a whole lot better than what happened to his little friend."

Wesley put his plate down on the porch floor. "What little friend?"

"Little Wilhelm, from over in that German community on the state line. His ma was so weak after her last childbirth, his pa brought the boy over there to that orphanage for a few weeks while he and the older kids put in a crop. He seemed to thrive some over there, put on weight right away. They fed the little ones pretty good at that place, but all of a sudden, he was dead."

Without warning, Wesley's foot automatically kicked forward and sent his half-full beer bottle rolling off the porch towards the cornfield. Uncle Charley didn't comment on the wasted beer but went on remembering things long forgotten.

"He got along with your little brother right away. I came over to visit after your Pa brought you boys there. Those two were always playing together. Course he was kinda shy, being used to hearing mostly German at home. He'd say 'vasser' for water or call your brother 'Villy' like people from those German countries do when they're trying to talk in English."

Remembering the two little boys brought on a smile as he talked, even once or twice, a chuckle. "Pretty soon Willard started copying the way the German boy talked. And the way little Wilhelm was puttin' on weight, and you listened to their baby talk, you might be hard put to tell which one was which."

Just then, Wesley recalled Doctor Malenday's words, spoken to him, it seemed, decades ago: "Sometimes, for some reason, he'd say Vill or Villy." This moved him to ask, "Uncle Charley, did the family have a funeral for the boy?"

"Not a real one, because those orphanage people said he had some catching disease, so they had to bury him. Course when the fire hit, everything was gone. Just some charred makeshift gravestones and nothing underneath—a few skeletons maybe."

Uncle Charley straightened up and cocked his head. "Wessie Boy, I think I hear your folks calling you. You come see us again soon, you hear?"

"Hey, Bro," Cleve hollered. "We want to get back before dark. Ol' Bill's gonna ride with me. Your car's too full."

As he ran off to join his family, Wesley kept telling himself, "Little kids pick up what other little kids say; little kids pick up what other little kids say."

With Wesley following behind in the Packard, and Rae scared to death for her husband, the motorcycle bounced along the worst road in the county. It looked, at first, as though Willard didn't know how to hold on, but when the Harley hit a deep pothole, almost hurtling him down a steep embankment and setting Rae to squealing, he wrapped his arms around Cleve's waist, pushing the rest of him tightly against his back.

That night Willard announced he would sleep in the attic with Wesley and Cleve so Rae could have the entire single bed they slept on the night before in Lilly's old room. Wesley, walking down the hallway from the bathroom, heard Rae whisper to her husband as he came in for a quick goodnight kiss. "We can't go on like this, Bill, at least I can't."

Easing himself closer to the bedroom door, Wesley glimpsed Willard taking his wife by the shoulders. "There's nothing to worry about," he told her, "because I have this plan...."

At that moment, Wesley had to move further down the hall so as not to be discovered. The last word he heard from the bedroom was something sounding like, "truth."

The truth! The truth about what? And what is this plan Willard has so she won't have to worry? Maybe she's going to have a baby. Could they not go on without telling us that? Oh, God, what if Cleve's been right all along? The truth. The truth that this guy is not our brother? And if he isn't, then our youngest brother might be ... might be dead, like Benny.

Shaken and bewildered, Wesley forced himself to join Cleve and Willard in the attic where they crawled onto cots lined up near the window like the three Tooper boys did before Cleve and later Benny went into Service. As Willard joined in telling stories and jokes, Wesley's misgivings almost disappeared. He couldn't tell stories like that and not be a Tooper. But long after the traffic on Schuyler Avenue died down to almost nothing, he still lay awake.

Maybe I heard it wrong. What rhymes with truth? Tooth does. And booth. Don't forget couth. Maybe she told him not to be uncouth. Hell, he couldn't be uncouth if he tried. Maybe she's got a wayward sister named Ruth and feels we have a right to know about her family. That's crazy! I heard it wrong. There's no doubt about it. Please, somebody, tell me I heard it wrong.

The next morning, Wesley took Cleve aside. He couldn't bring himself to repeat what Uncle Charley told him or what Rae told Willard the night before. All he could do was stammer, "What ... what do you think about him now, Big Brother?"

"I didn't come here because I finally believe he's the youngest son of Clara and Ed Tooper. I came here to watch him. He's smart, Wes, and so is that fancy doctor. I did a little detective work of my own lately and found out Malenday is having some financial problems."

"Financial problems? Are you sure, Cleve? Do you know how much?"

"I'm pretty damn sure, although I don't know how much. But I saw Pa give the kid another money bill yesterday. I only caught a glimpse of it, but it wasn't just a fiver—either a ten or a twenty. And who knows what Pa slips in with his letters that we don't know about, damn it. What's really got me hot under the collar is that him and Ma were saving up to buy a radio."

"But Cleve, Willard's going to medical school. He's got a wife to look after. Hell, I'll buy the folks a radio if they want one."

"For Christ sake, that's not the point! Pa's got patents on inventions that could bring in money over the years and he's drawing royalties on some, like the railroad coupling, right now. It might not be much, but it's more than that old Edwards couple back in St. Paul can give the kid. He even has to help them sometimes. And now Malenday doesn't have as much dough as he had before. So Billy Boy could use some cash from our pa, who thinks he's his real father."

With the burden from the day before magnified by what Cleve told him, Wesley could hardly choke down his breakfast. Somehow he managed to paste a grin on his face and nod his head when appropriate. He felt like an innocent child, having accepted things so readily. Now it turned out he didn't even know his older brother as much as he thought he did. Not only was he shocked by what Cleve found out about Dr. Malenday, but overwhelmed that he had carried out an investigation on his own.

Cleve's mood seemed the opposite of Wesley's. More outgoing than usual, he made sure their guests had enough breakfast. "More eggs, Bill? Did you get enough bacon, Rae? You can't have breakfast here without toppin' it off with Ma's cherry pie." After they finished eating, he organized a hike to the top of the hill overlooking the quarry where the Tooper boys used to put large rocks under their arms and dive far down into the water seeing how deep they could go.

"I'll make sure Willard doesn't try that," Rae said, looking warily over the edge.

Willard and Cleve decided to follow a meandering stream down to a little pool where they might spot some fish. "I'll show ol' Bill here how to catch 'em with his hands," Cleve said.

Wesley, his head clouded with doubt, stayed with Rae while she picked flowers in the woods.

"Look at this mulberry tree," she marveled. "Its leaves are so big, you can turn up the edges and float them like little boats. They don't go under. See?"

"Yes, I see, Rae. But why are you dropping them in the water? They'll just wash away and you'll never see your little boats again."

"I thought it might be fun to watch them come back."

"Jeez, Rae, they can't come back. They'd have to go upstream. The current will just pull them farther and farther until they're gone for good."

Rae took hold of his arm with both hands. "Well, dear Bro, let's just wait and see."

Not too much time had passed until they heard someone tramping through the brush. It was Willard carrying all the makeshift boats. Water dripped from his pants, his shoes, and Wesley thought, even from his eyes. Seconds later he realized that they were tears, like the ones glistening on his own cheeks.

"I remembered her, Wes," Willard said, "her touch and her voice reading to us. 'Boats,' I kept hearing her say, 'boats.' Rae thought it might be from a Robert Louis Stevenson children's poem. We looked it up in the library and found the ending: 'Away down the river, a hundred miles or more, other little children shall bring my boats ashore.' That's how, all at once, I knew you were my family."

"And today, you're … you're one of the children bringing the boats ashore?"

Willard nodded.

Then Wesley heard Cleve crashing through the brush and saw him wrap his arms around Willard, coughing so no one would think he was crying.

"Cleve," implored Wesley. "Do you know this poem? You were at school when she read it to us."

Cleve blew his nose into a handkerchief Mary made sure he always carried. "Don't you think Hazel and I were little once? She read it to us before the rest of you."

Wesley turned to Rae. "And is this the truth you thought you should tell us—that he's without doubt our brother because he remembered the poem our mother read to us?"

"The poem we never told him about," Cleve added.

Rae shook her finger at Wesley. "Naughty boy, were you eaves-dropping?" Then her face so full of mirth quickly changed to one of concern and then to sympathy. "Oh poor, dear Bro. What you must have been thinking. I'm so sorry."

Wesley wondered how she could feel sorry for him when he had such an idiotic smile on his face. He tried to look sad, then stern, but he couldn't get the smile off. It was like he had the face of Harpo Marx—eyes saucer-wide and a face full of constant wonder. If he had a horn like Harpo's, he would run to each person he loved and toot out his happiness. He would toot out that everything would work out for everyone there if they just "took patience." And he wanted to toot out that the right girl was not far down the line for him, that he wouldn't let attractiveness alone lead him into a romance this time. He would be honest with her, not hold anything back like he did with Lillian Mae.

Managing to wipe off his Harpo face, he glanced at the cloudless sky. "Well," he said, shutting one eye briefly as if winking at Benny, "it looks like all the boats are in."

About the Author

In 1957, high school junior, DOT TOOPER, and young musician, Pete Lund, fell in love-at-first-sight at a street dance in Eagle River, Wisconsin. The following summer, they rambled through Wisconsin's North Woods becoming inspired to write about its beauty and history. They soon married and majored in English in college, both receiving masters degrees.

After successful teaching careers, raising two kids, and buying a resort (originally a logging camp), they wrote and performed over five hundred songs about the North Woods logging past and beyond, recording under Gnarly Wood Records.

Dot's goal, besides writing a sequel to *Dark Brown is the River*, is to continue performing their songs like "Blueberry Summer" and "Wisconsin's Raftsmen." She says, "I do this in memory of my husband who passed on in 2015 from Parkinson's Disease and who taught me so much."

Made in the USA
Las Vegas, NV
12 September 2022